"SOFIE."

The wanting in his voice made her heart skip a beat. At her nod, he lowered his head to her neck. His tongue slid over her skin, sending a tingle down her spine. She leaned into him at the touch of his fangs, closed her eyes as pleasure moved through her. And for that moment, she felt what he was feeling—the way her blood warmed him, strengthened him, satisfied his hunger.

She shivered as his tongue sealed the tiny wounds in her throat.

He hugged her close for a moment, then tilted her face up. "Are you okay?"

"Fine."

Taking her by the hand, he led her to the sofa and pulled her down beside him.

"I felt you," she said, a note of wonder in her voice.

Ethan frowned. "What do you mean?"

"In my mind. I felt you there. It was weird. Kind of like I was you for just a moment. I knew what you were feeling, thinking."

Other titles available by Amanda Ashley

Published by Kensington Publishing Corporation

TWILIGHT DESIRES

AMANDA ASHLEY

ZEBRA BOOKS
KENSINGTON PUBLISHING CORP.
http://www.kensingtonbooks.com

ZEBRA BOOKS are published by

Kensington Publishing Corp.
119 West 40th Street
New York, NY 10018

All Kensington titles, imprints, and distributed lines are available at special quantity discounts for bulk purchases for sales promotion, premiums, fund-raising, educational, or institutional use.

Special book excerpts or customized printings can also be created to fit specific needs. For details, write or phone the office of the Kensington Sales Manager: Attn.: Sales Department. Kensington Publishing Corp., 119 West 40th Street, New York, NY 10018. Phone: 1-800-221-2647.

Zebra and the Z logo Reg. U.S. Pat. & TM Off.

First Printing: September 2018
ISBN-13: 978-1-4201-4738-4
ISBN-10: 1-4201-4738-2

eISBN-13: 978-1-4201-4740-7
eISBN-10: 1-4201-4740-4

10 9 8 7 6 5 4 3 2 1

Printed in the United States of America

Chapter One

Hands shoved into the pockets of his jeans, Ethan Parrish strolled the dark streets of Morgan Creek. It had been two months since Rylan Saintcrow turned him into a blood-sucking vampire. Two hellish months, and he was still trying to wrap his mind around the reality of what he'd become, and what he'd lost.

He blew out a sigh. It wasn't just food and drink he'd had to give up. It was his whole way of life. It was gone. All of it—his old life, his family and friends, not to mention his job. Damn! He had just received a raise and had been due for a well-earned promotion to vice president in charge of sales. Well, he could kiss that good-bye, too, along with everything else. Hard to keep a day job when you couldn't show up until after sundown.

Some people are born to be vampires, Saintcrow had told Ethan shortly after turning him into a fiend. *You're not one of them.*

As far as Ethan was concerned, truer words had never been spoken. And yet, the alternative—walking out into the sunlight and being turned into a living torch—was unthinkable.

Shit! Fate must be having a good laugh at his expense.

He had never liked horror movies, always been afraid vampires were real, and had been squeamish at the sight of blood. And now he was a creature of the night, complete with nice, sharp fangs and eyes that turned red with the lust for blood.

Like his lovely cousin, Holly.

He still couldn't believe she had *asked* to be turned. Why would anyone in their right mind want to be a vampire? Holly had given him some overly dramatic sob story about it being the only way she could be with her vampire husband, Micah Ravenwood, forever.

Ethan shook his head. How could anyone willingly give up their humanity? It was beyond his comprehension.

Sure, Holly had told him it wasn't so bad, that he would get used to it . . . yada yada yada.

When he reached the bridge that separated the town from the highway, he turned around and started back toward the house he'd chosen as his current residence. Morgan Creek had once been home to a pack of vampires who had kept ordinary people trapped here against their will. Though the prisoners had supposedly been well-treated and provided with food, housing, and entertainment, they had been no more than a ready food source for the vampires.

Ethan came to a halt, hands clenching, when he saw Saintcrow sitting on the front porch. "What the hell are you doing here?"

"Nice to see you, too. Kadie and I are leaving. Seems my wife's decided she wants to go to Scotland."

From what he'd heard, Kadie had also chosen to be a vampire rather than live without the love of her life. How anyone could fall in love with a vampire, let alone a master vampire like Saintcrow, remained a mystery.

Ethan lifted one shoulder and let it fall. "Good riddance."

Saintcrow blew out a sigh of exasperation. "I've taught

you everything you need to know to survive. The rest is up to you."

"Right."

"Do you remember what I told you?"

"Yeah, yeah. Don't hunt where I live. Don't kill my prey. Don't wait until the pain is excruciating before I feed. If I kill anybody except to save my own life, you'll know it and you'll destroy me."

Saintcrow shook his head. "I think I should just destroy you now and save us both a lot of aggravation."

"I'll be good, Dad," Ethan said, his voice heavily laced with sarcasm. "You and Mom have a nice trip." He flinched as his sire's power brought him to his knees. Rylan Saintcrow was a master vampire and not to be messed with. He would be wise to remember that, he thought, as Saintcrow vanished from his sight.

Ethan shook his head as he stared at the place where Saintcrow had been standing only seconds before. "Sad to be all alone in the world," he muttered.

And what the hell was he supposed to do now?

Ethan walked through Morgan Creek under a canopy of stars. The town was, for all intents and purposes, a ghost town, now inhabited by one lonely fledgling vampire. Holly and her husband had left a couple of days before to continue their honeymoon. Kadie and Saintcrow had left late last night.

Strolling down the main street of the old business section, he passed a grocery store, a library, a restaurant, a tavern. Farther down the street, he spied a movie theater and a gas station. If the place was his, he would have leveled everything except the houses, built a luxury hotel with a pool and a handful of exclusive shops and turned the place into a winter resort.

But it wasn't his, and he didn't have that kind of money.

Feeling lost and alone, he pulled his cell phone from his back pocket, then frowned. Who was he gonna call? His parents? They'd want to know where he was and why they hadn't heard from him in the last few weeks. What could he say? *Hey, Mom, Dad. You're probably wondering why I never made it to Cousin Holly's wedding, or why I haven't called. Well, that's an interesting story . . .*

He pinched the bridge of his nose. How did you tell the people you loved that you'd been turned into a vampire against your will?

And what about women? Sure, Kadie loved Saintcrow and Holly seemed smitten with the guy she had married, but Ethan was pretty sure women who liked vampires were rare . . . or maybe not. He recalled Holly telling him about some girl . . . what was her name? Sally? Sandy? No, Sofia. His cousin had told him Sofia *loved* vampires.

Well, there was one way to find out if that was true. He sent a quick text to Holly, asking for Sofia's number, then sat on the curb to wait for an answer.

Chapter Two

Sofia Ravenwood read Holly's text for the second time.

Remember my cousin?
The one I said I'd introduce you to?
Well, Ethan would like to meet you.
Should I give him your info?
Before you make up your mind,
you should know he's a vampire.

Sofia punched in her sister-in-law's number.

Holly answered on the first ring. "I've been expecting your call."

"Ethan's a vampire? When did that happen?"

"At the wedding. He was attacked outside. That's why he never showed up. Saintcrow found him."

"And he turned him?"

"It was either that or let him die."

Sofia stared at her bedroom wall. What would it be like to wake up and find out you weren't you any longer? Micah seemed to have gotten used to it. And so had Holly.

"Sofie? You still there?"

"What? Oh, yeah." There had been a time when she'd

thought she wanted to be a vampire. When Micah found out, he had made her promise she would let him know if she ever wanted to join the ranks of the Undead.

She'd had reason to change her mind since those days. It happened when the guy she had been dating handed her over to his vampire master. But for Micah's interference, she would have become prey. There had been a lot of changes since that night, she thought, glancing around. Her room, once painted a dark gray and covered with vampire posters, was now pink and white. She had stuffed all her goth clothing in the back of her closet, along with her black lipstick. "Did Ethan want to be a vampire?"

"No. I saw him shortly after he was turned, and he wasn't at all happy about it. But he seemed to have accepted it. More or less."

"Does my brother know you're trying to set me up with your cousin?"

"Not yet. What should I tell Ethan?"

"I don't know. Is he in control of his hunger?"

"Naturally, I called Saintcrow to ask him that very thing before I texted you. He said Ethan's got a handle on it and you should be safe enough."

"*Should* be? Great."

"Just get yourself a sharp wooden stake and some holy water," Holly said, laughter evident in her voice. "Would it help you make up your mind if I reminded you he's tall and blond with gorgeous brown eyes, and that he played football in college?"

"You're a lot of help. I don't know, Holly. He's almost eight years older than I am."

"He's lonely, Sofie. And so unsure of himself, not that I blame him. I mean, his whole life has turned upside down."

"Oh, all right," she said with an aggrieved sigh. "Give him my number and we'll see how it goes. But if he tries anything, I'll sic my big brother on him!"

* * *

Ethan stared at his cell phone. Now that he had the girl's number, he was having second thoughts. He didn't know anything about her—age, appearance, likes and dislikes. What if she had no more personality than a lump of coal and didn't enjoy any of the things he did?

Time to call Holly.

"Hey, Ethan," she said brightly. "Did you call Sofia yet?"

"Nah."

"Why not? You asked me for her number, remember?"

"Yeah, but I don't know anything about her, except she's supposed to like vampires."

"I'll send you her photo. She just turned nineteen . . ."

"Nineteen!"

"I know, she's young, but she's pretty and fun and you won't have to hide what you are with her. I'm not suggesting you guys get married, you know. Hang on a sec, I'm sending her photo. It's from our wedding."

Ethan whistled under his breath when he saw the girl's picture. She had black hair and dark eyes, a winsome smile and a killer figure.

"I knew you'd like her," Holly said smugly. "Ethan?"

"Maybe this isn't such a good idea. I mean . . ."

"What?"

"She looks good enough to eat," he muttered. "Literally. Stop laughing!"

"Sorry."

"Sure you are. So, how's being a vampire working out for you?"

"I'm fine, Ethan, really. Yes, there are adjustments to be made and things I miss, but I would have given up anything and everything to be with Micah."

Ethan had never known anyone, including his parents, who were happily married. His friends changed wives as often as they changed their underwear. Sometimes more often. In his set, marriage vows had been a joke. Couples promised to be faithful and the next thing he knew, they were cheating on each other. The last thing Ethan had in mind was marriage. But he was desperate for some female companionship. "Must be nice to feel that way about some-body," he said quietly.

"It is. If you call Sofie, let me know how it goes, okay?"

"Sure. Thanks, Cuz."

"Cheer up, Ethan. It'll get better, I promise."

"I'll hold you to it."

"You do that. Good night."

Ethan raked his fingers through his hair, took a deep breath, and punched in Sofia Ravenwood's cell number.

Sofia stepped out of the shower, wrapped a towel around her wet hair, and grabbed her phone off the toilet tank. When she didn't recognize the number, she figured it was some telemarketer. They always called at the worst possible times. Somewhat irritably, she said, "Hello?"

"Sofia?"

The voice was deep and sexy and totally unfamiliar. "Yes. Hello? Is anybody there?"

"It's Ethan Parrish. Holly's cousin."

"Oh, hi. She told me you might call."

"Yeah." He cleared his throat. "I was wondering if you'd like to go out sometime."

"Sure, when?"

"How about tomorrow night, around eight?"

"Works for me." Tomorrow was Saturday, which meant she had plenty of time to do her chores before she needed to get ready. "Where are we going?"

"Anywhere you want except out to dinner."

The sound of her laughter was warm and sultry. "How about a movie?"

"Okay by me."

Sofia gave him her address and said good-bye, then bit down on her lower lip. What would her family say when she told them she was going out with a vampire? Sure, they loved and accepted Micah, but he was family. Of course, so was Ethan, she supposed, since Micah had married Holly. Still, her parents, one of her sisters, and her brother-in-law had been terrorized by a vampire and her minion not long ago.

She slipped into her sleep shirt, pajama bottoms, and slippers, then dried her hair. Did Ethan look as sexy as he sounded? Was she taking a horrible chance, going out with a fledgling vampire? What if he got a sudden, irresistible craving for blood?

She took several deep breaths. "You'll be fine," she told her reflection as she braided her hair. "You've got a bottle of holy water and a nice, sharp wooden stake. What could possibly go wrong?"

Ethan whistled softly as he strolled down the dark, deserted streets of Morgan Creek. He had just made a date with a beautiful girl—his first date since he had become a bloodsucker.

On the plus side, she was familiar with vampires. If one date turned into two, he wouldn't have to make excuses for why he couldn't see her during the day, or why he couldn't come to dinner.

On the minus side, he couldn't see her during the day, or take her out to dinner.

But that was a worry for tomorrow.

Tonight, he needed to hunt, something that should have

been repulsive but was remarkably satisfying. The fact that the idea didn't gross him out grossed him out.

It still came as a shock, how easy it was to transport himself to the nearest town, find a suitable female, and quench his hellish thirst. What wasn't easy was stopping. But whenever he was tempted to take it all, he had only to remember Saintcrow's threat to destroy him if he took a life.

Ethan was a nervous wreck as he dressed for his date with Holly's sister-in-law. He hadn't been this unsure of himself when he was sixteen and went on his first date with Connie Shoemaker. He had always had more than his share of self-confidence where women were concerned. He'd never had any trouble getting dates in high school or college, and certainly not since then.

But the old Ethan didn't exist anymore. And he still wasn't sure who the new Ethan was.

He ran a comb through his hair, slapped on some cologne, looked up Sofia's address on his phone, and transported himself to her location, a second-floor apartment in a four-story building.

He took several deep breaths. And rang the bell.

Sofia smoothed her hand over her hair before she opened the door, felt her jaw drop when she saw the man standing in the hallway. Holly had said he was handsome, but this guy was gorgeous with his shaggy blond hair and dark brown eyes. His shirt emphasized his broad shoulders, his jeans clung to slim hips and long, long legs.

"Sofia?"

And that voice—like chocolate over black velvet. "Ethan?"

He nodded.

"Hi." Taking a step back, she said, "Please, come in, vampire."

He flashed her a wry grin, felt a shimmer of preternatural power as he crossed the threshold. "I thought you lived with your parents."

"I did." Closing the door, she led him into the living room. "I got a job a couple of months ago and moved here to be closer to work. Sit down, won't you?"

He sat on the sofa, hands resting on his knees.

"Can I get you a glass of wine?"

"Sure, thanks." It was the only thing—besides blood—he could keep down. He glanced around the room while she went into the kitchen. The walls were a sunny yellow, the curtains white, the floor hardwood. The furniture didn't match, but it all seemed to blend together. Family photos hung on one wall.

"Tell me about yourself." She handed him a goblet filled with dark red liquid, then sat in the green plaid chair across from the sofa.

He swirled the wine in his glass. "I'd rather not talk about my past, if that's okay with you. None of it matters anymore. As for the here and now . . ." He shrugged. "I'm still trying to find my way."

"Of course. I understand." Although she didn't, not really. She couldn't imagine what it would be like to just wake up and be a vampire. Holly had chosen to be turned. She had known what she was getting in to. But Ethan . . . her heart went out to him. He really seemed lost.

"Holly said you liked vampires."

"I used to be obsessed with them."

"And now?"

"I still think they're fascinating."

Ethan snorted.

"Well, it's true! I even asked my brother to turn me, although I'm not sure I want that anymore." In as few words as possible, she told him about Leticia Braga's attack on her family. "After that, I sort of changed my mind."

"I can see how that could happen. So, if you're over your obsession with the Undead, why did you agree to go out with me?"

She shrugged. "Holly asked me to," she replied candidly.

"So, it's a pity date," he said dryly.

Sofia laughed. "In a way. But mainly I was curious. She had told me about you. She even promised to introduce us at the wedding, but you never showed up."

"Yeah." He sipped his wine, remembering that night. "I was attacked and bitten by a vampire. Saintcrow—do you know him?" At Sofia's nod, he said, "Well, Saintcrow found me. He turned me into a vampire and took me to some ghost town."

"Morgan Creek?"

"You've heard of it?" he asked, surprised.

"Micah told me about it."

"Right. Well, Saintcrow kept me there for a couple of months to teach me how to be a bloodsucker."

Sofia didn't miss the bitterness in his voice. "I'm sorry," she murmured, although it seemed woefully inadequate. "Do you still want to go to the movies?"

"If you want, or I can just leave."

She reached out, her hand covering his. "Don't go."

Ethan stared at her hand. It was small and warm. No woman had willingly touched him in months. He looked up, his gaze meeting hers. Was he imagining things, or had something magical just sparked between them?

Chapter Three

Sofia stared at the screen, although she had no idea what the movie was about. She had spent the whole time sneaking glances at Ethan, admiring his strong profile, trying to imagine what he was thinking, feeling. Micah had made her promise that if she ever decided she wanted to be a vampire, she would let him be the one to bring her across. Something about it being important who your sire was. Good sires stayed with their fledglings, taught them the ropes, so to speak, made sure they understood the ins and outs of vampire life. Micah's sire hadn't done that. According to Micah, neither had Saintcrow's. She thought it likely Saintcrow had decided to teach Ethan because he knew exactly what it was like to be abandoned by the one who made him.

She had met Saintcrow. The fact that he was compassionate enough to look after Ethan surprised her. Granted, she didn't know the master vampire very well, but he seemed a formidable creature with few scruples. Still, she was eternally grateful to him for saving the lives of her family from that monster Leticia Braga.

She slid another glance in Ethan's direction, startled to

find him staring back at her. Heat warmed her cheeks. Caught in the act!

Their gazes met and held for stretched seconds and then, giving her plenty of time to back away, he leaned toward her.

Sofia's breath caught in her throat as his lips brushed hers. They were cool, softer than they looked.

He pulled back, his gaze searching hers before he leaned in again, his hand cupping her nape as his mouth covered hers a second time.

The world as she knew it came to a screeching halt. The theater fell away. She heard nothing, saw nothing, as she sank into his kiss. The wine he'd had earlier lingered on his tongue, intoxicating her still further. She cursed the armrest between them. Then again, maybe it was a good thing. Otherwise, she might have climbed onto his lap.

She wasn't aware that the movie had ended until the lights came up and someone behind them shouted, "For crying out loud! Get a room!"

Face hot with embarrassment, Sofia shrugged out of Ethan's arms. "Let's get out of here."

Cheeks burning, she hurried out of the theater.

Still not certain what had happened—certainly nothing that had ever happened before—Ethan followed her. He had kissed dozens of women in his time, but he had never experienced anything like that. Even now, he couldn't explain it, but it had been far more than just a kiss. Had she felt it, too, that almost mystical sense of connection? Or was he just imagining something magical because he was feeling so damn lost and alone?

Ethan cleared his throat. "In my other life, I would have suggested we go get something to eat, but . . ." He shrugged. "Would you like to go get a drink?"

Not quite trusting her voice, Sofia nodded.

"Any place in particular you'd like to go?"

"There's a nice place right down the street."

Side by side, not quite touching, they strolled down the sidewalk.

"It's a beautiful night," Sofia remarked.

"Yeah." He had never really appreciated the night until he became a vampire. His preternatural senses made him aware of sights and sounds that had been denied him as a mortal man. The night itself seemed alive, as if he could reach out and touch it. One of his new powers allowed him to sort of meld into the darkness until he became invisible. Sometimes, when he was inside, the night called to him, entreating him to come out and bask in the darkness, bathe in the moon's light.

"We're here."

Ethan halted abruptly, only then realizing Sofia had stopped several paces behind him. Turning, he closed the distance between them and opened the door to the night-club.

Like all clubs, this one was dimly lit. Round tables ringed the dance floor; the bar, long and curved, anchored the far end of the room. An old rhythm-and-blues tune wafted from speakers mounted near the ceiling.

"Do you come here often?" Ethan asked as they made their way to an empty table.

"Not often, no."

He held her chair for her. "What can I get you?"

"A tequila sunrise, please."

"Be right back."

Sofia noticed his taut backside as he walked away, but her mind still lingered on the kisses they had shared in the theater. She had been kissed before, though not terribly often. Her parents had been rather strict, especially with their two youngest daughters. Plus, she had four older brothers who had been very protective of their little sister. Sofia wasn't sure what had happened when Ethan kissed her, but it had been . . . magical, she thought. That was the only word to describe it. All it had taken was one touch of his lips to hers and she had been lost. But the last kiss . . . there was no earthly way to describe its effect on her senses.

"Here you go."

She smiled as she accepted the glass he offered, glad he couldn't read her mind. "Thank you."

He sat across from her and, to her chagrin, she found herself imagining them at home, alone in her room. In her bed . . . What on earth was she thinking? She didn't even know the man, and he certainly didn't know her. What was it with him anyway? She had never been attracted to a man so quickly before. Being alone with Ethan Parrish when there was a bed in the vicinity was definitely *not* a good idea.

And then she frowned. Was she really attracted to him? Or was it just his inherent vampire allure she found so irresistible? She had read about that kind of thing in books. It was supposed to be something all vampires possessed. It made it easier for them to lure their prey.

Prey! Was that what he saw when he looked at her?

Ethan frowned, confused by the wary look in Sofia's eyes, the sense of apprehension suddenly radiating from her. "Is something wrong?"

"I don't know." She sipped her drink to avoid looking at him.

"Sofie, what's going on?"

"I'm sure I don't know what you mean."

"I'm sure you do."

"Do you think of me as prey?" she blurted out, then clapped her hand over her mouth.

"What?"

"I . . . nothing . . . it was in a book I read."

Ethan frowned. "What book?"

"I've read a lot of books about . . ." She lowered her

voice. "About vampires and how they all have this built-in charisma that makes it easy for them to attract their victims and . . ."

"*Built-in charisma*?" He stared at her as if she were speaking a foreign language.

Sofia nodded. "It's true. Ask Micah or Saintcrow."

"So, that's what you think?" he asked incredulously. "That I'm exerting some kind of super sexual power to entice you to my lair?"

Sofia blinked at him, then burst out laughing.

"What's so damn funny?" he asked gruffly.

"I'm sorry, but it all just sounds so silly when you put it like that," she said and then frowned. "Unless that's what you're really doing."

Ethan shook his head, then pushed away from the table. "Come on. I'll take you home."

"Wait."

"Why?"

"Sit down, please."

Somewhat reluctantly, he did as she asked.

"It's just that, in the theater, you kissed me . . . and now, sitting here . . ." Sofia knew she was blushing, something she had done frequently this evening. "I've just never been this attracted to someone I just met."

"Yeah? Well, me either."

"Seriously?"

"Dead serious." He grinned as he realized how that sounded. "Why did you want to be a vampire?"

"I've been intrigued by them ever since I was a little girl. I think it all started when I saw that old George Hamilton movie. He was funny and handsome, and as I grew older, I realized he was also very sexy. And I loved the whole never-getting-old thing and being able to turn into a bat and . . ." She stuck her tongue out at Ethan when he started laughing.

"I've never met a woman like you. Most little girls want to be supermodels or Wonder Woman. You want to be a bloodsucking creature of the night."

"Is that how you see yourself?"

He shrugged. "It's what I am."

"Well, let's see. Do you go around killing innocent people?"

"Of course not."

"Do you kidnap children?"

"No."

"Are you committing unspeakable acts of terror?"

Ethan laughed despite himself. "You're something else, you know that?"

"So are you." She smiled as something warm and intimate passed between them. "This isn't going to be easy, is it?"

His eyes grew dark, intense. "Nothing worth fighting for ever is."

"Do you think I'm worth fighting for?"

"Definitely."

"You probably won't have to fight very hard," she murmured. And knew she was blushing again.

"Would you like to dance?"

She nodded, her heart skipping a beat at the thought of being in his arms.

The club's dim interior added to a feeling of intimacy, as did the music, which was soft and slow as he led her onto the floor and took her in his arms. She had no trouble following his lead. She had always wondered how people could gaze deeply into each other's eyes without laughing. Now she knew.

Ethan pulled Sofia closer. He was completely smitten with her. She was beautiful and funny and seemed totally at ease with what he was. For a few minutes, he had forgotten he wasn't human, but now, holding her close, all his hunting instincts kicked in. The rhythm of her heartbeat, the scent of the blood flowing warm and sweet and satisfying through her veins.

He cursed under his breath as the hunger he'd thought under control roared to life. His fangs ran out, and he knew his eyes had gone red. He wanted her. Heaven help him, he wanted her more than he had ever wanted anything.

With a hoarse, "I've got to go!" he spun away and left her standing there, alone, in the middle of the dance floor.

Chapter Four

"I don't know what the heck happened tonight," Sofia lamented. Cell phone in hand, she curled up in a corner of the sofa, one foot tucked beneath her. "One minute we were gazing into each other's eyes and the next—poof!—he was gone."

"Didn't he *say* anything?" Holly asked.

"He said he had to go, and he wasn't kidding. He left me stranded on the dance floor."

"Well, I'm just guessing, but he might have felt like he was losing control."

Sofia frowned. Losing control? Of course! She smacked her forehead with the palm of her hand. "I must be an idiot."

"Why do you think that?"

"It's so obvious. I mean, I've read enough books and had enough talks with Micah to know what stirs a vampire's hunger."

Holly snickered. "I'm guessing there were some sparks between you."

"Sparks!" Sofia exclaimed. "We could have started an inferno."

"Well, there you go. So, do you like him?"

"You have no idea. I've never felt this way about a guy so soon. How do I know if it's even real?"

"I guess you'll just have to go out with him again."

"I'm not sure that's a good idea."

"Why not? He seems to have a handle on things."

"If that was true, he wouldn't have gone storming out of the club."

"I'd say that proves he does. After all, he didn't bite you or anything."

"Well, he was darn close to it. His eyes went red just before he left. I know what *that* means!" Sighing, she murmured, "I don't know whether it's a good idea to see him again or not."

Ethan stalked the dark streets of the city, his hunger growing with every step he took. He knew he should feed. Saintcrow had warned him that waiting was dangerous, that if he waited too long he might accidentally kill his prey. Saintcrow had also warned Ethan that, if he killed anyone except to save his own life, he would destroy him. Well, hell, maybe that was the answer!

He had been so sure he was in control tonight. He had fed before he went to Sofie's, but somewhere on the dance floor, his control had slipped away and all he could think about was sinking his fangs into her throat.

He turned the corner at the end of the street, coming to an abrupt halt when Rylan Saintcrow materialized in front of him. Ethan bit off a curse. "What the hell are you doing here? Aren't you supposed to be in Scotland?"

Saintcrow lifted a brow. "Did you think I wouldn't know what's troubling you?"

Ethan stared at him. How was that even possible when Saintcrow had been thousands of miles away?

Saintcrow tapped a finger to his temple. "I made you,

remember? I'll always know when you're in trouble. Or when you need help."

"Great." Ethan started walking again.

Saintcrow fell in beside him. "Do you really think destroying you is the answer?"

"You don't know what I'm going through."

"The hell I don't. I've been there, and I didn't have anyone to help me through it."

"I don't know what you can do," Ethan muttered.

"You haven't killed anyone yet. You left before you attacked Sofia. I'd say you're doing okay."

Ethan ran a hand over his jaw. "How do I separate my hunger from my lust?"

"I grant you that's not easy."

"Tell me about it. I made sure to feed before I went to see Sofia. It didn't help."

"Sure it did. You had the strength to leave before you did anything rash. So, you and Sofia. Holly's quite the little matchmaker."

"Yeah."

"It's only been a couple of months," Saintcrow said. "Don't be so hard on yourself."

"I miss my old life," Ethan said, his voice tinged with anger. "I'm used to being busy, spending time with my family, hanging out with old friends. I've lost all that. But the worst of it is, there's nothing to replace it with."

"Hogwash."

"What's that supposed to mean?"

"If you want to work, work. There are a lot of night jobs out there. You can travel the whole world. If you miss your family, go visit them. You like Sofia. She seems to like you. She already knows what you are, so you don't have to worry about hiding the truth from her. And because she has a vampire in the family, she already knows what to expect. So stop feeling sorry for yourself. How are you fixed for cash?"

"I've got some put away."

"Well, then, get the hell out of Morgan Creek. Go find a place here in the city. It's not good to spend so much time alone."

"You speaking from experience again?"

Saintcrow nodded. "If you need anything, let me know."

"Yeah," Ethan said gruffly. "Thanks."

Saintcrow clapped him on the shoulder. "I've gotta go. Kadie wants me, if you know what I mean."

"I can guess," Ethan said with a wry grin. But he was talking to himself. Saintcrow was already gone.

A thought took Ethan back to Morgan Creek and the house he'd chosen as his lair. Sitting on the front porch, gazing up at the vast midnight vault of the sky, he thought about what Saintcrow had said. His sire was right. Vampire or mortal, life was what you made it. He had sulked long enough. He had always been able to accomplish whatever he set his mind to. It was time to accept that his old life was over. Like it or not, he was a vampire now. He could move with incredible speed, dissolve into mist. See and hear sights and sounds hidden from mortal eyes. He would never grow old or sick. All good things. Assuming an older vampire didn't destroy him and he didn't run afoul of a hunter, he might live for centuries, like his sire.

Tomorrow night, he would call Sofia and hope she could find it in her heart to forgive him for leaving her standing on the dance floor without so much as a good-bye or an explanation.

* * *

He called Sofia as soon as he woke Sunday night.

No answer.

He waited an hour and called again.

No answer.

A third call.

Still no answer.

The message couldn't be any clearer.

Swearing softly, he shoved his phone into his back pocket.

Maybe it was time to forget about Sofia, leave Morgan Creek, head for home, and see how much of his old life he could salvage.

Nodding, he willed himself to his house in Oakland. The grass hadn't been cut in weeks. Newspapers littered the front porch, but his mailbox was strangely empty. He was about to go into the house when he heard someone calling his name. Turning, he saw his next-door neighbor hurrying toward him, a grocery sack in her hand.

Ethan groaned softly. Grace Chapman was a recently divorced woman in her mid-forties. She had been flirting with him ever since her husband moved out eight months before.

"Ethan, honey, where have you been?" She thrust the sack into his hands. "I collected your mail," she purred. "The box was overflowing."

"Thanks, Gracie. I appreciate it."

She walked her fingers up his arm. "I just made dinner. There's enough for two."

"Not tonight. I . . . I had a long flight and I'm beat." Hoping to forestall any more questions, he said, "Maybe tomorrow, okay?"

She winked at him. "I'll hold you to it." She gave his arm a squeeze, then sashayed back home.

Thinking she was a complication he really didn't need,

Ethan climbed the porch steps, gathered up the papers, and unlocked the door.

Flicking on the lights, he glanced around. The place looked the same—white walls, tan carpet, leather furniture, a shelf filled with old football trophies and plaques, a picture of his parents. Every surface was covered with dust. Good thing the plants were plastic.

He dumped the mail on the table inside the door. He sorted through it—mostly junk and bills now past due. There was an invite to a friend's wedding. Leaving the bills on the table, he tossed the rest back into the grocery bag.

He started toward the back door. What was that smell? He followed it into the kitchen, to the refrigerator, and swore softly when he opened the door. Spoiled milk. Rotten eggs, cheese, and lunch meat. He dumped the milk down the sink, emptied everything else into a large plastic garbage bag, then started on the cupboards. With a shake of his head, he tossed in a loaf of blue bread, along with a box of moldy doughnuts, peanut butter, potato chips, and everything else he would never need again, and carried it all out to the trash.

Returning to the house, he stood in the middle of the living-room floor and realized his house made a lousy lair. Too many windows. A lock a five-year-old could pick.

Tomorrow night, he'd go online to see if he could find something more suitable.

But now, he needed to feed.

Ethan had just mesmerized his prey when his cell phone rang. Muttering, "Not now," he bent toward the woman's neck, then paused. What if it was Sofia?

Yanking the phone from his pocket, he checked the number, and hit Answer. "Hey, Sofie."

"Sorry I missed your calls," she said, a smile in her

voice. "I spent the day with my folks and I forgot to charge my battery and couldn't find my charger. So, what are you doing?"

Ethan frowned. Should he tell her the truth? Why not? They had no future if she couldn't handle the truth. "I was about to have dinner."

There was silence on the other end. And then she laughed. "Sorry. I didn't mean to interrupt."

"Hang on a minute." Gazing into the woman's eyes, he spoke to her mind, freeing her from his hypnotic spell and sending her on her way. "All done. So, what's up?"

"Nothing. I was just bored and . . ." She blew out a breath. "You left in a hurry the other night and I wondered why."

"Don't you know?"

"I think so. I guess I just wanted to make sure it wasn't anything I said or did."

"It wasn't." Should he try to explain how he'd felt, holding her, wanting her, desperate for her blood? Would she understand or be totally freaked out? He reminded himself that she had a brother who was a vampire. Surely nothing he said would come as a shock. Still . . .

"I talked to Holly. She said you were probably afraid you were losing control . . ."

"She was right," he said, his voice flat.

"She also said if you were really out of control, you wouldn't have been able to leave."

"Is that what she said? How the hell would she know? I might have killed you."

"But you didn't."

"Yeah," he muttered under his breath. "Not this time."

"What?"

"Nothing."

"Ethan? I'd like to see you again."

"I don't know why."

"Don't you want to see *me* again?"

He groaned deep in his throat. What kind of question was that?

"Ethan?"

"Of course I do." He plowed his fingers through his hair, torn by his yearning to see her and fear for her life. "I don't want to hurt you."

"Don't worry. I'll bring along my trusty wooden stake and a bottle of holy water."

He laughed despite himself, and she laughed with him.

The sound touched something deep inside him. "How about next Friday night?"

"It's a date."

Chapter Five

When Ethan woke Monday night, he called a Realtor to make arrangements to put his house up for sale. With that done, he went out in search of prey. Remembering Saintcrow's advice about not hunting where you lived, he transported himself to a small town in Arizona. He told himself his choice had nothing to do with Sofia being in the same town.

Walking the streets in search of an easy mark, he paused in front of an abandoned building. From the looks of it, it had once been a warehouse.

Strolling around the perimeter, he saw there was only one small barred window on the second floor. The glass was missing. There were two doors in the back—one large one with a loading dock and a smaller entrance beside it. Both were made of solid iron.

Dissolving into mist, he floated upward to the window and between the bars. Resuming his own form, he looked around. This floor was divided into what had probably been individual offices, he thought. All the rooms were empty now.

He walked down the metal staircase to the main floor.

It was a large empty space save for a long wooden table. A perfect lair, he mused, looking around. All it needed was a sofa, a chair, a bed. And a big-screen TV if he could find a way to get electricity to the place.

"Home sweet home," he murmured.

Pleased with his find, he went in search of prey.

Sofia curled up on her bed, book in hand. She kept her phone within easy reach, hoping Ethan would call. But as the minutes ticked by and the hour grew late, she turned off her phone, put her book aside, and slid under the covers.

Staring into the dark, she whispered, "I won't cry. I won't cry. I. Will. Not. Cry."

Standing on the sidewalk in front of Sofia's apartment building, Ethan stared up at her window. Opening his preternatural senses, he heard her whispering, "I won't cry, I won't cry." He frowned, wondering what had her so upset.

He hadn't intended to come here tonight. He had been on his way home—intending to sneak in the back door to avoid Gracie—when he suddenly found himself in front of Sofia's place. He shook his head. When had he started lying to himself? He had come hunting in Arizona because Sofia was here, and he had wanted to be close to her. And now he was in front of her complex.

Closing his eyes, he concentrated on rising to the building's second floor and then onto the balcony outside her bedroom. Taking a deep breath, he rapped on the French door.

A light immediately came on inside. A moment later, the slats of the blinds on the door parted and he saw her staring out, wide-eyed with alarm.

She blinked and blinked again when she saw him.

He cocked his head to the side, a half smile on his lips.

He heard the click of the lock and the door opened, revealing Sofia in a pair of hot-pink PJ bottoms and a flowered t-shirt.

"What are you doing here?" she exclaimed. "Do you know what time it is? You practically gave me a heart attack!"

"I'm sorry. I was thinking about you, and the next thing I knew, I was standing outside your building."

She grabbed her robe from the foot of the bed. "Well, since you're here, you might as well come in."

He crossed the threshold and closed the door behind him. Her room was decidedly feminine, from the frilly pink-and-white spread to the lacy curtains at the window. The furniture was white, the walls a pale pink, the floor hardwood.

Sofia sat cross-legged in the middle of the bed, head cocked to one side. "I never expected to see you tonight."

He shrugged one shoulder. "I never expected to be here." There was only one chair and he took it. "What was it you didn't want to cry about?"

She stared at him, her eyes wide, a hint of color flooding her cheeks. "You heard that?"

He couldn't help wondering why she was blushing, and then he frowned. Did her tears have something to do with him? "Sofie?"

"It's none of your business." She refused to meet his gaze. And her cheeks grew redder.

"It is if it has something to do with me."

"It was a girl thing, and it's over now."

It was obvious she wasn't going to tell him. "Would you rather I left?"

"No," she said quickly, then bit down on her lower lip. "I feel like you're mad at me, but I don't know why."

"Oh, if you must know, I was just disappointed because

you didn't call tonight. I know it was stupid, but I guess I was feeling kind of down and . . ." Before she realized he had moved, he was beside her on the bed, his arm around her shoulders.

"I'm sorry I didn't call," he said quietly. "I'm sorry you were feeling blue earlier." His fingers lightly stroked her cheek. "I'll call you every night if you want. Or every hour. Well," he said, with a grin, "every hour I'm awake, that is. And if you want, I'll take you out tomorrow night and buy you a dozen roses or a hot fudge sundae or anything that will put a smile on your face."

It was the sweetest thing anyone had ever said to her. "Really?"

"Really."

Feeling her heart swell with love, she threw her arms around his neck and kissed him. The next thing she knew, they were lying side by side, their legs tangled, her body pressed intimately against his. She went weak all over as his tongue skated across her lower lip, then dipped inside.

Gasping, she pulled away, one hand pressed to her heart. "Whoa, cowboy. We need to slow down."

Sitting up, Ethan took several deep breaths as he fought the urge to give in to the desire to make her his, to taste the sweetness of her life's blood. He flinched when she laid a hand on his back.

"Are you all right?" she asked tremulously.

"I will be," he said. "Just give me a minute."

Her hand slid away from his back as she sat up. "Is there anything I can do?" she asked, and immediately wished she could call back the words. She knew exactly what he wanted from her.

And maybe that was the answer.

"Ethan?"

"Yeah?"

"Would it help if you took a little . . . drink?"

He turned to face her. "Are you serious?"

"I just thought . . . I mean, maybe if you . . . um . . . tasted me, it would help. Somehow."

His gaze moved to her throat. Her heart was beating double-time. "What if I can't stop?"

She reached into the drawer of her bedside table and withdrew a sharp wooden stake.

"Well, that will certainly slow me down," he muttered. "Are you sure about this?"

"No, but I'm willing to give it a try." Pushing her hair out of the way, she turned her head to the side, giving him access to her throat, and closed her eyes.

Ethan took a deep breath as he folded his hands over her shoulders. She smelled so good . . . her hair, her skin. Her life's blood. He pictured it, flowing like a river of crimson through her veins. Bending his head, he ran his tongue over the smooth skin on her neck, then bit her as gently as he could.

Her blood trickled over his tongue, warm and salty-sweet. He closed his eyes, relishing the taste, the way even that little bit flowed through him, easing his hellish thirst— even as it filled him with a kind of interior stillness he hadn't known since Saintcrow turned him.

He ran his tongue over the tiny wounds in her throat, then kissed her cheek.

Frowning, she opened her eyes. "I thought you were going to drink from me?"

"I did."

"I didn't feel any pain."

"Why would you?"

"Well, you bit me, didn't you? I thought it would hurt, but all I felt was a kind of warmth." She looked at him, her brow furrowed. "Why didn't it hurt?"

"Because I didn't want it to."

Her eyes widened. "And if you wanted it to?"

"Hey, I can make it as painful as you like."

"No, that's okay. So, did it help?"

"Oh, yeah. Thank you."

She yawned behind her hand. "You're welcome."

"I should let you get some sleep. I'll call you tomorrow night. I promise."

Her smile was like sunshine in his soul. "Good night, Ethan."

Rising, he watched her crawl under the covers. Bending down, he kissed her lightly. "'Night, Sofie. Sweet dreams."

She sighed and turned onto her side. Her eyelids fluttered down and she was asleep.

Whistling softly, he went out the balcony door, feeling better than he had in months.

In the morning, Sofia woke smiling and then, as her mind cleared, she sprang out of bed and ran into the bathroom. Standing in front of the mirror, she turned her head from side to side. Had it all been a dream? Had Ethan actually bitten her last night? There were no telltale marks.

Making her way back into the bedroom, she sat on the edge of the mattress. He had tasted her blood—only a little, he'd said. It hadn't hurt at all. That had surprised her. What was even more surprising was that she didn't feel any different. She wasn't sure what she'd expected to feel, but surely something as life-changing as letting a vampire drink from you should have left some kind of . . . of . . . she didn't know what.

A quick glance at her phone told her she had slept through her alarm and was late for work.

She took the shortest shower in history, dived into her

clothes, grabbed her purse and her keys, and ran out of the apartment.

She found her boss, Mr. Moore, waiting for her in her office, his arms folded over his chest, a dour expression on his face.

"I trust you have a good excuse for your tardiness," he said, staring pointedly at the clock on the wall behind her desk.

Summoning her most winning smile, she said, "My alarm failed to go off."

"I trust you'll buy a new one."

"Yessir! Right after work. Assuming I still have a job?"

He burst out laughing.

After a moment, she joined in. She had been employed as Mr. Moore's personal assistant at the accounting firm of Donaldson and Moore for five months and she never knew what kind of mood Mr. Moore would be in from one day to the next. Sometimes he was as jolly as Santa Claus; at other times he was the Grinch.

"Get to work, Miss Ravenwood," he said, tapping his finger on his watch. "Time is money."

Sofia spent the morning screening phone calls, scheduling meetings for her boss, and answering his correspondence. Every time her phone rang, her heart skipped a beat, which she knew was silly in the extreme because Ethan didn't have her work number, and even if he did, he wouldn't be calling during the day.

She went to lunch with Mr. Donaldson's PA, Karen Stuart. Karen was in her mid-fifties, widowed, with three sons, two of whom still lived at home. She was always trying to fix Sofia up with her youngest, Jimmy, who was two years older than she was. Jimmy was a good-looking young man, with short brown hair and a crooked smile. Unfortunately, he was also a dyed-in-the-wool nerd with an affinity for "World of Warcraft" and "Doom."

Karen mentioned her son again during lunch.

"I'd really like to see my Jimmy dating a nice girl," Karen said, stirring cream into her coffee. "The girl he's dating now is a horrible influence on him."

"I'm sorry," Sofia said, "but I'm seeing someone."

Karen sighed dramatically. "I just know she's going to get him in trouble. If you break up with your young man, promise me you'll give my Jimmy a chance."

"I promise," Sofia said with a smile, and hoped it was a promise she would never have to keep.

Sofia shut her computer down at five, turned on her cell phone, and headed for home.

Her phone rang shortly after she walked in the door.

"Hey, beautiful, what are you doing?"

Just hearing Ethan's voice made her smile. "Taking off my shoes. What are you doing?"

"Wishing you were here."

"Where's here? You've never told me where you live."

"I've got a house in California. I just put it up for sale."

"Oh, why?"

"I decided it would be easier to move than to try to explain my sudden lifestyle change to my friends and neighbors."

"I never thought about that. Where are you moving to?"

"I found a place on the other side of town."

"My town?" she asked hopefully.

"Yeah. Do you mind?"

"Of course not." Sofia settled into a corner of the couch,

one leg tucked beneath her. "So, what's it like, this new house of yours?"

"It's just an old place that needs a lot of work."

"Sounds wonderful," she said dryly.

"I don't need much—just a place to sleep."

She clamped her lips together to keep from suggesting he move in with her. As much as she liked Ethan, moving in together was a big step, one she wasn't ready for. One she might never be ready for.

"You still there?" he asked.

"Yes. Are we still on for Friday?"

"You bet. What are you doing tonight?"

"Nothing; why?"

"How'd you like to go furniture shopping with me?"

"Sounds like fun. I *love* to shop."

"Pick you up in five?" he asked.

"Make it fifteen. I want to change clothes."

"Fifteen it is," he agreed, and ended the call.

Hurrying into her bedroom, Sofia changed out of her dress and heels and into a pair of jeans and a sweater. She brushed her teeth, ran a comb through her hair, applied fresh lipstick. She had just slipped on a pair of sandals when the doorbell rang.

It could have been anyone, but she knew it was Ethan, and it wasn't just because she was expecting him. She just *knew*. Was it because he'd tasted her blood?

Still pondering that, she opened the door. "Hi."

He whistled softly. "You look great."

She made a face at him.

"Honest." The jeans fit her like a second skin, the sweater outlined every delicious curve.

"So, what are we shopping for?" she asked, locking the door.

"Just the basics. Sofa, chair, bed. TV."

They took the elevator down to the parking garage.

Ethan whistled when he saw her car—a new Mustang with a convertible top. "Nice."

"You drive," she said, tossing him the keys.

He held her door for her, walked around the car, and slid behind the wheel. "You've got good taste in cars," he remarked as he started the engine and pulled out of the garage.

"You like Mustangs?"

"Yeah. I had one a year older than yours."

"What happened to it?"

"I don't know. Last time I saw it, it was parked outside the church where Holly got married. I guess it was stolen, because none of the impound lots I called had it."

"Wow, bummer."

"Yeah. I really miss that car." He braked at a stop sign. "So, where's the closest furniture store?"

"They have some really nice stuff here," Sofia said as Ethan pulled up in front of Finnegan's Furniture Outlet and parked the car. "And lots of choices."

Ethan killed the engine, got out of the car, opened her door for her.

A bell rang as they stepped inside. The furniture was laid out in sections—bedroom, living room, dining room, kitchen, kids' stuff.

"Shouldn't be too hard to find what you're looking for," Sofia remarked, smiling up at him.

She was right again. The sofa was easy. Ethan found a dark brown leather couch and matching chair he liked right away. He was fussier about the bed. He wanted something king-size and firm, and there were dozens to choose from.

"Which one do *you* like?" he asked after they had looked at everything twice.

"That one." The headboard was of carved oak.

Ethan looked at the bed, then at Sofia. She felt her cheeks grow warm under his gaze. She didn't have to be a mind reader to know he was imagining the two of them intimately entwined on the mattress.

"I'll take it," he told the salesman. "And that small dresser, too." He paid the bill and arranged for the furniture to be delivered the next night.

"Are you going to show me your new place?" she asked as they left the store.

"It's not much." He opened the car door for her.

"I'd still like to see it."

"All right."

She frowned as they left the city behind. "You found a house way out here?"

"It's not a house exactly."

She lifted one brow as they turned a corner. "What is it exactly?"

"An abandoned warehouse," he said, pulling into the parking lot behind the building.

"You're going to live *here*? Did you buy this place?"

"No. Judging from the rust and the dust, it's been abandoned for a long time. I figured I'd stay until I find a better place or until someone comes along and tells me to move." He didn't think that was likely to happen anytime soon. And if it did . . . hell, he'd worry about that if and when the time came.

"What about electricity? And water?"

"The water's still on. I can live without electricity, I guess." Although he'd need it if he wanted a TV in the place.

"Right. I forgot. So, do I get a tour?"

"Maybe next time. You wouldn't be able to see anything anyway."

"It's just as well," Sofia remarked. "It's getting late and I have to work tomorrow."

Ethan nodded. For her, the night was winding down. For him, it was just beginning.

"Thanks for going with me," he said as he pulled away from the curb.

"Thanks for asking me."

They drove the rest of the way in companionable silence. When they reached her place, he parked the car in the garage, held her hand in the elevator, walked her to her door.

"I'll call you tomorrow night," he said. "Oh, here." He dropped the keys to the Mustang into her hand.

She unlocked the apartment door, stepped inside, and switched on the light in the entryway. He paused a moment, then followed her inside and drew her into his embrace.

Ethan rested his forehead against hers. She felt so good in his arms, her slender body soft and pliable where his was hard and unyielding. He kissed her then, lightly at first, then longer, deeper. He needed her, he thought. She calmed the anger that still burned deep inside—anger at Saintcrow for turning him against his will, for stealing his life and everything that had been familiar. He knew it was foolish to blame Saintcrow when he should be blaming the vampire who had attacked him and left him for dead. Had that never happened, he would have met Sofia at the wedding, a mortal man who could hold her and kiss her without yearning to sink his fangs into her flesh and drink her dry.

He groaned as that need grew. "Sofie."

At her nod, he lowered his head to her neck. His tongue slid over her skin, sending a tingle down her spine. She leaned into him at the touch of his fangs, closed her eyes as pleasure moved through her. And for that moment, she felt what he was feeling—the way her blood warmed him, strengthened him, satisfied his hunger.

She shivered as his tongue sealed the tiny wounds in her throat.

He hugged her close for a moment, then tilted her face up. "Are you okay?"

"Fine."

Taking her by the hand, he led her to the sofa and pulled her down beside him.

"I felt you," she said, a note of wonder in her voice.

Ethan frowned. "What do you mean?"

"In my mind. I felt you there. It was weird. Kind of like I was you for just a moment. I knew what you were feeling, thinking."

He lifted one brow. "Really?" He wasn't sure he wanted her wandering around in his head. Some of his thoughts, especially those about her, were best kept private. "Has that ever happened before?"

"No."

He frowned, wondering why this time had been different. "I'd better go so you can get some sleep. I'll call you tomorrow night." He kissed her lightly. "Sweet dreams, sweet Sofie," he murmured.

And he was gone.

Chapter Six

Yawning, Sofia stretched her arms over her head. At last, it was Friday. She had hoped to see Ethan Wednesday night but discovered she was expected at a co-worker's wedding shower she had completely forgotten about.

Thursday night was her father's birthday and she couldn't skip that. She had been tempted to invite Ethan, but after the recent trouble with Leticia Braga, she wasn't sure how her family would react. Micah had lied to them about what he was for years, and even though they had accepted it, she doubted her parents would be thrilled at the thought of their youngest daughter dating one of the Undead. Accepting a son who was a vampire was one thing. A son-in-law was another.

But now it was Friday. She shut down her computer at five o'clock sharp, bid a quick good night to Mr. Moore, and was out the door and running for the elevator. Eager to get home and get ready for her date with Ethan, it was all she could do to keep from putting the pedal to the metal. She didn't know where they were going or what they were going to do, but it didn't matter as long as they were together.

But when she got home, her sister, Rosa, was inside, waiting for her.

"What's wrong?" Sofia asked, sitting on the couch beside Rosa.

"Nothing. Everything."

"Well, that clears things up," Sofia muttered. "Come on, 'fess up."

Rosa sighed dramatically. "I got fired today, and . . . Frankie broke up with me."

"Well, I'd love to feel sorry for you, but you hated your job. And Frankie's a jerk. So, I'm thinking we should celebrate with chocolate."

Rosa scowled at her a moment, then grinned. "I'd love something dark and rich."

"I have just what you need. Come on."

Sofia's phone rang on the way to the kitchen. "Go on, Rosie, I'll be there in a minute." When her sister was out of the room, she answered the phone. "Hi."

"Are we still on for tonight?"

"I'm not sure. My sister's here."

Ethan dragged a hand over his jaw. "I guess that means I'm persona non grata."

"I'm sorry, but, well, she's kind of down right now."

"Hey, I understand."

"It's not like that. It's just that . . ." Sofia broke off as Rosa stuck her head around the door. "Do you want hot fudge on yours?"

"Silly question."

Rosa looked at her, one brow raised, clearly wanting to know who was on the phone.

Sofia made a shooing motion with her hand.

With a knowing grin, Rosa went back into the kitchen.

"You still there?" Ethan asked.

"Yes. See you tomorrow night?"

"Sure; what time?"

"As soon as the sun goes down."

Chuckling, he ended the call.

"All right," Rosa said, carrying two bowls filled to the brim with chocolate ice cream topped with hot fudge and whipped cream. "Who are you going to see tomorrow night? You never told me you were dating anyone."

"Just a guy."

"Well, duh, I figured that," she said, following Sofia back to the couch. "Details, girl. I want details."

Sofia shrugged. "I met him a few days ago. He seems nice."

"Well, they all seem nice in the beginning."

"Careful, Rosie, your bitterness is showing."

"Is he anyone I know?"

"No."

"So, what's he look like? How old is he? What does he do for a living?"

"He's got dark blond hair and the most gorgeous brown eyes. He's twenty-six and at the moment, he's unemployed."

"Twenty-six!" Rosa exclaimed, grinning. "An older man."

"Not *that* much older."

"So, when do I get to meet him?"

"I don't know."

Rosa waggled her eyebrows. "Maybe I'll just stop by tomorrow night when the sun goes down . . ." Her eyes widened. "Sundown? Oh, Sofie, he's not a vampire, is he?"

"Why on earth would you jump to such a conclusion?"

"Why do you think? Does the name Micah mean anything to you?"

"Just because I'm meeting him after dark doesn't mean . . . oh, hell," she muttered. "He's Holly's cousin. Ethan. Saintcrow turned him at the wedding."

Rosa shook her head. "I was just kidding about him being a vampire. Sofie, what are you thinking? Have you forgotten that awful Braga creature and what she did? Mama still has nightmares about it."

"Ethan's not like that. Promise me you won't say anything to the family. I mean, it might not last, so there's no sense worrying everybody."

"I don't know . . ."

"If you say a word, I'll tell Daddy who really put that dent in his new car."

"Okay, fine, I promise!" Rosa said petulantly. "But I still want to meet him."

Chapter Seven

Sofia was on edge all day Saturday. It didn't bother her that Ethan was a vampire. She could learn to live with that, but she still couldn't help wishing he was just an ordinary guy, that she could call him and wish him good morning, that they could go out to breakfast and spend the whole day together.

She changed the sheets on her bed, did the laundry, took her car to the car wash. On the way home, she stopped at the store to buy groceries for the week, and all the while, she wished Ethan was beside her. If they stayed together, she would never cook him dinner, never share a meal with him. True, there were lots of things they could do together after the sun went down—go for moonlight strolls, take in a movie, wander through the mall.

At five o'clock, she took a long shower, washed her hair, shaved her legs. It took her thirty minutes to decide what to wear, twenty minutes to do her hair and nails, and she was ready to go five minutes before the sun went down.

Ethan knocked at the door ten minutes later, his hair still wet from his shower. He stepped across the threshold, took her in his arms, kicked the door shut with his heel, and kissed her until she was breathless.

"Did you miss me?" he asked with a knowing grin.

"Maybe a little."

"Wow, I can't wait to see what it's like when you miss me a lot."

Rising on her tiptoes, she wrapped her arms around his neck and pulled his head down toward her. "Shut up and kiss me again."

He was all too willing to oblige.

When they came up for air, Sofia blew out a sigh. "Okay, we need to slow down."

"If you say so."

"I do. So, did your furniture get delivered?"

"Yeah. The place is so big, it still looks empty. I'm still trying to figure out a way to get some electricity in there so I can have a TV."

"Good luck with that. I don't see how you can get the electric company to turn on the power when you're not the owner."

Ethan frowned. "There might be a way around that," he drawled. It was easy enough to mesmerize his prey. If he could do that, it shouldn't be too difficult to hypnotize workers into believing he owned the place.

"What way?"

"I'll tell you after I see if it works." For a moment, he thought she would argue, but, apparently, she thought better of it.

"So, what do you want to do tonight?" she asked.

He shrugged. "Anything you'd like to do is fine with me."

She looked thoughtful for a moment, then said, "I think we should go bowling."

"Bowling?"

She nodded.

"You're not afraid to be alone with me, are you?"

"Yes. You're far too tempting. Let's go."

* * *

"What else do you want to do?" Ethan asked. They had gone to the bowling alley only to find out that some league was having its tournament and there were no lanes available.

"Let's just go for a walk," Sofia suggested. "There's a nice park not far from here. It's well-lit at night."

Ethan shrugged. "A walk it is."

It took only minutes to reach their destination. Hand in hand, they strolled along wide cement paths lined with lacy ferns and flowers.

"I've never been here at night before," Sofia remarked. "It's pretty, isn't it?"

"Yeah." Drawing Sofia toward him, he stepped aside to allow a couple of joggers to pass. The faint scent of her perfume wafted to him on the breeze, along with the scent of her hair and skin. And her blood. Always the blood, he thought. Would there come a time when being with her didn't spike his hunger? When he could take her in his arms with no thought other than to hold a beautiful young woman?

She looked up, her gaze meeting his. Her hair shone blue black in the glow of a nearby light. Unable to resist, he slid his hands into the heavy mass. It fell through his fingers like ribbons of dark silk.

In her apartment, in the park, it didn't matter where they were. He wanted her.

"Come on," he said, taking her by the hand. "Let's go get a drink."

They stopped at the first nightclub they saw. Like most clubs, the interior of Roxy's was dark and intimate. Dim lighting, soft, sensual music, booths with high backs that offered a degree of privacy.

Another bad choice, Ethan thought as he slid into the booth beside her.

"Sofia? Hey, *chica*, is that you?"

A waiter with a wide smile stared down at Sofia. "Long time no see," he said, winking at her.

Sofia shrank back against Ethan, her face suddenly pale.

"Mateo," the waiter said. "Don't you remember me? I'm a friend of Jack's."

She nodded, her body trembling. She had seen him with her former boyfriend, Jack, a few times. He had even made a pass at her once or twice. He was a good-looking guy with black hair and dark eyes, but something about the way he had looked at her, as if he couldn't wait to pounce on her, like a cat on a mouse, had always made her wary.

"I haven't seen Jack lately," Mateo said. "Do you know if he left town?"

Sofia pressed closer to Ethan. "I don't know where he is."

"I haven't seen Cash, either. It's kinda strange, Jack and the boss both disappearing at the same time." Eyes narrowing, Mateo looked at Ethan. "You didn't have anything to do with it, did you?"

"Never met either one of them," Ethan said, steel underlying his voice.

Mateo grunted. "So, what'll you two have?"

Ethan ordered a glass of chardonnay, Sofia asked for a tequila sunrise.

"Who the hell was that?" Ethan asked when Mateo went to turn in their order.

"Just some guy I met once or twice. I used to date Jack, back in my goth period," she said. "Jack was kind of dark and edgy, and I found that appealing. Turns out he belonged to a vampire named Cash. One night, Jack took me to Cash's tavern . . ." She shuddered with the memory. "Anyway, if Micah hadn't found me . . ."

"You don't have to say any more." There was no doubt in Ethan's mind that Sofia's brother had killed Jack and destroyed Cash. "Too bad he didn't kill Mateo, too."

"Why would he kill Mateo? He never did anything."

"The guy's a vampire." Ethan grinned inwardly. He didn't miss the irony of wanting a vampire dead when he was one himself.

Sofia's eyes widened with shock. "Are you sure?"

"Oh yeah."

She shook her head. No wonder Mateo had inspired such fear in her. "I never would have guessed."

"That's the idea," Ethan said dryly. "Better for all concerned if we don't advertise it."

Sofia stuck her tongue out at him. "Very funny."

Mateo winked at her when he returned with their drinks. "Maybe we can get together sometime, *chica*," he suggested.

"I don't think so. I'm . . ."

"The lady's with me," Ethan said. "I suggest you stay away from her if you know what's good for you."

Mateo glared at Ethan, then turned on his heel and stalked away.

"You'd better stay away from that guy," Ethan said. "He's no good."

"Gee, you think?"

Chuckling, Ethan picked up his drink. And spat it out into his napkin.

"What's wrong?" Sofia asked.

"I think our waiter added a little something extra to the wine."

"Like what?"

"Ground oleander," Ethan replied. Not that it could hurt him. But it was a warning.

Sofia's brows shot up. "Oleander! But . . . that's poisonous."

"Yeah." Ethan's gaze swept the room, eyes narrowing

when he saw Mateo standing near the bar, a smirk on his face. Ethan grunted softly. They would meet again, he thought. And when they did, only one of them would walk away.

Sofia sighed as they left the club two hours later. She hated to go home. It had been nice chatting with Ethan, being in his arms when they danced, laughing together as they shared stories of their childhood. The only downside had been Mateo. Time and again, she had caught him watching her every move, like a snake stalking a rabbit. Once, she had seen him glaring at Ethan, his eyes filled with such loathing it had made her shiver.

It was still fresh in her mind as they walked back to the park to pick up her car. She wasn't surprised when they turned a corner and found Mateo waiting there, legs slightly spread, arms folded over his chest. Somehow, she had known they would see him again. He was a little taller than Ethan, though not as broad through the chest and shoulders.

Ethan came to an abrupt halt and stepped in front of Sofia. "You want to do this now?" he asked, glancing around. "Here?"

Mateo jerked his head toward the alley beside him. "In there."

Ethan's first thought was to tell Mateo to go to hell, then take Sofia home, but he quickly dismissed that idea. Whether he walked her back to her car or used his vampire powers to transport her home, it would be all too easy for the other vampire to follow. Better to get rid of the threat once and for all. "After you."

Mateo winked at Sofia. "This won't take long, *chica*."

Locking his gaze on Mateo, Ethan spoke to Sofia's mind. *As soon as we're out of sight, go home and lock the door.* He didn't wait for an answer. Still looking at Mateo, he said, "Let's get this over with."

Smirking, Mateo led the way into the alley.

Ethan followed, all his senses alert as he searched for some hint that Mateo had help hidden in the darkness, but he detected no one else lurking in the shadows.

When Mateo reached the middle of the alley, he whirled around, a faint shaft of moonlight glinting on the ten-inch blade in his hand.

Ethan snorted. "I didn't think you'd fight fair."

Mateo shrugged and lunged forward, the knife slicing toward Ethan's throat.

Ethan ducked it easily enough, feinted to the right, and drove his fist into the other man's face.

Dark red blood spurted from Mateo's nose. He let out an angry roar and charged again. And again.

Ethan avoided the blows. It soon became obvious Mateo wasn't the street fighter he thought he was, and just as obvious his preternatural powers weren't as strong as Ethan's and never would be, due to the fact that Ethan had been turned by one of the oldest vampires in existence. He dodged every blow easily, his own fists finding their mark every time.

Whether he was a coward or just smart, Mateo knew when he'd had enough. With a cry of frustration, he made one last swipe with the knife and vanished from the alley.

"Shit," Ethan muttered. "I doubt if I've seen the last of him."

After wiping his bloody hands on his jeans, he willed himself to Sofia's apartment.

Sofia paced the living room. Had she done the right thing in leaving Ethan? What could she have done if she had stayed? Calling the police had been her first instinct, but she had immediately squelched it, certain Ethan would not want the cops involved.

Her mind filled with images of the two vampires ripping each other to shreds. She knew vampires grew stronger with age, and Ethan was still a fledgling. She comforted herself with the knowledge that Saintcrow had sired him. Hopefully, being turned by a vampire who had lived during the Crusades would make him Mateo's equal, if not stronger.

She ran to the door when the bell rang, then hesitated. "Ethan?"

"Yeah, it's me."

She flung open the door, her gaze quickly moving over him. His clothes were spattered with blood, but he seemed unhurt. "Are you all right?"

"I'm fine." He followed her into the living room. "Mind if I wash up?"

She shook her head, relieved he hadn't been hurt. Or killed.

"Hey, I'm fine," he said again.

"I know, but I was so worried."

She followed him to the bathroom, stood in the doorway while he washed the dried blood from his face and hands, then ran a comb through his hair.

He grimaced at the crimson stains on his shirt, then took it off and tossed it in the wastebasket beside the sink.

Sofia stared at him, hands clenched to keep from running her fingers over his chest and down his arms. She didn't know if vampires worked out, but he must have done so at some point in his life, because he was buff to the max.

Ethan grinned when he looked in the mirror again and caught Sofia staring at him.

Cheeks flushing, she turned away. "Can I get you any . . . ?"

She bit off the last word, remembering she couldn't offer him cake or cookies or a cup of coffee. Only a glass of wine. The words *or your blood* whispered through the back of her mind.

Her skin tingled when he came up behind her. She could feel him standing there, close, so close, but he didn't touch her.

"I should go," he said quietly. "I'm sorry for the way things turned out tonight."

"It wasn't your fault."

He swore under his breath, thinking how foolish he had been to think he could have a normal relationship with Sofia, or with any woman, when so many things were against it, not the least of which was his infernal hunger. It was always there, sometimes resting beneath the surface, making him think he had it under control, sometimes clawing relentlessly at his vitals until he thought he might go mad with need . . . the way it was now, no doubt stirred to life by his fight with Mateo.

Sofia's scent filled Ethan's nostrils. The rhythmic beat of her heart, fast now that he was so near, was like sweet music to his ears. Her blood called to him, a constant temptation with its promise of relief from the craving that colored his every thought.

"Ethan?" She still had her back toward him.

And suddenly he couldn't face her. Silent as the clouds drifting across the sky, he transformed into mist and left her standing there.

She knew he was gone even before she turned around. Disappointment swept through her, followed by a quick rush of irritation. Why did he always run away? Sure, she had been scared earlier, but she wasn't some hothouse flower that would wilt at the first sign of trouble. And yes, she had been afraid when Mateo confronted them, but running away hadn't even entered her mind. She had known about vampires before she met Ethan, and what she hadn't known, she had learned from Micah. Day or night, she never left her apartment without a good stout stake tucked into her handbag and Micah's number on speed dial. A girl couldn't go through life being constantly afraid of what might happen, but a *smart* girl was always prepared.

Chapter Eight

Ethan materialized on the bridge leading to Morgan Creek. A deserted ghost town was just where he belonged, he thought as he strolled down the main street. There were no temptations in this dismal place, just the spirits of the men and women who had died here, if what Saintcrow had said was true.

Ethan had never believed in ghosts, but then, he had never really believed in vampires either, which made him wonder what other supernatural creatures might actually exist. Werewolves? Trolls? Zombies? Bigfoot? The Loch Ness monster? Hell, maybe they were all real.

He paused as a cold chill caressed his cheek. Odd, when there was no hint of a breeze. And then he chuckled. One of Morgan Creek's ghosts, maybe. Kadie was sure they lingered in the shadows of the town.

He passed a few businesses, all long empty, swore softly as he felt the same chilly sensation, stronger now, as the words *She's in danger* whispered in the back of his mind.

It wasn't his imagination, not this time. He focused all

his thoughts on Sofia and knew the ghost or whatever had tried to contact him was right. She was in danger.

With a muttered curse, he willed himself to her apartment.

The door stood open.

"Sofie!" he called, his voice edged with panic when he saw that someone had jimmied the lock. He didn't have to go inside to know she was gone.

Mateo! An indrawn breath carried his stink. Ethan swore again. How had the vampire gotten inside? Surely Sofia wouldn't have invited him in.

It was easy enough to follow the vampire's scent. It led out of town, twisted through a maze of new construction, and ended in a tavern that had obviously been out of business for several years.

Ethan slowed as he drew closer, his senses sweeping the area. Sofia was here, along with Mateo and another human whose scent he didn't recognize. Undoubtedly the stranger was the one who had burst into Sofia's apartment and dragged her outside.

Something he would live to regret, Ethan vowed.

He stood in the shadows, unmoving, as he determined Sofia's location. She was in a dark room. A basement, maybe, or a storage area. Mateo and his companion were in the tavern's main room.

Ethan frowned as he detected the heartbeat of a second female and then, a moment later, the unmistakable copper-tinged aroma of freshly spilled blood. He clenched his hands into tight fists. Was Mateo easing his hunger? Or was he baiting the trap?

Ethan licked his lips as the scent of blood grew stronger, the woman's heartbeat weaker. She was dying.

"Shit!" Gathering his power, Ethan propelled himself toward the tavern. He kicked the door open, broke the neck of Mateo's companion, grabbed the other vampire by the arm, and hurled him across the room.

Mateo crashed into the wall but quickly recovered. He smiled, fangs gleaming in the semidarkness. "Took you long enough," he said with a sneer.

Ethan wasn't in the mood for chitchat. Driven by his hunger and his fear for Sofia, he lunged forward, his hands curling around the other vampire's throat, driving him back against the wall.

Mateo struggled, his nails gouging Ethan's face and throat in a frantic effort to free himself.

"No way," Ethan snarled. Ripping the vampire's heart from his chest, he threw it across the room. It hit the far wall with a juicy splat.

The woman moaned softly as she struggled for breath. Ethan turned toward her. The scent of her blood, hot and fresh, drew him across the floor to her side. As though he had no will of his own, he dropped to his knees, his whole being focused on the steady stream of crimson leaking from the gash in her throat.

She was so near death, what would it matter if he drained her of what little life remained?

As from far away, he heard footsteps. A harsh gasp of shock. Someone calling his name.

"Ethan? Ethan!"

Sofia. It took him a moment to remember why he was there.

"Ethan?"

Guilt at what he had almost done rose up in him, and with it a deep sense of shame. "Are you all right?" His voice was harsh. He didn't look at her.

"Y . . . yes."

As she drew closer, he barked, "Stay where you are!" Dammit! How long had she been standing there? How much had she seen?

He took several deep breaths, then bit into his wrist. Forcing the woman's mouth open, he let his blood drip onto her tongue.

Sofia gasped. "What are you doing?"

"Saving her life, if she's not too far gone."

Sofia glanced around the room. Mateo lay in a heap on the floor, a gaping hole in his chest. The horrid man who had dragged her out of her apartment lay a few feet away, his head at an unnatural angle. And then there was Ethan, kneeling on the floor, his eyes almost as red as the blood dribbling into the woman's mouth. The stink of urine and death hung heavy in the musty air.

It was like some grisly scene from a slasher movie.

Stomach roiling, she ran behind the bar and retched in the sink.

When her stomach quieted, she wiped her mouth with the back of her hand, then stood there, listening. The woman had stopped moaning. Was she dead? Where was Ethan? Taking a deep breath, Sofia risked a glance over her shoulder.

The woman was still on the floor. Ethan sat beside her, head bowed, hands clenched at his sides.

"Ethan?"

"Give me a minute and I'll take you home."

"Is she going to be a vampire now?"

"No. She's just asleep. She'll be all right when she wakes up."

"How did you find me?"

"If I told you, you wouldn't believe it."

"Try me."

"I went back to Morgan Creek. One of the ghosts warned me that you were in danger."

"A *ghost* told you?"

He nodded. "I went to your apartment. You were gone. I followed Mateo's scent here." He shrugged, as if there was nothing more to say.

Suddenly cold, Sofia folded her arms over her chest. She could have been killed tonight. "Ethan."

He took a deep, calming breath, then stood. "Come on. I'll take you home."

"What about the woman?"

"I'll come back for her."

She tried not to notice the blood splattered over his face and clothing, tried not to flinch when he wrapped his arms around her. Taking a deep breath, she closed her eyes.

Traveling vampire-style was a little unsettling, like hurtling through time and space on a roller coaster. It left her feeling a little dizzy.

When she opened her eyes, she was standing in the middle of her living room, alone.

Keeping his mind carefully blank, Ethan returned to the tavern for the woman. Her eyelids fluttered open when he lifted her into his arms.

"Where do you live?" he asked.

Trapped in the web of his gaze, she gave him her address.

Outside her house, Ethan wiped all memory of what had happened from her mind, then carried her to the front door and rang the bell. When he heard footsteps, he willed himself back to the tavern. He dragged Mateo's body outside, where the morning sun would quickly disintegrate the remains. He left the dead man inside. Sooner or later, someone would find him.

Ethan thought briefly of going back to Sofia's to make sure she was all right, but then he remembered how she had looked at him, the revulsion in her eyes.

Sofia closed the door, shot the dead bolt home, then placed a chair under the knob. For a moment, she just stood there, wondering if she would ever again feel safe in her apartment, or anywhere else for that matter. She longed for a hot bath to wash away Mateo's touch but couldn't abide the thought of being naked and vulnerable.

She settled for washing her hands, face, and arms, then slipped into her nightgown. Leaving all the lights burning in the living room and bedroom, she crawled into bed, where she huddled under her blankets.

But every time she closed her eyes, she saw Mateo's friend coming through the door, remembered trying to fight him off, the sickly sweet scent of the drug on the rag he had pressed over her mouth and nose, waking up in the dark. She remembered using a hairpin to unlock the door, then creeping up the stairs.

And into the middle of a nightmare. She had never seen so much blood.

She had been relieved to see Ethan and yet repelled as well. She knew he had killed Mateo and the other man. She had little doubt that the night would have ended differently if Mateo had won the battle. Ethan had likely saved her from a horrible death. And yet . . . she knew the memory of what she had seen would stay with her forever.

Micah had tried to tell her what it was like to be a vampire.

Tonight, she had seen it with her own eyes.

It was a lesson she would never forget.

Chapter Nine

Ethan strolled the dark streets of Morgan Creek. After last night, he was pretty sure Sofia wasn't in any itching hurry to be with him again. He'd seen the look of revulsion in her eyes, sensed her horror at what had happened. Not that he blamed her. She'd seen things no mortal should ever see.

With a pithy curse, he shut her out of his mind. So much for dating, he mused glumly. He had given it a try. Now what? He had been a vampire only a couple of months. What did vampires do with their time? It didn't take long to hunt for prey, and once that was done, what was left? Sure, Saintcrow had suggested Ethan travel the world. Easy for him to say. The master vampire could be awake during the day. He had a beautiful wife who adored him. He was richer than Donald Trump. He had lairs all over the world.

Comparing himself to Saintcrow was ludicrous. Ethan shook his head. He had sold his home, which would leave him with a few thousand dollars after he'd paid off the Realtor and his loan. True, Saintcrow had said he could stay here as long as he wanted, but there wasn't a helluva lot to do in Morgan Creek, other than run old films in the movie theater.

He dragged a hand across his jaw as he passed the old gas pump. When he had first seen the town, he'd thought that, if it was his, he would level all the buildings and start from scratch. But now, with a second look, he changed his mind. He had dabbled a little in real estate, enough to realize that there was a certain rustic charm to Morgan Creek. The old gas pump was vintage. The tavern reminded him of a Roaring 20s speakeasy. The houses were good-sized and had been well cared for. If someone added a few modern conveniences, upgraded the carpets and the appliances, repainted the houses inside and out, they would make great summer rentals. The theater had recently been updated. With a good hotel and restaurant, and a pool that wasn't cracked, Morgan Creek could be turned into a profitable vacation resort. But, again, he didn't have that kind of money.

But Saintcrow did.

Pulling his cell phone from his pocket, Ethan called the master vampire.

Saintcrow answered on the second ring. "What's wrong now?"

"You said I could stay here as long as I like, right?"

"Yeah."

Ethan didn't miss the wariness in Saintcrow's voice. "How would you feel about giving me a loan?"

"For what?"

"I'd like to turn this place into a resort. Swimming in the summer. Skiing in the winter. I thought I'd renovate that old hotel and all the other buildings, especially the restaurant. The pool needs some work, too. The theater looks pretty good."

"So, after you turn the town into Shangri-la, who's gonna run it? You?"

"I guess I'd have to hire some help to work during the day, and . . ." Ethan paused when he heard Kadie's voice asking questions in the background.

"Kadie says do whatever you want, we'll pay the bills."

Ethan blinked several times, unable to believe his ears. "You mean it?" It was too easy, he thought. There had to be a catch.

"Just one thing," Saintcrow said. "Make that two things."

Ethan blew out a sigh. *Here it comes.*

"Don't touch my lair or tear down Blair House. Do whatever you want with the rest of the town. Oh, and Kadie says don't get rid of the old gas pump. And don't mess with the cemetery."

"About the cemetery—would it be okay if I replaced the old wooden fence with a wrought-iron one, and maybe replace some of the markers? Might make an interesting attraction for tourists."

Ethan heard the phone change hands, and then Kadie's voice came over the line. "If you make it modern and re-place all the old markers, it will just look like any other cemetery. I think you should leave it alone."

"You heard the boss," Saintcrow said. "Keep us up-to-date."

"Send photos!" Kadie called as Saintcrow disconnected the call.

Ethan slipped his phone back into his pocket, unable to believe the master vampire had pretty much given him the go-ahead to do whatever he wanted, except for sprucing up the old graveyard. And perhaps Kadie was right about that. It did have a certain rustic charm.

Whistling softly, he started toward the house he had stayed in after Saintcrow turned him, then paused. None of the houses in the residential area offered any kind of security while he was trapped in the dark sleep. If he was going to be here a while, he needed a secure lair, a place where he could rest without worrying about someone breaking in.

He glanced at the three-story mansion on the hill. Blair House. The Morgan Creek vampires had once lived there. Grunting softly, he ran effortlessly up the road to the house. There were a lot of things he didn't like about being a vampire, but being able to run faster than the human eye could follow wasn't one of them.

The door opened easily enough. The interior was dark and musty. The scents of the house's previous occupants, though faint, lingered in the drapes and the carpets, in the very air, as did the smell of old blood and death. People had died here, both human and vampire.

He strolled along the dark corridors, peering into the rooms he passed. They were little more than jail cells, he thought glumly, furnished only with narrow beds and antique dressers. The floors were cold and bare, the windows were covered with heavy drapes. From talking to Saintcrow, he knew the vampires had spent their waking hours in the town.

Eventually, he came to a narrow set of stairs that led downstairs. There was nothing at the bottom but an iron-barred door. It opened on silent hinges, revealing a large, square room. There was no lock on the outside of the door, but several on the inside. The floor down here was cement. An old-fashioned coffin lined in white silk stood against the far wall. A twin bed was pushed against the wall opposite. There was nothing else in the room. He certainly didn't want to spend his waking hours here, but definitely his days. He'd bring a bigger, more comfortable bed from one of the houses below.

Leaving Blair House behind, he strolled down the hill to the house he had used before, his mind filled with ideas for modernizing the town.

Chapter Ten

Sofia picked up her phone, looked at it a minute, then dropped it back on the table. Five days had passed since she had last seen or heard from Ethan. Several times a day, she had been tempted to call him, but she always resisted the urge. She wasn't sure why. Yes, she had been shocked at the carnage she had seen. Yes, she had known Ethan was a vampire and capable of almost anything. And yes, she liked being with him, and she had known what he was when she agreed to go out with him. Had he been human, she might easily have fallen in love with him. But he wasn't human, and even though she had known what he was capable of, knowing and seeing it in living color were two different things. And she just wasn't sure she could handle it.

Falling back on the sofa, she closed her eyes. She reached for her phone again but didn't pick it up, afraid if she did, it would start something she might regret.

Ethan sat on the front porch of the house in Morgan Creek. He had made a lot of progress in the last five nights. He had found a contractor in a nearby city who had been willing to drive out, look the town over, and meet with him later, after dark. They met, and Ethan had outlined his ideas.

The contractor, who had introduced himself as Alan Reed, had made a few rough sketches, said he could handle the work and knew people who could manage anything he couldn't. He also said he knew someone who could replaster the pool.

Ethan had been happy with Reed. With his preternatural senses, he knew the man was telling the truth. Reed had said he would need a deposit up front and Ethan had assured him the money would be in the man's account the following day.

"I'll get my crew together," Reed said. "It'll take me a couple of days to line up the permits and purchase the supplies we'll need."

They shook hands, and the contractor hopped in his truck and drove over the bridge to the highway.

A couple of days, Ethan mused. So far, so good, he thought, but he needed someone who could look after things while he was at rest. Someone to pay the bills, make decisions if necessary. Dammit, he hated being dead to the world when the sun was up!

He pulled his phone from his pocket and checked his messages. Not that he expected Sofia to call him after what had happened a week ago. He had started to call her a dozen times, but he'd chickened out every time. But damn, he missed her! He longed to hear her voice, see her smile, taste her kisses, inhale the warm womanly scent of her skin. He wanted to take her in his arms and make slow, sweet love to her until the sun came up.

Biting back an oath, he slammed his fist on the porch step, so hard he cracked the wood.

Lurching to his feet, he stalked into the darkness, his anger stirring the desire to hunt. To bury his fangs in human flesh and to hell with the consequences. He was a monster and he always would be. Better to end it now than spend the rest of his existence alone.

A thought took him to the next town. Saintcrow had vowed to destroy him if he took a life. And tonight was as good a time as any. He found his prey standing on a corner, waiting for the light to change. He hypnotized her with a glance and carried her to a deserted part of town, away from prying eyes.

"Come and get me, Saintcrow!" he bellowed, and lowered his head to her neck.

"Dammit!"

Kadie glanced up from the book she had been reading, startled by the vehemence in Rylan's voice. "What's wrong?"

"It's that damn-fool cousin of Holly's. He wants to die."

"What? Why?"

"No time to explain," he said.

Moments later, he stood at Ethan's side. One look at the deathly white pallor of his prey's face and Saintcrow knew he'd barely arrived in time. Without a word, he pulled Ethan away from the woman, caught her before she fell facedown in the dirt.

Fangs bared, Ethan growled at him.

Saintcrow let his own fangs run out, let his eyes go red. Let his power wash over the other vampire.

Ethan reeled back under the onslaught, then turned his head to the side. "Go on; what are you waiting for?" Before his sire could answer, Ethan's phone rang.

"You wanna take that before I rip your heart out?" Saintcrow asked.

Ethan yanked his phone from his pocket.

It was Sofia.

Taking a deep breath, he growled, "Hey, Sofie."

"Ethan, are you all right?"

"Yeah, I'm fine. Why?"

"I was watching TV and I had this terrible feeling you were in danger. I know it sounds silly. At first, I tried to ignore it, but it just got stronger. Are you sure you're all right?"

"Yeah." The sound of her voice washed over him, calming the monster within. "Can I call you right back?"

"Sure."

"All right," Saintcrow said as Ethan ended the call. "What the hell is this all about?"

"I want to finish this. Now. Tonight."

Saintcrow shook his head. "Last week you were gung ho to rebuild Morgan Creek." He shifted the woman in his arms. He'd have to give her some blood soon. "What happened between then and now?"

Voice curt, Ethan told him about his run-in with Mateo. "Sofia saw it all. She's never going to think of me as anything but a monster now."

"Is that why she called? To tell you that you're a monster?"

"You know why she called." There was no such thing as privacy when a master vampire was around.

"She was worried about you." Saintcrow bit into his wrist, pried the woman's mouth open, and dribbled some blood inside.

Guilt ate at Ethan's soul as he watched the woman swallow once, twice, three times. Color returned to her cheeks, but she didn't wake up.

Saintcrow sealed the shallow gash in his wrist. "It's been my experience that the female of the species doesn't worry about a man if she doesn't have feelings for him."

"Then why didn't she call sooner?"

"Why didn't *you* call *her*?"

"How do you know that I didn't?"

Saintcrow snorted. "You damn fool! I know everything

you do." He glanced down at the woman in his arms, then spoke a few quiet words. Her eyelids fluttered open and she stared at him, her expression blank. When he set her on her feet, she walked away without a backward glance.

"How'd you get here so fast? I thought you were still in Scotland."

"Kadie wanted to be in New Orleans for Mardi Gras. Great place to be a vampire," Saintcrow remarked with a grin. "Easy pickings among the tourists. A real smorgasbord."

Ethan shook his head in wry amusement.

"So, are we done here?"

"Yeah."

"Give yourself some time," Saintcrow said quietly. "And call Sofia. She's a good influence on you, like Kadie was—and still is—on me." He grinned again. "Never underestimate the power of a good woman."

Ethan laughed despite himself. "All right, Dad."

"Or the power of good blood." Lifting his arm, Saintcrow bit into his wrist and held it out. His eyes took on a faint red glow. "Drink."

Ethan tensed as Saintcrow's preternatural power rolled over him with all the strength of a tsunami. It was a fearsome thing, that ancient power, dark and heavy and compelling. There were centuries behind that power, yet it was more than age.

"Why?"

"Just do it."

Ethan stared at the dark red blood oozing from the shallow gash. He didn't remember much about the night Saintcrow had turned him, except gagging on the blood. Did he really want to drink it again? But Saintcrow seemed insistent, so he took hold of his sire's arm and drank.

The sheer power of Saintcrow's ancient blood exploded through every nerve and fiber of his being, more potent than anything he had ever known. It burned through his veins like hellfire. One taste and he wanted more. Wanted it all. If he drank enough, he would be invincible. Perhaps even able to walk in the daylight again.

"Enough."

Ethan heard the word, but it meant nothing to him.

And then Saintcrow's power slammed into him again.

Ethan dropped his sire's arm and reeled back. "You should bottle that stuff. Vampires would pay millions for it."

"I'll keep that in mind," Saintcrow said dryly.

Ethan licked the last drops of blood from his lips. It sizzled through him like heat lightning.

Saintcrow slapped Ethan on the shoulder. "You'll be all right now, fledgling. Call the girl."

And with that last bit of advice, the master vampire was gone.

Ethan stood there for several minutes, gathering his courage, then he pulled out his phone and called Sofia.

"Ethan. Hi."

"Did you want something?"

"I thought I did." Her annoyance came through loud and clear.

"I'm sorry, Sofie. I've just been going through a bad time."

"Is that why you never called me?"

"After what happened with Mateo, I didn't figure you'd ever want to see me again."

"At first, I didn't think I would," she admitted. "But then . . ."

"Then what?" He clenched his hands while waiting for her answer.

"I started missing you." Her voice was so quiet, only a vampire could have heard it.

"I miss you, too, Sofie. You have no idea how much."

"Are you coming back here?"

"I don't know. I had this idea about Morgan Creek."

"That place in Wyoming?"

"Yeah. I got to thinking it would make a great resort. Hiking and swimming in the summer, skiing in the winter."

"Oh?"

"Yeah. I talked to Saintcrow about it and he gave me the green light. Said he'd foot the bill."

"Wow, that's really generous of him."

"Well, I don't know about that. It's his town, after all."

"I never knew anyone who owned a whole town."

"Me either." He stared into the darkness a moment, gathering his courage. "Would you like to see it?"

"I don't know. Maybe." She fell quiet, thinking it over. "I would kind of like to see where Micah spent so much time."

"It's kind of late tonight," he said. "How about if I pick you up tomorrow as soon as the sun goes down?"

"All right."

"Dress warm. It's still cold here."

"I will. Good night, Ethan."

"'Night, Sofie."

Whistling softly, he willed himself back to Morgan Creek, thinking life was starting to look a whole lot better.

Rosa stared at her younger sister. "You're going where?"

"Morgan Creek. It's in Wyoming."

"Are you crazy? Isn't that where that awful vampire, Saintcrow, lives?"

"He's not there right now. No one's there but Ethan."

Rosa's eyes widened. "You really are crazy if you're thinking of going there alone! Good gosh, Sofia, have you lost your mind? Ghost town!" she exclaimed dramatically. "Vampire! Girl alone! Cue the scary music."

"I'm not afraid of Ethan."

"Well, from all you've told me, you should be. At least tell Micah where you're going."

"No! And don't you tell him either. He's on his honeymoon. If you call him, he'll come home. And Holly will hate me."

"She's too nice to hate anybody," Rosa said.

"Promise me."

"If Mom and Dad find out I didn't tell them, they'll disown me."

Sofia laughed. "No, they won't. You've talked your way out of way worse things than this. Anyway, I'll be fine."

Sighing with resignation, Rosa said, "All right. I won't say anything, as long as you call me as soon as you get back."

"It's a deal."

"Don't forget your wooden stake."

"No chance," Sofia said with an inward grin. "I never leave home without it."

Chapter Eleven

Saturday morning bloomed bright and clear. Despite her assurances to Rosa that she'd be fine in Morgan Creek, Sofia was a nervous wreck. She plunged into her chores with a vengeance—vacuuming, dusting, washing the windows. She went to the grocery store, stopped at the car wash, dropped in to visit her parents only to find they weren't home.

Back at her apartment, she took a shower, washed her hair, and spent forty minutes deciding what to wear, always conscious of time passing.

Ethan's knock came five minutes after the sun went down. Taking a deep breath, she grabbed her jacket and opened the door. "Hi."

"Are you ready?"

She nodded. What had she been worried about? She had let Rosa's fears get to her, she thought irritably. This was Ethan, looking handsome and harmless in a pair of blue jeans and a dark green shirt.

He put his arm around her. "Hang on."

She closed her eyes as she experienced the familiar sense of flying through time and space. When she opened her eyes again, they were standing in front of an old hotel.

All the lights were on inside, as well as in every other building as far as she could see.

"What plans do you have for the hotel?" she asked.

"New front, modern interior, that kind of thing. Why?"

"It has a lot of old-world charm. There are lots of up-scale hotels, but I was thinking, maybe you should modernize the plumbing and the kitchen equipment and that kind of thing but keep the antique feel of the exterior and the interior. But, I mean, it's your place."

"I think maybe you're right. So, do you want a tour?" he asked, taking her hand.

She blinked several times, then nodded.

The town looked like it had once been a nice place, she mused as they walked along.

"I was going to modernize everything," Ethan remarked. "But you've changed my mind. I think we'll try to hang on to the 1920s feel of the place as far as interiors and exteriors go, but modernize the amenities."

He planned to renovate the old hotel, the tavern, and the restaurant, but tear down the barbershop and the beauty shop and add those amenities as part of an addition to the hotel. He said the movie theater was in pretty good shape. The grocery store needed a lot of work, but he liked her idea of keeping the Roaring 20's atmosphere while bringing in modern cash registers, upgrading the freezers, shelves, and food storage.

She was surprised to see a library at the end of town.

"It's about the only thing that doesn't need work," Ethan said.

Beyond the library, there was only darkness.

She shivered as Ethan tugged on her hand. "Where are we going?"

"There's a park just ahead. I'll turn the lights on when we get there."

Biting down on the inside corner of her lip, she let him lead her into the darkness.

"Sofia, I'm not going to drain you dry and bury you in the park."

"What?" She came to an abrupt stop.

He dropped her hand. "I can tell you're scared. Come on; I'll take you home."

"No. No, I'm just letting my sister's fears get to me. I probably shouldn't have told her I was coming here with you. She wanted to call Micah."

"Call him if you want. I've got nothing to hide."

"He's on his honeymoon. Anyway, I'm fine."

He looked doubtful.

Smiling up at him, she took his hand. "Let's go."

The park was large, surrounded by tall trees. The pool in the center was empty, some of the plaster cracked.

"We'll have to fix that," Ethan said, hitting a switch that lit the lamps located at the park's four corners.

Sofia nodded, then shivered.

"Are you cold?"

"No." Frowning, she glanced around. "I felt something. Or I thought I did."

"I wouldn't worry. Probably one of the ghosts," he said casually. "Maybe the one who warned me you were in danger."

"How would a ghost I never met know I needed help?" She laughed softly, thinking how foolish that sounded.

"I don't know, but he—or she—was right on. The cemetery is farther down the road."

"I'm not sure I want to see that at night."

"Okay. Let's go back."

Returning to the town, they crossed the road. In the distance, Sofia could see streetlights. As they drew closer, she saw houses, all of them with lights burning inside. "Are there people living here?"

"Just me."

"Why are all the lights on?"

He shrugged. "I programmed them to come on when the sun goes down. Makes it seem less lonely."

Her heart went out to him, but she didn't know why. No one was making him stay here.

"Do you want to go inside one?" he asked.

"Sure." She couldn't help being curious. Micah had told her that men and women who had stumbled into this town hadn't been allowed to leave and had been forced to feed the vampires who lived here. The thought made her shiver.

"This is the house I was staying in," he said, leading her up a short red-brick path to a single-story house painted green with white shutters. He opened the door for her, then followed her inside.

"It's nice," she said, her voice tinged with surprise.

"What did you expect?"

"I don't know, but nothing like this." The house was old, there was no doubt of that, she mused as she wandered from room to room, just as there was no doubt it had been upgraded through the years. The carpet and the furniture were years out of style but still in good condition. A relatively new TV stood in one corner; the appliances were modern.

Sofia returned to the living room. "This doesn't seem like a very safe place," she remarked. "Of course, I don't guess very many people even know about it."

"I don't spend the day here. Neither did any of the other vampires."

"Oh?" She perched on the edge of the flowered couch.

"The humans lived in the houses down here." She flinched, making him think he should have left that part out. "Do you remember seeing a place up on the hill?"

Sofia frowned. "I don't think so."

"It's where the vampires used to spend the day. Iron bars

on the windows and the door. There's a secure lair in the basement."

"The basement." She lifted one brow. "Sounds real homey."

Ethan shrugged. "I don't need much during the day."

"Can I ask you something?"

"Sure."

"I don't know how to pose it tactfully."

He cocked his head to the side, his mind brushing hers. "You're wondering if I'd rather be dead than live like this."

Her eyes widened in surprise. "How did you know that?"

"I read your mind."

"Well, that's just rude!" she exclaimed, feeling her cheeks grow hot as she remembered some of her more erotic thoughts about him.

Ethan burst out laughing. She was one in a million, he thought. "If it makes you feel better, it's the first time."

"Well," she grumbled, "make sure it's the last!"

At home, while getting ready for bed, Sofia thought about everything Ethan had told her. It was disconcerting, knowing he could read her thoughts, which reminded her that he hadn't answered her question about whether he would rather be dead than live as a vampire. He didn't seem particularly happy about being what he was. There were times when she thought she detected a sense of despair, maybe even a desire to end his life. She hoped she was wrong.

She wondered who was going to keep an eye on things during the day, when he couldn't. Sighing, she slipped under the covers. It was none of her concern, but she wished him well. Maybe doing all that renovation would give him a sense of purpose.

* * *

The next week seemed to fly by. Sofia spent Sunday with her parents. She had warned Rosa earlier not to say a word about Ethan or the fact that Sofia was dating him, and especially about her visit to Morgan Creek.

At work on Monday, she had the feeling something was wrong. Mr. Donaldson's secretary, Karen, was unusually quiet.

On Tuesday, Sofia's boss didn't come to work.

On Wednesday, he told her the bad news. They were going out of business.

"I don't know what I'm going to do now," she told Ethan when he called her that night. "It's not going to be easy finding another job. I've only worked there for five months." She sighed dramatically. "You don't know anyone who's hiring, do you?"

"As a matter of fact, I do."

"Really? Who?"

"I need an accountant."

"That's great, but I'm not an accountant, just a personal assistant."

"Well, that's really all I need. Someone to pay the bills as they come in. Take notes if someone has a question, that kind of thing."

"I guess I could do that, but it's a heck of a long commute from Arizona to Morgan Creek."

"Yeah, I hadn't thought of that. Maybe you could stay here during the week and go home on weekends."

"I don't know . . ."

"Forget I suggested it. Listen, I need to go. Talk to you tomorrow night, okay?"

"Where are you going?" It was a silly question.

"Sofie, come on."

"Do you like it?"

He groaned low in his throat. She was killing him.

"I'm sorry. It's none of my business."

"It's not unpleasant," he said, choosing his words carefully. "I try not to think about what I'm doing. It's necessary, you know, something I have to do. Like taking insulin if you're diabetic. Except . . ."

Her heart skipped a beat as she waited for him to go on.

"Except when I drink from you."

"Why is that different?"

"I don't know, but it is. Do you really want to talk about this?"

"Well, it *is* kind of fascinating."

Her response reminded Ethan that she had once wanted to be a vampire. "Didn't you discuss all this with Micah?"

"Not really. He was always trying to talk me out of following in his footsteps," she said, a smile in her voice. "I read tons of books on the subject, but they were mostly about how to destroy a vampire, not what it was like to *be* one."

"Well, stick with me, kid," he said dryly. "And you'll learn more about bloodsuckers than you ever wanted to know."

He was probably right, Sofia thought as she disconnected the call.

She was tempted to take him up on his offer, but she didn't like the thought of staying in Morgan Creek day and night. Maybe it was silly, but she didn't want to be stuck in an old town, surrounded by construction workers, miles from civilization. Maybe she was being foolish, or chicken, but whatever it was, she just didn't want to be there with a bunch of burly guys while Ethan was at rest.

Too bad, because she really liked spending time with him. Maybe because it was thrilling and a little bit dangerous. Maybe because there was something dark and exciting in knowing that he thought her blood was special.

Or maybe it was just because he needed her.

Chapter Twelve

Ethan found Saintcrow sitting on the rail of the veranda when he stepped out of Blair House the following night. "What the hell are you doing here?"

Saintcrow shook his head. "Are you gonna ask me that *every* time I show up?"

Ethan laughed. "Sorry. It's just that it's always such a surprise."

"A good one, I hope."

"So, what *are* you doing here?"

"Well, if you must know, I'm bored. Kadie went to see her family, so I decided to come by and give you a hand during the day."

"Yeah?"

"The paperwork was taking too long, so I paid a little visit to the guy in charge of permits and got him to move things along. Your permits will be ready tomorrow morning and I'll be there to pick them up."

"I don't know what to say."

"*Thanks* will do. I also deposited some more money in your contractor's account, then called him and told him that I was your business partner and we want him to buy the best materials out there."

Ethan nodded. "That's great. I didn't know Kadie had any family."

"Mother, father, little sister, Kathy." He had saved Kathy's life by giving her some of his blood. "Her father's a doctor. Used to be a vampire hunter."

"You're kidding!"

"Nope. He took a shot at me once and hit Kadie instead. Almost killed her."

"And that's why you turned her?"

Saintcrow nodded. "Although it probably would have happened anyway, eventually."

"I can't believe you let her old man live after taking a shot at you."

"He's Kadie's father."

"So . . ." Ethan shook his head. "Mom and dear old Dad are okay with what you did?"

"They don't know. I wiped all memory of what happened from her father's mind, made him forget he used to be a hunter. Wiped her mother's memories, too. They have no idea we're vampires. We're just one big happy family now. Speaking of family, you've been spending a lot of time with Micah's sister."

"You got a problem with that?"

"I don't. Micah might, though, especially if you bring her across."

"Why would I do that?"

Saintcrow shrugged. "It can be a powerful temptation. She's young, beautiful. You obviously want her, and not just for her blood."

Ethan hopped up on the railing, one shoulder braced against a support post. "What is it with Sofia's blood?" he asked. "Why does it calm me the way it does?"

"I'm not sure. There's no science to back it up, but I think some mortals are inherently compatible with vampires."

"Like, made for each other?" he asked, somewhat sarcastically.

"Not exactly *made* for each other. Take me and Kadie. We met under less-than-pleasant circumstances. She should have hated me. And I guess maybe she did. She said it often enough." He smiled faintly at the memory. "But I wanted her the first time I saw her. And she wanted me, no matter how often she denied it. Just like you want Sofia. And she wants you."

"Yeah? How do you know?"

Saintcrow shook his head in exasperation. "How can you *not* know?"

"Okay, we're attracted to each other. I admit it. If I was just a man, maybe one day I'd ask her to marry me. But as a vampire, I've got nothing to offer her. If I had a shred of decency, I'd tell her good-bye and never see her again."

"But you won't," Saintcrow said, dropping to his feet. "Come on; let's make like vampires and hunt the night."

"One more reason why I should end it now," Ethan muttered. But they both knew he wouldn't.

Hunting with Saintcrow was always an adventure. The master vampire tended to be very picky about his prey. Ethan figured that, because his sire had been a vampire since the Crusades, the need to feed wasn't as urgent for him as it was for fledglings.

Saintcrow had decided they should hunt in Colorado. When asked why, he shrugged. "I like the mountains."

The streets were quiet this time of night. Saintcrow strolled toward a movie theater. He stopped a block away.

"One of the movies should be letting out in the next hour or so," he remarked.

"So, we're just gonna hang around here?"

"You got someplace better to be?"

"No, I guess not." Ethan rested a shoulder against the side of a building. Snowcapped mountains rose in the distance, like tall fingers pointing toward the sky.

Tensing, Ethan glanced at Saintcrow as a patrol car turned down the street, slowing as it passed by.

The master vampire's gaze was fixed on that of the cop behind the wheel. When he lifted his hand in a friendly wave, the cop waved back and drove on.

Saintcrow laughed softly. "Easy," he murmured, amusement in his voice. "So easy."

"You really like being a bloodsucker, don't you?"

"It amuses me from time to time."

"And the rest of the time? Do you ever miss being human?"

"I don't even remember what it was like."

Ethan frowned. "I don't believe that."

"No?"

Ethan shook his head. "If you didn't retain some of your humanity, you'd be a monster. A real monster."

"Maybe I am." Saintcrow jerked his head toward the crowd exiting the theater. "Dinner's ready."

It was remarkably easy to blend into the crowd. Ethan let Saintcrow choose their prey—two unescorted, well-dressed, middle-aged women. The master vampire was good, Ethan mused. His sire mesmerized them from behind, then directed them to turn down a dark, deserted street a block past the parking lot.

"Black or red?" Saintcrow asked.

Ethan glanced from one woman to the other. "I'll take the redhead."

With a nod, Saintcrow took the dark-haired woman by the hand and led her a short distance away.

Ethan turned his back to Saintcrow, then drew the red-haired woman into his arms. She stared up at him, her expression blank, her body limp. Hunger stirred inside him, but it was Sofia's face he saw as he lowered his head to the woman's neck, Sofia's blood he craved.

Chapter Thirteen

Sofia's mind was on what to have for dinner when she stepped out onto the street Monday night after cleaning out her office and came face-to-face with a tall man wearing a hooded sweatshirt and black pants. A lock of inky-black hair fell across his forehead; a thin white scar ran from the outer edge of his left eye, down his cheek, and disappeared beneath his shirt collar.

Murmuring, "Excuse me," she tried to step around him, only to find him blocking her path again, even though she hadn't seen him move.

"Sofia?"

She nodded, unable to look away from his eyes—deep black eyes that seemed to trap the breath in her lungs. Every instinct she possessed screamed that she was in danger.

"Relax. My name is Rylan Saintcrow. I know your brother."

Sofia blinked at him. This was the vampire who had befriended Micah and taken Ethan under his wing. She glanced around. Surely he wouldn't do anything when there were so many people passing by. "What do you want?"

"I want you to take Ethan up on his offer."

"I'd like to, but . . ." She shook her head. "I don't want to be alone in a ghost town with a bunch of men I don't know."

"I'll be there."

"That's great, but I don't know *you* either."

"When you come to work for Ethan, it'll give us a chance to get acquainted."

He held up his hand when she started to protest. "We can do this two ways," he said. "You can agree to come to Morgan Creek on your own or I can compel you to do it."

She didn't ask how. Just standing there, she could feel his power surrounding her. She had no doubt he could force her to do anything he wanted.

His smile was a trifle smug when he said, "So, all you have to do is give Ethan a call tonight and tell him you changed your mind. I'll arrange it so that I pick you up in the morning and Ethan can take you home at night. Does that suit you?"

Hating herself for not having the backbone to stand up to him, she nodded.

"One more thing. Let's not tell Ethan about our little chat, all right?"

She nodded again. Blinked. And he was gone.

Her encounter with Saintcrow left her feeling shaky inside and out. She had never been afraid of Micah, she thought, as she unlocked her car door and slid behind the wheel. But then, he was her brother. She hadn't really been afraid of Ethan either. But meeting Saintcrow had scared the crap out of her.

At home, she made a cup of tea and wished she had something stronger, but she wasn't much of a drinker and she didn't keep booze in the house.

She gave herself a stern talking-to, assuring herself that she would be all right, that Saintcrow wouldn't hurt her. Scary as he was, he had helped her brother, saved her parents. And now he was helping Ethan cope with being a vampire.

Taking a deep, calming breath, she picked up her phone and punched in Ethan's number.

He answered on the first ring.

"Ethan? Hi."

"Hey. What's up?"

"I've been thinking about your job offer."

"Yeah?"

Sofia paused. He didn't sound very happy to hear from her. Maybe she should just hang up, forget about Ethan, and go back to her normal boring but safe life.

"Sofie, you still there?"

"Yes. I was wondering . . . that is, if you still need me . . ."

"When can you start?"

"Tomorrow?"

"What changed your mind?" Silence crept over the line between them. "Sofie?"

"It's a woman's privilege, don't you know?"

"Uh-huh. What aren't you telling me?"

"Nothing."

"You're lying, Sofia. I can hear it in your voice."

She poured as much indignity into her tone as she could muster. "Ethan!"

"Saintcrow talked to you, didn't he?"

She started to deny it, but what was the point when he could read her mind? "Yes."

"Do you really want to come here?"

"He said he'd pick me up in the morning and you could take me home at the end of the day, so I wouldn't have to spend the night there. If that's agreeable, I'm willing to give it a try."

Ethan cursed under his breath. Damn his master for interfering. He could tell from the tone of Sofie's voice that she had strong doubts about working in Morgan Creek. No doubt Saintcrow had made her an offer she couldn't refuse.

"Ethan?"

"I'll see you tomorrow, Sofie. Dress warm."

"All right. Good night, Ethan." She disconnected the call, then stared at the phone. Why was he mad at her? she wondered. And then she realized he wasn't mad at her, but at his sire.

Ethan was fuming when he went in search of Saintcrow, but the master vampire was nowhere to be found. No doubt his sire had returned to New Orleans to be with Kadie.

Jaw clenched, Ethan stood in the middle of Morgan Creek's main street. His growing anger spiked his hunger. He needed to hunt, but not now. Any mortal he encountered while in this mood definitely would not survive.

Sofia. He needed Sofia. Just a little of her blood would calm his anger and his hunger. Dropping to his knees, he buried his head in his hands, murmuring her name over and over again.

Ethan? Ethan, are you all right?

His head snapped up. "Sofia?" He glanced left and right, expecting to see her there, even though he knew it was impossible.

Ethan?

I'm here.

What's going on?

What do you mean?

You called my name. I heard you. It was so clear, I looked all over my apartment for you.

Ethan shook his head. He'd tasted her blood, but she had never tasted his. How was it possible for her to hear his thoughts?

Are you all right?

No.

If you come here, I'll give you what you need.

Are you crazy? If you've been in my mind, you know it's not safe to be near me.

You won't hurt me.

His laugh was bitter. *How can you be so sure?*

You never have before. And if my blood calms you, why would you kill me?

Ethan shook his head. There was, he supposed, a certain logic to what she said. *Get your wooden stake. I'm on my way.*

Sofia worried her lower lip as she went into the bedroom and opened the drawer of the bedside table. The wooden stake rested inside, looking as harmless as any old piece of wood. But it wasn't. At Micah's insistence, she had taken it to a priest, who had blessed it and sprinkled it with holy water.

She lifted it carefully from the drawer. It fit her hand as if it had been custom made, which she supposed it had; Micah had carved it for her, a fact she found rather ironic.

She slid it into the pocket of her cargo pants, practically jumping out of her skin when the doorbell rang.

She took slow, deep breaths as she went to let Ethan in, reminding herself that he had never hurt her before, that when he'd felt out of control, he had fled her presence.

She unlocked the door, took another deep breath, and smiled. "Hey."

"Hey, yourself."

Stepping back, she said, "Come on in."

"In a minute. If I start to lose control, all you have to do is revoke my invitation and I'll have to leave."

"Really?"

"Yeah. I don't know why it works, but it does."

"Okay." She had never noticed it before, but there was a peculiar stirring in the air when he crossed the threshold. Was she somehow becoming more aware of the supernatural? And if so, why?

He followed her into the living room.

Feeling suddenly nervous, she sat on the edge of the sofa, one hand clenched in her lap, the other folded around the stake in her pocket.

Ethan stood several feet away, watching her. "Are you sure you want to do this?"

She nodded. "Let's get it over with."

He closed the distance between them, careful not to make any sudden moves. Sitting beside her, he slid his arm around her waist. "I won't hurt you."

"I know." The tremor in her voice told him she wasn't as sure of that as she wanted him to believe.

He stroked his knuckles over her cheek, then ran his tongue along the side of her neck. When she relaxed in his embrace, he bit her gently, closed his eyes as her life's blood flowed over his tongue, spreading warmth to every fiber of his being, calming the beast inside.

He needed only a little, but she tasted so good. Surely a little more wouldn't hurt, he thought. Just one more taste. Maybe two . . .

He jerked his head up when he felt the sharp point of a stake against his chest, hissed as it penetrated his shirt and bit into the skin beneath. Cursing, he lurched to his feet.

She stared up at him, her eyes wide with fright. "I'm sorry," she said tremulously. "But I was afraid you weren't going to stop."

"You did the right thing," he said, his voice tight.

She stared at his chest. Through the hole in his shirt, she could see where the stake had burned his skin black. "Does it hurt?"

"Like a sonofa . . . yeah, it hurts. Maybe this wasn't such a good idea."

"How do you feel?"

"I'll live. You'd better keep that stake handy when we're together."

"I will." She slid it back into her pocket, thinking she would have to call Micah and tell him that it worked. And then she reconsidered. Probably not a good idea to say anything to her brother about Ethan.

"You soaked it in holy water, didn't you?"

"I didn't. A priest did. And then he blessed it."

He had never heard of anybody doing that, but then, he hadn't been a vampire very long. There was probably a lot he didn't know.

Sofia laid a tentative hand on his arm, her gaze searching his.

Ethan frowned. Was he reading her signals right? Only one way to find out. Leaning down, he kissed her lightly, then more deeply as her arms went around his neck.

Groaning softly, he fell back on the sofa, carrying her with him, so that she lay sprawled across his chest. His hand delved into her hair, tangling in the long, silky strands. Her breasts were warm against his chest, her mouth on fire as they kissed again and yet again.

In a sudden move, he rolled over so that she was beneath him. Every instinct he had urged him to take her, to make her his.

She went suddenly still, her hands falling to her sides.

Smart girl, he thought. Too smart to fight him, knowing it would only excite his urge to hunt. But he wasn't so far gone that he couldn't stop. He eased to a sitting position and gathered her into his arms again. "Thank you for tonight," he said, his voice thick. He kissed her again, then gained his feet. "If you don't show up in the morning, I won't hold it against you."

She smiled when, instead of just vanishing from her sight, he left by the front door.

Ethan transported himself back to Morgan Creek, back to the house he'd been staying in. He flicked on the lights, even though he didn't need them to find his way around. He saw perfectly well in the dark.

Dropping down on the sofa, he picked up the remote and turned on the TV. Damn Saintcrow; why didn't he just mind his own business?

You are my business.

Get out of my head!

Then stop acting like an idiot. The two of you belong together.

Yeah? Since when? As I recall, you said we weren't made for each other.

Maybe you weren't, but you belong together. I can see that now.

Don't you think that's something Sofia and I should decide?

Just call me Cupid. I'll see you tomorrow night.

Ethan shook his head. Why was it so hard to stay mad at Saintcrow?

It's part of my charm. Saintcrow's voice again, followed by his laughter.

Unable to stop himself, Ethan laughed, too. And felt better for it.

Since Saintcrow had neglected to tell Sofia what time he would pick her up, she was dressed and ready by eight.

He showed up an hour later, wearing jeans, a gray sweatshirt with the hood pulled up, and a pair of dark glasses. "Ready?" he asked cheerfully.

"I guess so." Grabbing her handbag, Sofia stepped outside and locked the door behind her.

She tensed when Saintcrow's arm curled around her waist, closed her eyes as he transported her swiftly through time and space. She was slightly dizzy when he set her on her feet inside one of the houses.

"I set up an office in here," Saintcrow said, striding into the adjoining room.

Nodding, Sofia followed him. She didn't know what had been in the room before, but now it held a large cherry-wood desk, a padded desk chair, and a small TV.

"The computer is set up and ready to go," Saintcrow remarked, removing his sunglasses. "There's paper in the drawer, pens, pencils, that kind of thing." He handed her a checkbook. "All three of our names are on the account. Pay the bills out of that." Next, he handed her a credit card. "Anything you want for yourself—groceries, clothes, office supplies—pay for it with that. If you don't like this computer, get another one."

Sofia stared at him. "I can't have you buying things for me."

"Honey, I've got more money than I'll ever spend. As long as you're employed by me, buy whatever you want. Oh, I bought some new bedding, in case you ever want to spend the night here. There's food in the kitchen. I didn't know what you liked, so I bought a little of everything. There's a town east of here, about twenty miles, if you want to go shopping or out to lunch."

She raised her eyebrows. Did he expect her to walk?

Saintcrow chuckled. "There's a car in the garage. The keys are in it. There's gas in the tank."

"You're far too generous."

His gaze caught hers, dark and intense. "You make Ethan happy."

She didn't know what to say to that. Micah had told her

stories about Saintcrow, about how he had killed without compunction when he was first turned, that he had been ruthless, a predator without equal. She found it hard to reconcile the portrait her brother had painted of Saintcrow with the man who stood before her.

"The workers will be here in an hour. I gave the foreman my cell number. All we really need you to do is answer the phone and pay the bills." His gaze probed hers. "Are you gonna be all right?"

She nodded.

"If you need me, just call my name."

Sofia nodded again and blew out a sigh when he vanished from her sight. And then she pinched herself to make sure she was awake.

In the basement of Blair House, Ethan felt the dark sleep fall away as he caught Sofia's scent. She was here. Peace settled over him. She was here. Smiling faintly, he tumbled back into oblivion.

Chapter Fourteen

Sofia spent the morning getting acquainted with her computer. She added her email account. She sent her parents a text, telling them she had a new job, but didn't mention it was in Wyoming. She had a short email from Micah, saying he and Holly were in Tennessee and having a wonderful time.

She hit Reply, then sat there, wondering if she should tell her brother about Ethan. After several minutes, she decided against it. Instead, she typed a short note wishing them well and adding that she hoped to see them soon.

At lunchtime, she went into the kitchen. Saintcrow hadn't been kidding when he said he'd bought a little of everything. The pantry was filled with a variety of canned goods and condiments, bags of candy, potato chips, three kinds of bread, a new jar of mayonnaise and one of mustard, and anything else she could possibly have wanted. One cupboard held a set of dishes; she found silverware in a drawer, pots and pans in the cupboard under the marble countertop. The fridge was likewise crammed with several kinds of lunch meat and cheese, dairy products, and soda. She found four kinds of ice cream in the freezer.

"Good grief, I'll be fat as a pig," she muttered as she took out the makings for a ham and cheese sandwich.

After lunch, she went into the bedroom. She saw a package of new sheets—a very pretty flowered print—on the mattress, along with a matching spread and two brand-new pillows. The old bedding had been stripped away. There was no sign of it anywhere. Had he thrown it out?

The only other furniture was a four-drawer dresser and a pair of matching nightstands.

It didn't take long to make the bed. When she finished, she stood in the middle of the room, wondering who had lived here back in the days when the vampires ruled the town and the inhabitants were their prey. The house was nice enough, but even a pretty prison was still a cage if you couldn't leave.

She shuddered as the room suddenly grew cold. Ethan said there were ghosts in Morgan Creek. Had one of them once lived in this house? The chill was quickly gone, leaving her to wonder if she had imagined it.

Needing some air, she went out onto the porch. She couldn't see the town from this distance, but the sound of hammering was audible, along with the sound of an automatic drill of some kind.

Returning to the office, she sat at her desk. With nothing to do, she played several hands of solitaire, then jumped when the doorbell rang.

Going into the living room, she peered through the window, frowned when she saw a FedEx man on the porch.

Opening the door, she said, "Can I help you?"

"Delivery for Mr. Parrish."

"Oh, of course."

"Just sign here, ma'am."

She scrawled her name on the paper he handed her.

"Where do you want this?"

For the first time, she noticed several large cardboard

boxes stacked on the porch. "In here, I guess." She stepped out of the way as he carried them into the living room.

"Good day, ma'am," he said, taking his leave.

"Thank you."

Frowning, Sofia closed the door. She found a pair of scissors in the office, then, sitting on the floor in the living room, opened the first box. It held carpet samples. The second box held books of wallpaper samples. The third held swatches of drapery material. The fourth held brochures displaying various types of doors and shutters. The fifth held more brochures, these displaying floor tile.

She was perusing wallpaper samples when Ethan materialized in the room.

"Oh!" Startled, she blinked up at him. "Can't you make a noise or something before you just pop into the room?"

One corner of his mouth turned up in a wry grin. "Sorry." He dropped down beside her. "How was your day?"

"Fine. I can't believe Saintcrow. He gave me a credit card and told me to buy anything I wanted. I mean . . ." She shrugged. "I feel like a kept woman."

"Nah. It's just one of the perks of the job." He jerked his chin toward the samples on the floor. "Find anything you like?"

"Lots of things. Is the wallpaper for the hotel?"

"Yeah, why?"

"I really like this pattern." It was a pale blue and silver stripe.

"For which room?"

"Mine."

"Buy it."

"I don't know anything about hanging wallpaper."

"Me either. We plan to hire someone to do it when we're ready. It only takes a week or two for delivery."

Nodding, Sofia rose, pressing one hand to the middle of her aching back.

Ethan stood beside her. He hesitated a moment, then began to massage her shoulders.

Sighing, Sofia closed her eyes as his fingers moved over her back and shoulders, kneading gently. "That feels really good," she murmured.

He continued a few minutes more and then turned her in his arms, his gaze searching hers. "Is everything all right between us?"

"Why wouldn't it be?"

He shrugged. "Some of our nights together haven't ended too well."

She smiled up at him. "We'll find our way."

He nodded, hoping she was right, because he wasn't sure he wanted to live without her. "Come on; you must be tired. I'll take you home."

Traveling by Vampire Air was incredibly fast, but this was one time when Sofia wished it took longer. She was no longer certain about her relationship with Ethan. Was she just an employee now? They had shared some kisses. He had tasted her blood. He had admitted he wanted her. He knew she wanted him. But every time they seemed on the verge of taking the next step, something happened to prevent it. Was it fate trying to keep them apart? Or just bad luck?

All too soon, they were at her apartment door. She unlocked it but didn't go inside.

"Thanks for bringing me home."

"My pleasure."

She thought he looked as confused as she felt. "I guess I'll see you tomorrow night."

"Sofia."

Her heart skipped a beat. "Yes?"

"Where do we stand?"

She smiled inwardly. So, he didn't know either. "I'm not sure."

His fingertips slid down her cheek, curled around her nape. "I need you in my life, Sofie. We can be just friends if that's all you can handle."

"What does being *just friends* entail?"

He glanced briefly at the pulse beating in the hollow of her throat.

"So you want me to be a blood donor, is that it?"

He dropped his hand and took a step back. "It sounds pretty bad when you put it like that."

"How would *you* put it?"

"I told you before, there's something about your blood that eases my hunger. But it's more than that. Being with you . . ." He clenched his hands at his sides. "Being with you makes me feel less like a monster."

"Well, I guess that's better than bringing *out* the monster in you," Sofia muttered, and burst out laughing.

"What's so damn funny?"

Still laughing, she shook her head. It wasn't *that* hilarious, but for some reason she'd found it humorous. Maybe she was just tired and easily amused.

Feeling like a fool, Ethan glared at her.

Sofia took a deep breath. "I'm sorry; I couldn't help it. What you said was really very sweet. I don't know what the connection is between us, but I feel it, too. So, I'm suggesting we see where it takes us. And . . . and anytime you need to . . . you know . . . just tell me." Grinning, she met his gaze. "As long as I have a stake in my hand."

With a wordless growl, he pulled her into his arms and held her close.

Feeling utterly content, Sofia rested her cheek against his chest. A tickly sensation fluttered in her belly when his lips moved in her hair. Looking up, she cupped his face in her palms, went up on her tiptoes, and kissed him.

He kissed her back as if he was a drowning man and she was the only life preserver in sight.

She was breathless, mindless when he lifted his head.

"I don't see a stake in your hand," he said, his voice thick. "So you'd better go inside."

"Take what you need, Ethan."

He blew out a sigh, his eyes filled with torment and self-loathing.

"Don't argue with me." She pulled him inside and closed the door, then reached into her pocket and withdrew her stake. "Like the Boy Scouts, I'm always prepared."

With a low groan, he took her into his arms. His voice was filled with apology when he whispered her name.

And then he lowered his head and took what he so desperately needed. As always, her blood filled him, soothed him. Satisfied his need.

Lifting his head, he kissed her lightly. "Thank you."

"See you tomorrow."

Nodding, he kissed her again, and then he was gone.

Sofia hummed softly as she dropped the stake on the coffee table. This was, she thought, the strangest relationship she'd ever had.

Saintcrow picked her up at nine the next morning and transported her to Morgan Creek. He left her in the house that was now officially "the office," then went to check on the workmen at the hotel.

She was sitting on the floor hours later, surrounded by samples and swatches, when he materialized beside her.

"Found anything you like?" he asked, hunkering down across from her.

"I like this for the hotel lobby." She opened one of the wallpaper books and showed him a dark-red flocked sample.

Saintcrow shook his head. "That looks like it belongs in a brothel," he said, laughing.

"How would you know?"

"I saw something similar in a house of ill repute in Deadwood back in the 1800s."

"You did not! You did?"

"Yep. I guess the most famous madam in the old west was Julia Bulette. She ran a place in Virginia City called Julia's Palace. She was the first white woman in the town. She got to be quite famous before she was murdered. It's said Mark Twain was there when they hanged the man who killed her."

"Did you know her?"

"We met."

Sofia stared at him. He looked no more than thirty. It was hard to believe he had lived for hundreds of years.

"Fannie Porter was another famous madam. Ran a whorehouse in San Antonio. Butch Cassidy and the Wild Bunch were frequent visitors."

"Did you know her, too?"

"I saw her a couple of times," he said with a wink. "But we were never formally introduced."

Sofia closed the wallpaper book and opened another. What a life he had led. She could scarcely imagine all the things he must have seen and done, the places he'd been, the people he'd met. What was it like to stay forever the same while everyone around you changed, grew older, passed away?

He stared past her. "It's hard," he said quietly. "A lot of vampires can't adjust to the constant change. Some go mad when everything and everyone they know is gone."

"But not you."

"A lot of ancient vampires go to ground . . ." At her frown, he said, "They bury themselves in the earth."

Her eyes widened in horror.

"I know, it sounds morbid, but it's quite restful."

"You've done that?"

"Once, when I was badly burned. I went to ground to heal." He had stayed there, deep in the arms of Mother Earth, long after he'd recovered. He might have been there still if Kadie hadn't inadvertently entered Morgan Creek.

"Can I ask you something?"

"Ask away. I've got nothing to hide."

"Ethan says my blood soothes him, that it's different from anyone else's."

"And?"

"Blood is blood. I mean, isn't it all the same?"

"No. It was the scent of Kadie's blood that drew me from the earth. I knew as soon as I caught her scent that she would be mine. It happens that way sometimes. I don't know why, only that it's rare."

"So he's not just imagining it, or making it up?"

"No. I'll tell you what I told him. I think you two belong together. And what you've just told me confirms it."

Sofia thought about what Saintcrow had said long after he had taken his leave. Was she truly meant to be with Ethan? And if so, what did that mean for her future? If she stayed with him, she would age and he would not. And what about children? Could male vampires father children? What would it be like, watching herself grow older when he didn't? How long would he stay with her when she was eighty—should she live so long—and he looked like her grandson instead of her husband? Was that why Kadie had become a vampire? Why Holly had given up her humanity? Would she have to make that choice? And if so, would she?

Lost in thought, she didn't realize night had fallen until Ethan stepped into the room.

"What's wrong?" he asked.

"Nothing; why?"

"Sofia . . ."

She grimaced. That was another thing about being with Ethan. He always knew when she was lying. And if she didn't tell him what was bothering her, he'd just read her mind. How unfair was that?

His grin told her he knew what she was thinking. But then, didn't he always? So why did she have to say it?

He sat at the other end of the sofa, one arm flung across the back. "You might as well tell me."

"Saintcrow thinks we were meant to be together because . . . because of the way my blood affects you. And I was just wondering what it would be like, if we were . . . if we were serious about each other."

He lifted one brow. "What *would* it be like?"

"You know what I mean. Holly and Kadie both gave up everything to be with the men they love. Not just the big things, like children, but little things, like never being able to take a walk on a spring morning or feel the sun on their faces after the rain or going to church on Easter morning. Not that that's a little thing," she amended. "But just ordinary things people do every day without even thinking about it."

"Hey, you don't have to tell me. I lost a good job. Going to see my family or friends is just too complicated. At least Kadie and Holly chose this," he said bitterly. "I didn't." Rising, he paced the floor, his strides long and angry.

She watched him for several minutes. Then, hoping she wasn't making a mistake, she stepped in front of him.

He stopped abruptly, his gaze burning into hers.

Praying she was doing the right thing, she placed her hand on his arm. "I know how frustrating this must be for you," she said quietly. "But I'm here, and I'm not going anywhere, at least not for a while. So let's just see where being together takes us, okay?"

He groaned softly as he took her in his arms. Just holding her made the world look brighter. "Are you ready to go home?" he asked some time later.

"I guess so," she replied, though she was reluctant to leave him when he was feeling so down. "Maybe we could go out to a movie Friday night."

"Yeah, I'd like that."

"All right, then." Standing on tiptoe, she kissed him lightly. "It's a date."

Chapter Fifteen

Micah Ravenwood slid a glance at his bride as they strolled along the upper deck of the *General Jackson* riverboat. Holly had always wanted to see the Grand Ole Opry, Graceland, and Dollywood, so after leaving Morgan Creek, they had headed south.

"Where do you want to live when we go back?" he asked.

"I don't know." Holly paused at the rail to look out over the water. "Where would you like to live?"

"If it's okay with you, I'd like to get a place close to my folks. Now that they all know what I am, I'd kinda like a chance to make up for all the birthdays and holidays I missed."

"Sure, if you want."

"Is anything wrong? You've been awfully quiet the last few nights." It was a sure sign she was hiding something. He had asked her what was troubling her a couple of times, but she had put him off. He decided to try once more. "So," he said, his voice casual, "what's bothering you, Holly?"

"I don't know what you're talking about."

"Come on, Sunshine. You've been stewing over something for days. What is it?"

She nibbled on her lower lip, then said, all in a rush, "I haven't heard from Sofia and I'm a little worried."

"What are you worried about? Is there something I should know?"

Holly blew out a sigh. "No. Yes."

"Which is it? Yes or no?"

"Do you remember my cousin Ethan?"

"The guy Saintcrow turned at our wedding? That Ethan?"

She nodded.

"What about him?"

"Well . . . I . . . um, I was worried about him, being alone and all, and I had promised Sofia I'd introduce them at the wedding, and . . ."

"Wait a minute! Are you telling me you set my sister up with your cousin? Your cousin who's only been a vampire for a couple of months? *That* cousin?"

"Yeah."

"Are you out of your mind? Have you forgotten Sofia wanted to be a vampire not long ago? Have you already forgotten what it's like to be a fledgling? How hard it is to control your hunger? Dammit, Holly, why didn't you tell me what you were up to?"

"I'm sorry," she said, placing her hand on his arm. "I should have discussed it with you first."

"You got that right," he muttered. "So, what's got you worried now?"

"I'm not worried exactly, but I asked her to call me if they went out, and she never did, so maybe they never met."

"And maybe they did," he said darkly.

"You don't think . . . ?" She couldn't put the sudden fear that something had gone terribly wrong into words.

"He hasn't hurt her," Micah said, thinking how grateful he was that he had taken a little of his sister's blood. "I'd

know if he had. And he'd be dead now." Pulling out his cell
phone, he punched in his sister's number, then kissed Holly
on the cheek. "Thanks for finally telling me."

Sofia was getting ready for bed when her phone rang.
She frowned when she saw her brother's number. Hoping
he would hang up, she let it ring again. When it didn't stop,
she reluctantly answered. "Hi, Micah," she said cheerfully.
"What's up?"

"I don't know," he said dryly. "You tell me."

"What do you mean?"

"Cut the crap. Holly told me about you and Ethan."

"Oh." Wishing she had never answered the phone, she
sank down on the edge of the mattress, her mind racing.
How much did Micah know? Was he angry? Oh, Lordy, he
hadn't gone after Ethan, had he?

"I thought you were done with vampires."

"I was. I am. I mean . . ."

"You remember your promise, right? You're not thinking of doing anything that can't be undone, are you?"

"Of course not!" He didn't sound angry, she decided.
Just worried. "We've got enough vampires in the family
already."

"I think so, too."

"On the other hand," she said, just to tweak his tail,
"Ethan is awfully cute, and he loves my blood." She wor-
ried her lower lip when the phone went silent. "Micah?
Micah, are you there?"

Sofia knew she'd gone too far when Holly's voice came
over the line. "He's on his way to see you."

Uh-oh.

"You never called me," Holly said, a note of reproach in
her voice.

"I know. I'm sorry. I've just been so busy. Ethan decided to try his hand at rebuilding Morgan Creek."

"What?"

"Saintcrow lent him the money. I lost my job at the accounting firm and Ethan hired me to keep the books and answer the phone. Read the mail. Pay the bills, that kind of thing. Saintcrow picks me up in the morning and takes me to Morgan Creek, and Ethan brings me home at night."

"Wow. I didn't see that coming."

"Saintcrow's a little scary, isn't he?"

"He can be. But once you get to know him, he's really kind of nice."

"I've gotta go," Sofia said. "Micah's about to break my door down. Talk to you later. I hope."

Dropping the phone on the bed, she ran to open the door. "Micah, what are you doing here?"

"What do you think?" Striding into the room, he glanced around. "I came to make sure my little sister is all right."

"I told you I was."

"Yeah, well . . ." His gaze moved over her.

"Stop that!" she exclaimed as his mind brushed hers. "You have no right to be poking around in my head. I'm a big girl now."

"Well, you haven't gotten any smarter."

"Would you please just calm down?"

"He's drinking your blood and you want me to calm down? Really?"

"He doesn't take much. Just a little bit. He says it soothes his hunger. And I know it's true. Your buddy Saintcrow thinks Ethan and I are meant to be together."

"I'll kill him."

"Ethan?" she asked, her voice rising with panic.

"No. That meddling Saintcrow."

She snorted. "I'd like to see you try."

"What does that mean?"

"I've met the man. I've felt your power and I've felt his. No way you'd win."

"I might not be able to destroy Saintcrow, but I can mop the floor with Parrish."

"If you lay a hand on him, I'll never speak to you again."

Dropping down on the sofa, Micah cradled his head in his hands. "Sofia, do you know what you're getting in to?"

"No. But he needs me. And I think . . ."

He looked up, his gaze knife sharp. "You think what?"

"That I'm falling in love with him."

"Well, don't."

"Isn't this a case of the pot calling the kettle black? I mean, you fell in love with Holly and you turned her. Why would it be any different if Ethan turned me?"

Micah stared at her, eyes narrowed, thinking there was no good way to answer that question. And then he frowned. "For one thing, Holly was twenty-five, and she was dying. You're only nineteen. I told you before, you're too young to make a decision that's going to affect the rest of your life. A life that could be very, very long."

"So, if I was older, it would be okay?"

"I didn't say that." He reached for her hand. "I won't lie to you, Sofie. There are good things about being a vampire. But there are good things about being human, too. If you decide you want to spend the rest of your life with Ethan, I'll make the best of it. But think long and hard before you make a decision that can't be undone, before you give up your humanity and everything it entails. Promise me."

"Didn't I already promise you that once?"

He nodded. "Just make sure it's one you keep. And I'm telling you now, if he turns you without your permission, I *will* kill him. You might want to tell him that."

Chapter Sixteen

Sofia wasn't looking forward to going to work Thursday morning. She'd never had much of a poker face and she was pretty sure Saintcrow would know something was troubling her. And she didn't want to talk about it. Not with him. And definitely not with Ethan.

Saintcrow showed up at nine sharp. It took only minutes to get to Morgan Creek. He dropped her off at the house, gave her a long, probing look, and went to check on how things were going at the hotel.

He knows, she thought. *He knows something is wrong. Heck, he probably knows exactly what's bothering me.* Well, she couldn't be worried about it now. She had invoices to check and bills to pay.

She was sitting at her desk, running numbers, when she heard footsteps on the porch. Thinking it was one of the workers, she went to the front door. A woman with bright blue eyes and long brown hair stood there looking confused.

"May I help you?" Sofia asked.

"I don't know. I was driving by and . . ." She shook her head. "Something drew me across the bridge. I don't know why, but I had the feeling I'd been here before. That I'd seen this house before." She lifted a hand to her neck, her fingers running back and forth, as if she expected to find something there. She smiled self-consciously. "You must think I'm crazy."

Before Sofia could think of a reply, Saintcrow came striding up the walkway. "What's going on?" he asked, and then he frowned. "Pauline? Is that you?"

At the sound of his voice, the woman made a slow turn. And then she gasped. "It's you," she murmured. "I'm not crazy, after all."

Saintcrow muttered something in a language Sofia didn't understand. But profanity sounds the same in any language, and he was definitely angry. Taking the woman by the arm, he said, "I think we should go inside."

"No! No!" She flailed and kicked as he dragged her into the house.

"Saintcrow, what are you doing?" Sofia exclaimed as she followed them into the living room.

"Let me go!" Tears flooded the woman's eyes. "Let me go! I never told anyone!"

A wave of Saintcrow's hand slammed the front door. Sofia heard the click as the dead bolt slid into place. What the hell was going on?

Saintcrow pushed the woman into a chair. "Stay there."

The power in his voice raised the hair on Sofia's arms and sent chills down her spine.

"Pauline, how did you find this place?" His voice was softer now.

"I don't know. I started dreaming about it last month." Her face paled. "Dreaming about you." She lifted her hand to her neck again. "All of you."

"That's unfortunate."

Sofia didn't miss the threat in his voice.

Neither did Pauline. Unable to move, she stared at Sofia, her eyes filled with panic and a silent plea for help.

Sofia laid a tentative hand on Saintcrow's arm. "Can I see you in the other room?"

When he nodded reluctantly, she led the way into her bedroom and closed the door. "She's one of them, isn't she? One of the people you kept here?"

"So Micah told you about that, did he?"

"Some of it. I know you kept people to feed on." She couldn't disguise the disapproval in her voice. "Was there more to it than that?"

"I don't think you want to know."

"What are you going to do to Pauline?"

"I'm going to wipe away her memory of this place. And me."

"Why?"

"Why do you think?"

"So, it's all true."

He regarded her through narrowed eyes for several long moments. "Long before I met Kadie, Morgan Creek was a haven for a group of vampires. They came here to get away from hunters and because they hoped to find a safe place to live. I warded the town so any human who entered couldn't leave."

"You made them prisoners?"

He nodded. "They lived in these houses. We provided food and entertainment and anything else they wanted."

"Except their freedom."

He nodded again.

"And you fed on them."

He shrugged. "They were prey. The vampires I allowed to stay here weren't allowed to abuse them, or hurt them. Or kill them."

Sofia sat on the edge of the bed, her hands clasped tightly

in her lap. "How could you do such a despicable thing? What about their families?"

He met the condemnation in her eyes without flinching. "At the time, I didn't worry about those things. I had promised my protection to any vampire who came here if they followed my rules."

"You had no right."

"That's what Kadie said."

"Kadie was here?" She remembered what Saintcrow had said, about the scent of Kadie's blood drawing him out of the ground. Somehow, she hadn't put two and two together. "Did you feed on her?"

He nodded. "Vampire," he said, as if that explained everything.

"And she married you." Sofia shook her head. "How could she?"

"She fell in love with me. Is that so hard to believe?"

"After what you did? Yes."

"It was Kadie who made me realize what I was doing was wrong. I sent the vampires away and let the humans go, but first I wiped the memory of this place from their minds. Apparently, in Pauline's case, I'll have to do it again."

"That's cruel."

"I think she'll be happier, not remembering. Don't you?"

"If Ethan and I don't stay together, are you going to erase my memories, too?"

"Probably. It's a matter of survival, Sofia, nothing more."

Saintcrow returned to the living room. Reluctantly, Sofia followed him.

He knelt in front of the woman, his gaze—faintly red— trapping hers. "Listen to me, Pauline. You will forget everything that happened here today."

She stared at him blankly. "I will forget."

"You were never here. You've never heard of Morgan Creek. There are no such things as vampires."

"I was never here. There's no such thing as vampires."

"If you try to remember any of this, any of your past, it will cause you great physical pain."

"Pain."

"I'm going to take you home now."

"Home."

"How do you know where she lives?" Sofia asked.

"I read her mind. She lives in the same place she did years ago." Taking Pauline's hands in his, he pulled her to her feet, then wrapped his arm around her waist. "I won't be gone long. She doesn't live far from here."

Sofia blinked, and they were gone. He had kept people here against their will. Kept them from their homes and families. From friends, jobs. Basically stolen their futures. Fed on them. How had Kadie ever fallen in love with such a horrible man?

She didn't want to think about it.

She didn't see Saintcrow the rest of the day.

She was relieved when Ethan came to pick her up.

In the blink of an eye, she was home. "Do you want to come in?" she asked, unlocking the door.

"Sure."

Inside, Sofia kicked off her shoes, then went into the kitchen and put the coffee on. She stood at the counter, looking out the window, waiting for the coffee to brew. She didn't turn when Ethan came up behind her.

"I saw Saintcrow before I came to get you," he said. "He told me what happened."

"Did you know what he'd done?"

"Yeah. I didn't condone it, Sofie, and I wouldn't have done it."

"How could Kadie marry him? He's a monster."

"I guess you can't choose who you love," Ethan said. "But if you could, I'd choose you."

His voice, soft and low, seeped into the very heart of her. He was a vampire. True, he hadn't done the horrible things Saintcrow had done. But he might have, if Saintcrow hadn't taken him in, taught him what it meant to be a vampire, given him a place to stay.

Sofia sighed. Maybe Saintcrow wasn't quite as bad as she thought. Or maybe, deep down, they were all monsters.

She met Ethan's gaze. He didn't look like a monster, and he certainly didn't act like one. She dismissed his need for blood. He couldn't help that. She lifted a hand to her neck, a question in her eyes.

When he nodded, she tilted her head to the side and closed her eyes. His bite filled her with warmth. This was what the Morgan Creek vampires had done, she thought, with one big difference. Ethan didn't take what he wanted by force. And she was willing.

Raising his head, he hugged her close. "Is what Saintcrow did going to change your opinion of me?"

"Of course not. You had nothing to do with anything that happened here."

"So, we're still on for tomorrow night?"

She smiled up at him. "Of course. I'll bring a change of clothes with me."

"Until then," he said. And kissed her good night.

Saintcrow was late picking her up in the morning, leaving Sofia to wonder if he was angry with her for what she had said the day before. She could have lied to him, but he could read her mind, so it hardly seemed worth the trouble.

She could never condone what he and the other Morgan

Creek vampires had done. She had tried hard to make
excuses for him, to understand his decision to use people
as a permanent food supply, but she just couldn't. It was
wrong, no matter how you looked at it. She tried to imagine
what it must have been like, knowing you could never
leave, that you would never see your loved ones again, that
you were nothing more than a ready blood supply. How
had Kadie endured it? How had she fallen in love with a
man who could do such a thing?

She jumped when the doorbell rang, overcome with an
unexpected sense of guilt for what she had been thinking.
The Bible warned against judging others, but how could
she help it?

Hoping her face didn't betray her thoughts, she opened
the door.

Saintcrow's face was equally blank. "Sorry I'm late," he
said, his voice like ice over steel. "Are you ready?"

Nodding, Sofia grabbed her purse, a bag containing a
change of clothes and a sweater. Fighting off the urge to
shudder, she closed her eyes when Saintcrow put his arm
around her.

He left without a word as soon as they arrived at her
office.

Sofia dropped her things on a chair, then set to work
opening the mail. For the first time, she wondered if the
vampires had received mail when they lived here. And how
Saintcrow had arranged for mail delivery now. She shook
her head. She knew how he had managed it. He was a
master vampire. All it would take was one trip to the post-
master, a little vampire mind control, and Morgan Creek
would be on the map and on some mailman's route. There
were a number of bills, as well as several estimates for
refinishing the pool. On the spur of the moment, Ethan

had decided to add a playground area in one corner of the park.

She paid the bills that were due, put the estimates in a separate pile. In addition to the letters, several boxes arrived containing linens for the hotel.

She fixed a sandwich for lunch, washed it down with soda, and then, deciding she needed some exercise, left the house.

The sounds of men hard at work drew her toward the business district. The place swarmed with workers. A number of men were repairing the hotel roof. Others were pouring concrete in front of the tavern. Still others were demolishing the barbershop and beauty parlor. The library had a new coat of paint; the grocery store had been gutted. She was amazed at how much they had accomplished in such a short time.

She was about to go back to the office when she saw Saintcrow, agile as a monkey, shinny up a light pole to replace the old lamp with a new one taken from the bag hanging from his shoulder. Instead of coming down, he just sort of flew across six feet of ground to the next pole, and so on down the street, until he had replaced all the lamps.

Muttering, "He should be in the circus," she walked away from the town, curious to see the park in the daytime, and the cemetery Ethan had mentioned.

The park had once been beautiful, she thought, though now many of the plants were wilted, the grass more brown than green. The pool in the middle looked worse in the light of day.

When she found a wrought-iron bench beneath a tree, she sat down and found herself wondering again what being trapped here had been like. How dehumanizing it must have been, to know you were seen as nothing more than food. Did the people ever try to resist? Were they punished for refusing? Or did the vampires just mesmerize them and take what they wanted? At least the people had a respite during the day, when the vampires were at rest. Saintcrow had provided a theater and a library for entertainment, a grocery store for the necessities of life—human life. Had the people formed friendships with one another? With the vampires? She shook her head. That seemed unlikely. How could you be friends with a creature who thought of you as prey?

Her thoughts came to an abrupt halt when Saintcrow materialized beside her. "Instead of wondering, why don't you ask me?"

"Is there any way to keep you out of my mind?"

"If you have enough control, you can try to build a wall around your thoughts to block me."

She looked skeptical.

"It can be done. Takes a lot of practice. To answer your question, the people here formed close friendships with one another. After I agreed to release everyone and the vampires were gone, some of the women chose to stay. Your brother fell in love with one of them. Always surprised me, what with her being so much older and everything."

Sofia stared at him in disbelief.

"You didn't know about Shirley?"

"Did she love Micah?"

Saintcrow nodded.

"What happened to her?"

"She passed away."

Sofia sat back, stunned by the news that her brother had fallen in love with an older woman, and the woman had loved him in return. She didn't recall Micah ever mentioning anyone named Shirley; if he had, she'd forgotten. Did Holly know?

Saintcrow slapped his hands on his thighs. "I'll see you tomorrow. Kadie will be rising soon."

Alone again, Sofia gazed into the distance, wondering how many other women had fallen in love with vampires.

And how many had lived to regret it.

Chapter Seventeen

Friday was pretty much like Thursday. With one exception. She had a date with Ethan. The butterflies in Sofia's stomach grew more frantic as the hours went by. At five p.m. she closed and locked the front door, then went into the bedroom to get ready. She showered and washed her hair, laid out a pair of white slacks, a silky dark blue shirt, and heels, then went into the kitchen to find something to eat, because dinner with a vampire was out of the question—unless she was dinner.

She fixed a bowl of tomato soup and a toasted cheese sandwich, wolfed down a candy bar to bolster her courage, then returned to the bedroom, where she combed her hair and applied her makeup.

She had just brushed her teeth and put on her lipstick when the doorbell rang, sending the butterflies in her stomach into overdrive.

She took a deep, calming breath, felt it catch in her throat when she opened the door. Ethan looked gorgeous in a pair of black slacks and a pale gray shirt.

He whistled softly when he saw her.

Heat flooded Sofia's cheeks. "Thank you."

"You look . . ."

"Good enough to eat?" she asked, a smile teasing her lips.

Ethan grinned at her. "That's exactly what I said when Holly sent me your photo."

"You did not!"

"I did. And it's still true. Are you ready?"

"Ready." Grabbing her purse, she closed the door and followed him down the steps. A turquoise Dodge Viper with black racing stripes waited at the curb. "Wow. Is that yours?"

"It's the car Saintcrow left in the garage."

"Really?" As much as she loved her Mustang, she had always wanted to own a Viper.

Ethan held the door open for her. "It's a beaut."

Sofia nodded as she slid into the seat and sank into the embrace of butter-soft black leather.

Ethan climbed behind the wheel and switched on the ignition. He whistled with appreciation as the engine purred to life. "Hang on," he said, and hit the gas.

The car roared down the street, across the bridge, and onto the highway.

Sofia laughed as they flew down the road. "Where are we going?"

"There's a town not far from here."

Sofia nodded, remembering that Saintcrow had once mentioned the place.

A short time later, she spied lights in the distance. Ethan eased off the gas as they approached the town. It was Friday night and the sidewalks were teeming with couples and families.

He parked the car and they joined the crowd. Being surrounded by so many people made it easy for Sofia to pretend they were just a man and a woman like any other as they strolled toward the theater. She slid a glance at Ethan, wondering for the first time if it was difficult for him to be in the midst of so many people.

He bought their tickets and they went into the lobby.

"Do you want anything?" he asked.

She glanced at the long line at the concession counter and shook her head. "I've got candy in my bag." At his amused look, she said, "Never leave home without it."

Women and chocolate. He had never understood it.

They found two seats in the center section. Even though he was surrounded by hundreds of people, his whole being was focused on the woman beside him. Her scent engulfed him, the beat of her heart thundered in his ears, her nearness aroused his desire. It had been a long time since he'd had a woman. As the theater went dark, he glanced at Sofia, imagining her in bed beside him, caressing him. What would it be like, making love to a woman now that he was a vampire? Would he be able to control his lust? His hunger? Or would he sink his fangs into her tender flesh and rip her to pieces? Vampire sex was something his sire had neglected to mention in How to Be a Vampire 101.

With an effort, he forced himself to block everything from his mind but the action on the screen.

Sofia slid a look at Ethan. He sat stiffly beside her, his jaw clenched. Was he sorry he had asked her out? She had expected him to put his arm around her, maybe hold her hand, but he seemed oblivious to her presence. Which was too bad, because she was acutely conscious of him beside her. She didn't know if it was his cologne or just his own masculine scent, but it was driving her crazy.

She was glad when the movie was over.

Outside, she avoided his gaze.

"It's still early," he said. "Would you like to go get a drink?"

"Would you?"

He frowned at her. "What do you mean?"

"Nothing. I could use a drink."

"There's a nightclub just down the street. I think you might like it."

"All right." Maybe she was overreacting, Sofia mused, as they made their way to the club. Maybe he hadn't been ignoring her; maybe he'd just been caught up in the movie.

The Fandango was your usual, run-of-the-mill nightspot—dimly lit, a small dance floor surrounded by booths and tables. Standing at the bar, Ethan ordered a glass of cabernet; Sofia asked the bartender for a tequila sunrise.

"Did you enjoy the show?" he asked as they waited for their drinks to arrive.

"Not really."

"No? I thought it was pretty good."

"You must have."

He frowned at her. "What do you mean?"

"You watched it like there was going to be a test later. I felt like . . . never mind."

"Like what?"

"Like I was alone."

Damn. "I'm sorry, Sofie." He picked up their drinks. "Come on; let's go sit over there." He led the way to a booth in the back, slid in beside her. "Sitting there in the dark, I couldn't think of anything but you. Holding you. Making love to you."

"And that's a problem?"

"Isn't it?"

"I'm not sure of anything except that I'm not ready to go there just yet."

"Me either, but not for the reason you're thinking."

"I'm not thinking anything."

"No? You haven't wondered what it would be like, making love to a vampire?"

She made a vague gesture. "Not really. I mean, we've just met."

"Well, I've thought about it. I haven't had a woman since Saintcrow turned me."

"Oh. Oh! I'm sorry, I didn't know . . ."

"Wait! I don't mean I can't. I just don't know what it's like, or if I can control myself so that I don't hurt you. Or worse."

Sofia picked up her glass and took a long drink. She hadn't thought that making love to Ethan might put her life in danger, but now that he mentioned it, she was surprised it hadn't occurred to her. He was a hunter, after all, and she was prey.

"Would you like to try dancing again?" he asked as the band broke into something soft and slow.

"Only if you promise not to bolt out the door."

"Not sure I can promise that. So, are you game?" He swore under his breath as Sofia burst out laughing. "Sorry," he muttered. "Wrong choice of words."

"I would love to dance with you, Mr. Parrish," she said, partly because she wanted to be in his arms, partly out of a bizarre sense of curiosity to see what would happen.

The lights dimmed as he led her onto the floor. As always, there was something magical about being in Ethan's arms. Even knowing what he was, she wanted nothing more than to be close to him, to inhale his musky scent, to feel his lips moving in her hair.

He drew her closer, so that his body brushed hers with every movement. Desire sparked between them, the same desire she saw when she looked up and met his gaze.

Lowering his head, he kissed her, his tongue sweeping over her lower lip. It sent a shaft of heat sizzling through her, quickened her senses, made her even more aware of his body touching hers. She tensed when his fangs touched her throat, relaxed as a wave of sensual pleasure swept over her. He was drinking from her, here, on the dance floor.

And she didn't mind at all.

He took only a little, as always, and murmured, "I'm sorry," when he lifted his head.

"Don't be," she said, with a crooked grin. "It kept you from running away."

"Sofia."

"Hmm?"

His arm tightened around her waist. "I think I'm falling in love with you." His words were met with stunned silence. Dammit, he should have kept his mouth shut. "Sofie, say something."

"I think I might be in love with you, too."

They were, he thought, the sweetest words he had ever heard. Oblivious to the fact that the music had stopped, or that people were staring, he cupped her face in his hands and kissed her, silently thanking fate or Cupid or whoever was in charge of such things that she hadn't run screaming from his presence.

Sofia's cheeks grew hot as the sounds of cheers and applause rippled through the room. Taking Ethan's hand, she tugged him off the dance floor and into the relative privacy of their booth.

As soon as they were seated, he took her in his arms again. She snuggled against him, her head resting on his shoulder. For the first time, she had an inkling of why Holly and Kadie had risked everything for the men they loved.

It was close to midnight when they returned to Morgan Creek. Ethan parked the Viper in front of the garage, then opened Sofia's door and handed her out of the car. "I guess I'd better get you home."

"I decided to spend the night here, in Morgan Creek."

"Oh?"

She nodded. A curl of pleasure unfurled in the pit of her

stomach when he took her hand as they walked toward the house that was now her office. "I thought maybe you'd stay the night with me."

He lifted one brow.

"I didn't mean that! I just thought you'd keep me company for a while, and then we could spend tomorrow night together. If you want to."

Giving her hand a squeeze, he said, "Believe me, I want to."

"It's settled, then."

She hadn't bothered to lock the door, figuring only the workers and the mailman knew Morgan Creek even existed. As soon as she switched on the lights, she knew she should have turned the dead bolt.

Ethan thrust Sofia behind him when a man stepped out of the shadows. "Who the hell are you?"

"Who the hell are *you*?"

Ethan took a deep breath. *Vampire.* "What are you doing here?"

"I'm looking for someone."

"Yeah? Well, there's no one here but us."

"You're lying, fledgling," the other vampire said. "I want to know what's going on here. And what you've done with Saintcrow."

"What are you talking about?" Ethan asked.

"This used to be his town."

Ethan nodded. "It still is. We're just doing a little renovation."

The other vampire snorted. "And I suppose you're part of *we*?"

"As a matter of fact, I am. Now who the hell are you?"

"Nolan Browning. I lived in Morgan Creek for over half a century." He prowled around the room as if he had, indeed, been there before. "Good times, they were." He glanced at Sofia. "Always something good to eat."

"She's mine," Ethan said, his voice little more than a growl of warning.

"No problem," Browning said with a shrug. "Now that you know who I am, I'll ask you again. Who are you?"

"Name's Parrish. Saintcrow's my sire."

As Ethan had earlier, Browning took a deep breath. And all the tension drained out of him. "So, where is he?"

"I don't know. He doesn't answer to me."

"Or anyone else," Browning muttered.

Sofia clutched Ethan's arm as a faint ripple stirred the air.

"Actually, I answer to Kadie," Saintcrow said, materializing behind Browning. "What brings you here?"

Browning spun around. "I ran afoul of a master vampire and I need a place to hole up. I thought maybe I could hide behind the wards on the bridge, but . . . I guess times have changed."

Saintcrow shrugged. "Some things, perhaps. One thing that hasn't changed is that the people in my town are under my protection. Human or vampire. You know what I'm saying?"

Browning glanced over his shoulder at Sofia.

She cringed as his hungry gaze moved over her.

A snarl rose in Ethan's throat. There was nothing human about it.

"Nolan!"

Browning looked back at Saintcrow. "I understand."

"Ethan, why don't you spend the night at my place as long as Browning is here? Nolan, you can stay up at Blair House for a few days, and then I want you gone."

"Are you kicking me out?"

"If you want to think of it that way, yes."

Browning nodded. "It's your town," he muttered. "Mind if I have a look around?"

"Help yourself." Eyes narrowed, Saintcrow watched Browning leave the house.

Ethan followed his sire's gaze. "My gut tells me you don't believe a word he said."

"I don't know what game he's playing, but I can smell a lie a mile away and he's not hiding from anybody." Saintcrow looked thoughtful a moment, then said, "Take Sofia with you when you go up to my place. She'll be safer there."

"You don't trust him," Ethan said flatly. It wasn't a question.

Saintcrow smiled, showing a hint of fang. "Like he said, times change. Sometimes old friends become new enemies. It pays to be prepared until we find out which way the wind blows. I'll see you later."

Sofia was shaking inside when Saintcrow left the house. She wasn't stupid. She had caught the underlying currents of distrust in the conversation between Saintcrow and Browning. The fact that Saintcrow thought she would be safer spending the night in his lair proved something was going on, something she didn't quite understand.

Ethan pulled her into his arms. "Hey, don't worry. I won't let anything happen to you."

"I want to go home."

"Didn't you hear Saintcrow? He thinks you should stay here tonight."

"I'll be safe in my own house. Browning can't cross the threshold. And why would he want to come after me anyway?" Even as she asked the question, she remembered the feral look in the vampire's eyes.

"Browning might not be able to cross the threshold," Ethan said quietly. "But any vampire worthy of the name can compel humans to do his bidding."

Her eyes widened as she realized what he meant. A stranger in Browning's thrall could break into her house and drag her outside. It had happened before, with Mateo.

"I'm sorry, Sofie. I never should have gotten you tangled up in my life. But I swear, I won't let anyone hurt you."

"I know." Resting her cheek against his chest, she prayed it was a promise he could keep.

Chapter Eighteen

Heeding Saintcrow's advice, Ethan transported Sofia to the master vampire's house. Made of weathered gray stone, it had turrets at all four corners, which made her think of an ancient English castle, though she had never seen one with thick iron bars covering the front door and all the windows. She couldn't help thinking the place looked like something out of an old, scary movie.

Muttering, "Home sweet home," Ethan opened the door for her.

Sofia shivered as she stepped into the lion's den. She didn't know what she had expected—tapestries and antique furniture, perhaps—but the interior was lovely. Dropping her handbag on a small table in the foyer, she turned in a slow circle. The sofa and love seat were modern and obviously expensive. Only the fireplace seemed to be as old as the house. Large enough to hold a horse and rider, it dominated the room. But it was the suit of armor in the corner that captured her attention. Saintcrow was ancient. Had that armor been his? Had he worn it in the Crusades? The thought that it was possible was mind-boggling.

"This is quite a place," she remarked.

"Yeah." Ethan had known Saintcrow was rich, but seeing

this made it real. He had seen that sofa in a magazine. It hadn't been cheap. It made him wonder just how much money his sire had, and how he'd acquired it. "Do you feel like exploring?"

"Haven't you been here before?"

"No." Taking her hand, he said, "Come on. Let's go upstairs and find you a room for the night."

Sofia got a quick look at the kitchen as they passed by. She was somewhat surprised to find it outfitted with modern appliances, including a microwave and a toaster. "Do you think Saintcrow bought all this stuff for Kadie before he turned her?"

"It's the only explanation that makes sense," Ethan said, although that wasn't necessarily true. Some vampires stored bagged blood in refrigerators and warmed it in microwaves, but he doubted Saintcrow was one of them.

With some trepidation, Sofia followed Ethan up the wide stairway to the second floor.

She opened the first door on the left at the top of the stairs. It was a nice-enough room, she thought. The walls were off-white, the rug a deep forest green. Matching drapes hung at the single barred window. The four-poster bed looked like an antique.

Curious, she walked down the hallway, peeking into each room. All were decorated much the same as the first one. Only the colors were different.

"Did he keep a harem?" she wondered aloud.

"Beats me."

"I'll take the first room," Sofia decided. "Where are you going to sleep?"

"I'll take the one next to yours."

A narrow stairway led to the third floor. "The turret rooms must be up there," Sofia said. "Come on; I've always wanted to see one."

Ethan followed her up the winding stone staircase.

She felt a twinge of disappointment as she looked in the first room. It was round and empty, as was the second one. Apparently, Kadie hadn't been interested in remodeling up here. The third room contained a narrow cot and an old wooden chair that looked like it would break if anyone sat on it.

Sofia paused to stare at the black iron cross on the wall across from the bed. Had Saintcrow once been a religious man? Or was it merely a decoration that held no meaning?

The last room held a bed, a table, and another rickety chair. A floor-to-ceiling tapestry that looked hundreds of years old covered the far wall. The colors were faded, the edges frayed.

"It's still beautiful, isn't it?" she murmured.

"Yeah." Ethan took a step forward, his eyes narrowing. The tapestry depicted a knight in chain mail mounted on a rearing black stallion. He held a sword in one hand and a shield in the other. "Am I imagining things or is that Saint-crow?"

Sofia moved up beside him. "I think it is." Reaching out, she ran her fingers over the red cross emblazoned on the knight's surcoat, took a quick step back when a peculiar grinding noise came from behind the tapestry. "What was that?"

"I don't know." Moving to the edge of the drapery, Ethan pulled it away from the wall.

Sofia's eyes widened when she saw a narrow doorway. "Where do you think it goes?"

Ethan shrugged. "Only one way to find out."

She held her breath as Ethan opened the door. In the dim light from the window, she saw a long, winding staircase.

"What is it?" Sofia asked. "Where does it go?"

"I think Saintcrow's lair is down there."

She backed away as visions of the vampire asleep in his

coffin filled her mind. Turning on her heel, she hurried down the stairs to the living room.

Ethan closed the door, then followed her.

He found Sofia sitting on the sofa, face pale, her arms folded over her breasts. "Every time I think I've got a handle on the whole vampire thing, something new comes along and spooks me. I never thought of myself as a coward, but then, I never knew vampires were real."

"And now that you know, everything's changed?"

She nodded. "I guess once you've seen the wizard behind the curtain, you can't pretend he isn't there." Reaching for Ethan's hand, she pulled him down beside her. "In spite of everything, I'm glad Holly brought us together."

Ethan nodded, then kissed her lightly, hoping she would always feel that way.

"Browning can't walk in the daylight, can he?" Sofia glanced at the bed, thinking she should have brought a nightgown with her. But then, spending the night had been a spur-of-the-moment decision.

"I don't know," he said, "but I don't think so. I'm sure Saintcrow would have mentioned it."

Sofia looked around the room. She told herself there was nothing to fear. No one could get into the house.

"Are you all right?"

"I don't want to sleep in here alone."

Ethan nodded slowly. "Okay."

"Do you have a problem with that?"

"I don't, but you might."

"Why?" Comprehension dawned as she watched him search for an answer. "Oh!" she exclaimed. "Are you gross during the day?"

"Nothing like cutting right to the chase," he muttered.

"But to answer your question, I don't know. The subject never came up. And I've never seen a vampire at rest."

"Oh." She worried her lower lip with her teeth. What if he looked really dead, all pale and shriveled? Did he stop breathing?

Ethan pinched the bridge of his nose. Then, shoving his hands in his pants' pockets, he sent a mental question to Saintcrow. *What do vampires look like at rest?*

He immediately heard his sire's amused laughter echo in his mind. *Don't worry, you won't look like a corpse. Your skin will look a little paler, your breathing stops, but other than that, you just look like you're asleep. Nothing will wake you, unless you're in danger.*

Sending Saintcrow his thanks—and hoping he could believe him—Ethan said, "Mostly, I'll look like I'm asleep."

Sofia smiled, obviously relieved. "Then you'll stay?"

He nodded. Dawn was hours away, but she was ready for bed now. How was he going to lie beside her and not take her in his arms? "I'll wait downstairs. Call me when you're ready to turn in."

She closed the door after him, then went into the bathroom. There was no shower, only a tub. But what a tub. It was round and blue and deep. She found a bottle of bubble bath in the cupboard. Minutes later, she was submerged in bubbles. Resting her head on the back of the tub, she closed her eyes. Life had certainly taken an unexpected turn. Who'd have thought, when she'd agreed to go out with Holly's cousin, that she would find herself falling in love with him? Or staying in the home of an ancient vampire?

When the water cooled, she stepped out of the tub, dried herself with a thick terry towel, and got dressed, wishing again that she'd brought a nightgown. But then, maybe it was just as well that she hadn't, since Ethan would be resting beside her. The thought sent a little thrill of excitement down her spine.

Although it was quite late, she was suddenly wide awake. Barefooted, she tiptoed down the stairs, then thought how foolish it was. Ethan would know she was coming long before she got there.

She found him stretched out on the sofa, his arms folded behind his head. He had taken off his boots, laid a fire in the enormous hearth. "Cozy," she murmured.

Sitting up, he patted the place beside him.

Sofia bit down on her lower lip. She had been alone with him before, but this was different somehow. She had nowhere to run, no one to call for help if he suddenly lost control.

He lifted one brow, as though amused by her sudden trepidation.

And her fears dissolved. This was Ethan. He would never hurt her. She sank down on the sofa, a little frisson of heat spiraling through her when her thigh brushed his. "I've never seen a fireplace that big."

"Me either." He slid his arm around her shoulders. "You smell good," he murmured. "Like roses."

"Oh. I thought . . . it's the bubble bath."

Laughter rumbled in his throat. "You thought I meant your blood, didn't you?"

She nodded as a flush warmed her cheeks. "Sorry."

"That smells good, too," he said, nuzzling the side of her neck.

"Have you fed lately?"

"Earlier tonight. Why? Are you worried?"

"Maybe. A little."

His laugh turned wicked. "Beautiful young maiden, pure and untouched, all alone in the wicked vampire's lair."

She jammed her elbow into his side. "Stop that!"

"Okay. Geez, I was just kidding."

"Yeah, well, it's a little too close to the truth, don't you think?"

"Especially the beautiful part."

"I didn't mean that."

"I know. But you are beautiful, Sofia. The most beautiful woman I've ever known. And the sweetest . . . make that the nicest, so you don't mistake my meaning again," he said with a wry grin.

She stared up at him, pleased by his words. Her heart skipped a beat when he captured her lips with his. Leaning back, he turned slightly as he drew her into his arms, his mouth moving slowly over hers in a long, lazy kiss that warmed every fiber of her being. His fingers played in her hair. She moaned low in her throat when his tongue swept over her lips.

She didn't remember moving, but somehow, they were lying side by side on the floor in front of the fire. She closed her eyes as Ethan rained kisses on her cheeks, her forehead, lingering on her lips, the pulse beating rapidly in her throat.

Caught up in the heat of the moment, she slid her hands under his shirt, reveling in the touch of his bare skin. When he rose over her, his eyes burning hotter than the flames, she realized, too late, that she had inadvertently sent him the wrong signal.

"Ethan . . ." She shook her head. It was too soon. She wasn't ready to take their relationship to the next level.

He drew back, a groan erupting from his throat.

"I'm sorry . . . I . . . I can't. Not yet."

Eyes closed, he rested his forehead against hers. "I thought . . ." He sucked in a deep breath. "It's all right."

He sounded like he was in pain. "Are you . . . okay?"

His answer was a wordless grunt. And then he rolled onto his side, carrying her with him, his arm draped over her waist.

"Are you mad?"

He opened one eye. "No. Just . . . no." With a shake of his head, he sat up. He didn't know which was worse—his hunger for her blood or his need to bury himself deep within her. He kissed the tip of her nose, then rose to his feet in a single fluid movement. "I need some fresh air," he said, his voice thick. "Good night."

"'Night." She stared after him as he left the room, wishing she had the nerve to follow her heart, but she couldn't ignore the little voice in the back of her mind warning that once she surrendered her virginity, there was no way to get it back.

Kadie curled up against Saintcrow, her hand resting on his chest, her head on his shoulder. A cozy fire burned low in the living room hearth of their New Orleans place. It was the only light in the room. "What do you think Browning really wants? I mean, why did he come back after all this time?"

"I don't know. But that story about running afoul of a master vampire is a load of crap."

"Do you think he went there just to find you?"

He shrugged. "Doesn't make much sense."

"Maybe he thought he'd defeat you and take over the town."

"I'd like to see him try it."

"My hero."

He brushed a kiss across the top of her head. "I can see why he'd want to go back. They had it pretty easy there back then." He let out a mock groan when she punched him in the arm. "Yeah, yeah, I know, my bad. But, morality aside, life was good for the vampires." He caught her hand before she could hit him again. "And I met you there, Kadie Andrews Saintcrow, love of my life."

"And such a *long* life."

"It didn't really start until I met you."

"Rylan." She melted against him, her heart swelling with love.

"No regrets?" It was a question he asked from time to time.

"Not one." Looking up, she met his gaze. "I have a bad feeling about his being there."

"Not to worry, Kadie, my sweet."

She nodded. He was the oldest vampire in the world. Powerful. Virtually indestructible. So why was she still so apprehensive?

Chapter Nineteen

Nolan Browning strolled through the town, pausing to investigate the changes being made in the hotel, the tavern. He was surprised Saintcrow had decided to renovate the place. To what end, he had no idea. Saintcrow didn't strike him as the type of man to take up innkeeping as a hobby—unless he intended to turn Morgan Creek back into the vampire haven it had once been. Ah, those were the days. A secure lair to rest in. Always a good meal. No hunters breathing down their necks.

He shook his head. Kadie would never allow Saintcrow to resume that lifestyle, but he thought it was an excellent idea. Had, in fact, come here hoping to find the town abandoned so he could start his own hideaway with prey of his own choosing. He licked his lips as he thought of that pretty little human female. Sofia. Young and innocent, she would provide nourishment to a hungry vampire for a good long time. And satisfy other needs, as well.

If he could find a way to defeat Saintcrow, the town would be his. He dismissed Parrish out of hand. The fledgling was too young and inexperienced to cause him any trouble.

Browning strolled through the park, thinking about

the past. There were few of the original Morgan Creek vampires left. Lilith was gone. Saintcrow had dispatched Kiel years ago for attacking Kadie. Trent Lambert had been destroyed by Leticia Braga. That left Quinn, Darrick, Felix, and Wes.

Nolan shook his head ruefully. The five of them together didn't have enough power to take down a master vampire. Saintcrow had existed far longer than all of them put together. With age came added strength and increased power. The master vampire could crush them all with a glance.

Browning looked up at the house on the hill, reluctant to give up his plan to take over the town. He was tired of living among humans, tired of worrying about some hunter taking his head while he rested. He had been happy in Morgan Creek, but if he was determined to take the town away from Saintcrow, he needed backup. But where to find a vampire old enough, strong enough, to defeat the master of Morgan Creek?

Chapter Twenty

Saturday morning, Sofia woke with a start. She had been dreaming, but she couldn't remember what it had been about. And for a moment, she couldn't remember where she was either. Jackknifing to a sitting position, she glanced around. She was in a room in Saintcrow's house. But where was Ethan? He had been beside her last night. She remembered waking up several times and finding him there.

Frowning, she slipped out of bed, put on her shoes, and went downstairs. When her stomach growled, she blew out a sigh. There was no food here, which meant a fairly long, hungry walk to the office, but there was no help for it.

She murmured, "Bless you, Ethan," when she saw the Viper parked in front of the mansion.

Sliding behind the wheel, she rolled down the windows and started the engine. She let it idle a minute, listening to the engine's low growl.

And then she flew down the hill. It took only moments to reach the outskirts of the town. As she drew nearer, she heard the distant sound of hammering. Unlike many construction companies, the Advantage Construction crew didn't take weekends off, although she normally did.

With regret, she pulled the car into the driveway and cut the engine. She didn't know where Saintcrow was, although she assumed he must be here on weekends. Someone had to be available in case one of the workers needed something.

She shut off the engine, thinking that one of these afternoons, she was going to get behind the wheel and take a long drive.

Going into the house they now called the office, she double-locked the front door, then went into the bathroom. She had taken to leaving a few changes of clothes in the bedroom closet. After her morning ablutions, she slipped on a loose-fitting shirt and a pair of yoga pants, then went into the kitchen to make breakfast. After pouring herself a second cup of coffee, she went out to sit on the porch stairs.

It was a beautiful morning, the sky a bold, clear blue decorated with a few scattered white clouds. Darker clouds loomed above the mountains, making her wonder if it would rain later.

It was so peaceful here, she mused. Hard to believe men and women had once been kept in this place to feed a coven of vampires. Looking around, it was easy to visualize children playing in the park while their mothers looked on. She imagined families going to the movie theater on a Friday night, walking to church on Sunday morning . . .

Reality wiped away her bucolic vision. There was no church in Morgan Creek. Had the people prayed in their homes, or had they given up all hope, all faith, when their prayers to be rescued went unanswered year after year? Had they wanted a church and been denied one? What was it like to have your liberty stolen? There had been no freedom of choice here—only slavery for the helpless men and women who had sought shelter and found bondage instead. How had they survived? How would she have survived if she had been unfortunate enough to be one of them? Would she have fought against the vampires? Tried to escape? Or just given up?

"You would have learned to cope. Mortals have an amazing capacity to adapt to their circumstances."

Startled by Saintcrow's abrupt appearance, Sofia almost tumbled down the stairs. "What are you doing here?"

"Kadie's at rest," he said with a shrug. "I was bored."

Sofia shook her head. She didn't believe that for a minute. From what Micah had told her, the vampire and his wife were practically joined at the hip. "Why are you really here?"

"You won't like it."

"I'm sure of that!"

He gave her an arch look. "I don't want you going back to your place for a while."

"What? Why not?"

"Browning is up to something. Until I know what it is, you're safer here."

She thought about arguing, but then she remembered what Ethan had said about vampires being able to compel humans to do their bidding. "What do you think Browning wants?"

"I'm not sure. Like I told Kadie last night, I think he wants to take over the town. But he'd have to defeat me to do that."

"Could he? Defeat you?"

"You tell me." He unleashed his power for the space of a heartbeat.

It was a frightful feeling, like being weighed down by an unseen force. For that brief moment of time, she was completely at his mercy, her will subject to his. Fear washed through her, and with it a fleeting sense of imminent destruction. And then it was gone.

Sofia stared at him as the last ripples of power faded, certain that no creature on earth could defeat him.

Saintcrow grinned inwardly. She was right. No single vampire could conquer him. But more than a dozen or so, working together, might be able to accomplish it. But he saw no reason to tell her that.

The rest of the day passed in spurts. Sometimes she was very busy—answering the phone, straightening out a discrepancy in the plumber's bill, writing checks—leaving her to wonder if every Saturday was as hectic. Sometimes she sat at her desk, staring out the window, wishing away the hours until she could see Ethan again.

Saintcrow came and went a couple of times, making her wonder how he had spent his days before Ethan decided to renovate the town. Until she met Saintcrow, she had never known vampires could be awake during the day. Micah had told her that only ancient vampires could walk in the sun. How long did it take to become ancient? Fifty years? A hundred years? A thousand? If so, the master vampire had a long time to wait until Kadie could share the day with him. And Ethan . . . he hadn't even been a vampire for a year yet.

Sighing, she propped her elbows on the desk and rested her chin on her folded hands. She was falling hard for Ethan. If she decided to continue seeing him, she would have to make a lot of adjustments in her life. So, she guessed the big question was, would it be worth it?

The answer that immediately came to mind was, *Yes. Yes. Definitely yes!*

And that settled that.

* * *

Ethan rose with the setting of the sun. He closed his eyes and opened his senses, smiled when he realized Sofia was still in the office. He'd wondered, in spite of Saint-crow's admonition that she should stay in town, whether she had convinced him to take her home.

Rising, he took a quick shower, pulled on a pair of jeans and a t-shirt, and willed himself to the office.

He found Sofia at her desk, straightening a pile of papers. He whistled softly. "You even look good from behind."

She glanced at him over her shoulder, one brow arched. "I'll bet you say that to all the girls."

"No way."

Like magnets inexplicably drawn together, they moved into each other's arms.

"You were gone when I woke up," Sofia said, a note of censure in her tone.

"I know. I'm sorry. I stayed as long as I could."

Her brow furrowed. "What does that mean?"

"You're a hell of a temptation, you know. Lying there beside you all night . . ." He shook his head. "I'm not made of stone."

She curled her hands around his biceps and squeezed. "Are you sure about that?"

"You know what I mean."

Sofia nodded. Being close to him made her want things better left unexplored, too.

"So, you about through here?" he asked.

"Yeah. I was thinking of driving into the next town for dinner." She hesitated. "Do you want to go with me?"

"I'm sure as hell not letting you go alone."

She smiled up at him, eyes twinkling. "I thought you'd say that."

"Yeah? What am I thinking now?"

She widened her eyes, then slapped him lightly, play-fully. "Shame on you!"

He grinned at her. "I bet you're thinking the same thing."

Lifting her nose in the air, she said, "You'd lose."

"Yeah?" His gaze bored into hers. He didn't have to read her mind to know what she was thinking. He could smell her desire for him on her skin.

"All right, all right," she exclaimed. "Guilty as charged."

"I know a way we can both get what we want," he said, his voice a husky purr.

"I'm sure you do!" Going up on her tiptoes, she kissed his cheek. "But I'm starving."

"So am I, darlin'," he growled. "So am I."

"Me first," she said with a saucy grin, and hurried out the front door.

She chose an Italian restaurant, where she ordered rigatoni with marina sauce and a glass of red wine.

The waitress looked at Ethan, a question in her eyes.

"Just a glass of wine, thanks."

With a nod, she went to turn in their order.

Ethan wrinkled his nose against the strong scent of olive oil, basil, oregano, garlic, and Romano cheese.

"Maybe you should go for a walk," Sofia suggested when she saw his expression.

"I'm not leaving you alone." He shook his head. "Italian food used to be my favorite. Now I can't stand the smell."

"Why didn't you say something?"

"I don't want you giving up things you like on my account."

He fell silent when the waitress returned with their drinks and a basket of warm breadsticks.

Ethan lifted his glass. "To you, Sofia Ravenwood. For giving me something to live for."

Lifting her own goblet, she touched it to his. "To you, Ethan Parrish, for bringing a dash of excitement into my life."

Gazing into each other's eyes, they took a drink.

Sofia's dinner arrived a short time later. Her meal was delicious, but she didn't comment on it. She ate as quickly as possible, aware of Ethan sitting across the table, looking at everything but her.

When she put her plate aside, certain she couldn't eat another bite, he insisted she have dessert. He also insisted on paying the check.

"But you didn't even eat," she protested as they left the restaurant.

"Doesn't matter. I've never let a girl pay for her own dinner in my life, and I'm not about to start now. Besides," he said with a grin, "I can deduct it as a business expense." He held the car door for her, then paused. "I know how much you love this car. Do you want to drive home?"

"Are you sure you don't mind, Mr. Macho Man?"

"Well, it might tarnish my manly image, but I'm willing to risk it for you."

Ever the gentleman, he walked her to the driver's side and opened the door before taking his place in the passenger seat. Throwing her a look of mock terror, he clutched the door handle when she started the car.

"Very funny," Sofia muttered as she put the car in gear and stomped on the gas.

The Viper peeled out, leaving a layer of rubber behind.

"Geez, Sofie!" Ethan exclaimed. "I may be hard to kill, but you're not."

He figured it was the right thing to say because she immediately eased off the gas. "One of these nights we'll have to find a long stretch of deserted highway," he remarked, settling back in his seat. "Someplace where you can really open her up."

"Sounds like fun."

"If this bomb had a bigger front seat, I'd suggest we find a dark spot and make out."

"Make out?" Sofia laughed. "Do they still call it that?"

"I don't know, but you know what I mean."

"Do you think that other vampire—Browning—is still in Morgan Creek?" Sofia asked, changing the subject.

"I don't think so."

"I don't like him."

"Smart girl."

"Saintcrow thinks he wants to take over the town. What do you think?"

"I doubt if Saintcrow is wrong very often."

"Doesn't it just blow your mind that he's lived so long? I can't even imagine it." She slid a glance in his direction. "You could live as long as he has. Do you ever think about that?"

"Sure. But I can't help wondering if it's a good thing. I mean, as long as he's lived, he must have seen everything, done everything, been everywhere. What is there left to do that he hasn't already done?"

It was a good question, Sofia thought as she drove across the bridge. One she hadn't really thought about.

She parked in front of Saintcrow's lair, smiled at Ethan as he came around to open her door. A gentleman vampire, she thought with an inward grin as she stepped out of the car.

She had never lived with a man, or had one stay the night in her apartment, and even though they weren't doing anything in bed other than sleeping, there was something incredibly intimate about spending the night in the same house.

Excitement fluttered in the pit of her stomach as he

closed and locked the door behind them. When they moved into the living room, a fire sprang to life in the hearth.

Startled, she turned to look at Ethan. "Did you . . . ?"

He winked at her. "Yeah. I thought you might be cold."

"How?"

He shrugged. "I don't know, really. I think it and it happens. Kind of cool, actually."

Nodding, she turned her back to the flames. Even though it was really cold outside tonight, she'd noticed it was always chilly in Saintcrow's lair.

"I guess you're ready to turn in for the night," Ethan remarked.

"Not really. It's still early. Why?"

"I was just hoping to have your company a little longer."

"We could talk awhile." She settled on the couch, her smile an invitation for him to join her.

"What do you want to talk about?"

"I don't know." It was hard to think with his thigh brushing hers. All her senses went into overdrive at his nearness. "Um, well, what kind of plans do you have for the future?"

"That's what you want to talk about? My future?"

"You must have given it some thought. I mean, you could live forever. What are you going to do with all that time?"

"I've never thought much past tomorrow since Saintcrow turned me. There aren't many job opportunities for a vampire. Sure, that TV vamp Nick Knight was a cop and managed to work nights, but I always wondered how he went through the academy, and how he avoided going to court. I guess he could have mesmerized his captain into giving him the night shift, but how did he learn to be a cop without going through the training? It was just TV, not real life," he added ruefully. "I guess it didn't have to make sense."

"Maybe he got turned after he became a police officer?"

"Maybe. What about your future, Sofie?" he asked, his gaze holding hers. "What do you want out of life?"

"The same things as a lot of women, I guess. A home and a family. A man who loves me . . ."

"I love you," he said, his voice whisper soft.

"Ethan . . ."

"I know. You don't want to tie yourself to a vampire. I don't blame you."

"It's not that, exactly. I mean, we hardly know each other. But that's not it either. Holly seems happy enough, and I know I wanted to be a vampire once, but not so much anymore. I'll get old and you won't and . . ."

"Shh. It's all right. I'm not asking you to give up your life for me. Just a few more weeks, until the work here is finished, and then . . . we'll say good-bye."

The word *good-bye* seemed to echo in the back of her mind. At the thought of never seeing him again, a single tear slid down her cheek.

"Hey, Sofie, don't."

His words only made her tears come faster.

He huffed a sigh, then gathered her into his arms, his hand stroking her back while her tears dampened his shirt-front. He kissed her cheek, the top of her head, and then, unable to help himself, he ran his tongue along the side of her neck. The temptation to drink from her, to drink it all and make her what he was, was nearly overpowering. She would stay with him then, he thought. With her by his side forever, being a vampire wouldn't be a curse but a blessing.

As if she knew what he was thinking, she pulled away. Murmuring, "Sorry," she wiped her cheeks with her fingers. "Ethan?"

The trepidation in her voice warned him that his eyes

had gone red and he turned away from her, ashamed of his thoughts. He had been made vampire against his will. How could he even think of doing it to the woman he claimed to love? What kind of monster was he?

"Ethan?"

"It's late," he said, his voice almost a growl. "You should go to bed. And lock the door."

She didn't argue. Nor did she give in to the sudden urge to run out of the room. Never a good idea to run from a predator. Instead, she rose slowly to her feet and walked calmly up the stairs to her room, where she locked the door, then threw herself across the bed as more tears came.

She had known she was falling in love with Ethan, but it wasn't until he talked of never seeing her again that she realized how much she really cared for him, and how big a hole his absence would leave in her heart.

Chapter Twenty-One

Sunday was a horrible day. It dawned cold and rainy. Sofia drove to the office/house where she spent her days. After showering, she fixed a quick breakfast and then, unable to face another minute alone in Morgan Creek, she drove to the next town and went to an early movie.

After the show, she grabbed a burger and fries from a drive-through. Glancing at her watch, she decided she had enough time to take in a second movie and still get back to Saintcrow's before dark.

It was still raining when she left the theater. She made a quick trip to the mall, where she bought a nightgown, a robe, and slippers, Earlier, she'd asked Saintcrow to go to her place and pack her a suitcase, but he'd neglected to bring anything for her to sleep in. She made one more stop for some take-out chicken before heading back to town. The weather perfectly suited her mood, she thought as she crossed the bridge. She had cried herself to sleep last night and it had showed in the mirror this morning. There were dark shadows under her eyes, but not as deep or dark as the ache in her heart.

She parked the car in front of Saintcrow's place, went inside, and locked the door. She felt as if she was being watched as she turned on all the lights in the spooky old house. Sitting on the sofa, she picked at her dinner, then put it aside.

What was she going to do about Ethan? She could stay with him for a few years, but the longer they were together, the more difficult it would be to leave him.

She could let him turn her into a vampire. . . . She tried to imagine herself living only by night, stalking innocent victims, stealing their blood, maybe accidentally killing one or two . . .

Sofia shook her head. Why had she ever thought she wanted to be a vampire?

She could just end her relationship with Ethan now and go home. But she quickly rejected that idea, too.

There seemed no easy answer, she thought, blinking back her tears. No way to find a happily-ever-after ending with her vampire.

Ethan stood out of sight in the hallway, growing more and more discouraged as he caught snatches of Sofia's troubled thoughts. Maybe he should make it easy for her and just disappear. Saintcrow would look after her if she decided to stay on as his bookkeeper until the renovation was complete. And if she wanted to leave, the master vampire could probably find her another job. There seemed to be no end to his sire's talents.

As usual, anger roused his hunger and, with it, the desire to kill something. Frustrated, he willed himself out of the house, then strolled down the hill, his curses filling the air. He didn't need a mortal lover. And he didn't need his sire. Who the hell was Saintcrow, to tell him what he could and couldn't do? The vampire was ancient. No doubt he had killed dozens, maybe hundreds of people in the past. What gave him the right to tell Ethan he couldn't take a single life?

He let out a gasp of mingled surprise and pain as a pair of strong hands locked around his throat from behind.

"I'm the one who holds your next breath in his hands." Saintcrow's voice, soft, compelling—his breath as cold as the grave against the back of Ethan's neck.

Ethan clawed at the fingers digging into his flesh, but to no avail. It was like trying to pry open a steel trap.

"You want to take a life?" Saintcrow asked. "Very well. Come with me."

Before Ethan could answer, he found himself in a dark alley, though with his preternatural vision, he saw everything clearly—the overflowing trash cans, the wizened old man clad in rags, sucking the last drops of cheap wine from a bottle.

"Take him," Saintcrow said. "I give him to you."

Ethan grimaced. The man smelled worse than the garbage.

"What's the matter?" Saintcrow asked with a sneer. "Not good enough for you?"

Saintcrow grabbed Ethan's forearm, and when the world stopped spinning, he found himself standing in the middle of a high-class nightclub. He frowned when he realized no one in the room was moving. The patrons stood as still as statues.

Saintcrow pointed at a young woman. She was flawlessly beautiful, with a wealth of long blond hair and deep blue eyes. The red dress she wore outlined a figure as perfect as the rest of her.

"Is she more to your liking?" his sire asked. "She's yours."

Ethan shook his head.

"Come, don't be squeamish. You wanted to kill something." Saintcrow took the woman in his arms and sank his fangs into her flesh. At his touch, whatever spell she'd been under vanished. But she didn't fight, merely stood acquiescent in Saintcrow's arms, her eyes unfocused.

The scent of warm, fresh blood filled Ethan's nostrils, drawing him toward the woman. He caught her in his arms when Saintcrow shoved her toward him. "Drink, vampire. Drink it all."

Ethan stared at his sire. Was this a test? He didn't care. His fangs descended, and he buried them in the woman's throat. Her blood was warm and rich, and as he drank, he caught snatches of her past, experienced her joy, her pain, her hopes for a long and happy life with the man she loved.

The hunger burning inside him urged him to take it all, every last crimson drop. But he couldn't do it. He sealed the wounds in her neck, then thrust her away from him. "She won't die, will she?"

"No. She'll be a little light-headed, that's all." A wave of Saintcrow's hand and the spell in the room was broken. No one seemed aware that anything unusual had taken place. "Let's go."

They left the club by the back door.

"Well," Saintcrow said, "what happened? I thought you wanted blood."

"I couldn't do it," Ethan said flatly.

"Why not?"

"You know why not."

"Because you're not a born killer," Saintcrow said. "In most cases, becoming a vampire doesn't change who you are."

"You've killed."

Saintcrow nodded. "I was born to it. You were not."

"So, if I'd been on my own and found some random woman, I wouldn't have taken her life?"

"Under normal conditions, no. But there could be extenuating circumstances that you might not be able to resist. If you're in desperate need of blood to survive, or badly wounded, your sense of self-preservation will kick in."

"If I'd killed that woman tonight, would you have destroyed me?"

"I wouldn't have let it go that far. But my warning still stands. I made you. Any life you take is ultimately my fault."

Ethan nodded, deeply relieved by Saintcrow's assurance that he wasn't a murderer by nature.

"You ready to go back?"

"Yeah." He didn't like the idea of Sofia being alone in Morgan Creek, with no one to protect her.

A thought, and Ethan materialized in front of the hotel moments after his sire.

"Have you heard any more from Browning?" Ethan asked.

Saintcrow shook his head. "If we're lucky, we've seen the last of him."

"But you don't think so?"

"No. But I'm not going to worry about it now," Saintcrow drawled with a wicked grin. "There's a pretty woman in my bed in New Orleans, eagerly awaiting my return."

Ethan nodded, wishing he could say the same.

Hands shoved into his pants' pockets, Ethan materialized inside the living room of Saintcrow's house. He hadn't really expected Sofia to be waiting for him, but he was disappointed just the same.

He made his way up the stairs, heading toward the turret room. He paused on the second floor, his feet carrying him to Sofia's bedroom. He frowned when he heard nothing but silence from the other side of the door. He knew before he looked inside that she wasn't there.

Fear shot through him. Closing his eyes, he opened his senses, searching for her heartbeat. He was stunned when her scent led him up to the turret room.

"Sofie?"

Sobbing his name, she stepped out from behind the tapestry and fell into his arms.

"What are you doing up here?"

"I woke up and you were gone. I heard someone trying to open the front door and I ran up here because I couldn't think of anywhere else to hide. Was it you?"

"No. Come on; I'll take you to your room."

She clung to his hand as they made their way down the stairs.

"Stay here and lock the door." He kissed the tip of her nose. "Don't worry. I'll be right back."

He waited until he heard the click of the lock before going down to the living room. Materializing on the front porch, Ethan opened his preternatural senses again, his eyes narrowing as he caught an unfamiliar smell. It wasn't Browning. It wasn't another vampire. But it wasn't entirely human either.

He followed the scent down the hill toward the town until it disappeared across the bridge. Brow furrowed, he transported himself back to Saintcrow's.

Sofia opened the bedroom door when he called her name. "Did you find anything?" she asked anxiously.

"No, but someone was definitely here."

"Was it that vampire? Browning?"

"No. I think we should spend the rest of the night in Saintcrow's lair."

She looked at him in horror. "Why?"

"Just a safety precaution until we figure out who's been prowling around."

Fighting to overcome a growing sense of trepidation, Sofia put on her new robe and slippers and followed Ethan to the turret room. He held the tapestry aside for her, opened the door, then took her hand in his.

"There aren't any lights down here, so stay close."

Sofia's apprehension increased as they made their way down the spiral staircase. She couldn't see anything as Ethan moved forward. Her footsteps echoed loudly in the all-encompassing darkness.

"We're in a tunnel," Ethan said, sensing her unease. "It's pretty long."

"A tunnel?"

"Yeah, it runs under the house. The door at the end leads to Saintcrow's lair."

"Have you been spending your nights there?"

"Yeah." After what seemed like forever, he said, "We're here." He opened the door. "There are matches on the table if you need them," he said as he lit a candle with no more than a quick look.

Sofia glanced around. She wasn't sure what she had expected. Certainly not what she saw—a large room with pale gray walls. An old-fashioned wardrobe stood across from a king-size bed covered with a thick black quilt. Several wrought-iron wall sconces held fat black candles.

"Nothing to be afraid of," he assured her as he closed the solid oak door and slid a heavy wooden beam in place to lock it.

Sofia stared at him. Nothing to be afraid of? She was trapped in an underground lair with a vampire.

Her discomfort was a palpable presence in the room. "I'll sleep on the floor," Ethan said.

"No! No need. The bed's big enough for two. Besides,

we've shared a bed before." Sofia folded the quilt and laid it across the foot of the bed. The sheets were black silk.

She ran her hand over the pillowcase. Real silk. Saint-crow's doing? Or Kadie's?

Removing her robe and slippers, she slid under the covers. The silk was shivery cool against her skin.

Her heart skipped a beat when Ethan stretched out on his back beside her. She was glad he'd left the candle burning.

"Get some rest, Sofie."

She closed her eyes. Took several slow, deep breaths. "I can't sleep."

"Come here." Ethan drew her close, his arm curling around her shoulders.

Sighing, she snuggled against him. Vampire or not, he comforted her on so many levels. His scent was appealing, his presence intoxicating, his hair soft against her cheek. She closed her eyes, all the tension draining out of her.

Ethan was here.

She was safe.

Ethan knew a moment of regret as sleep claimed her. She had snuggled against him so willingly, so trustingly, he had dared hope they might make love before he succumbed to the sun's light. He supposed it was just as well that nothing had happened. Things were already complicated enough. But he wanted her in every way a man—and a vampire—could want a woman.

Lying beside her was torture of the sweetest kind. The scent of her hair, her skin, her blood aroused his senses. The warmth of her body, so close to his, was almost painful.

Closing his eyes, he let the slow, steady beat of her heart lull him into oblivion.

* * *

"Well, this is a hell of a sight."

Sofia woke with a start at the sound of Saintcrow's voice, let out a gasp when she saw him standing beside the bed. Fear that something might be wrong mingled with her embarrassment at being caught in bed with Ethan. She darted a glance at him, but he lay still and unmoving.

"Meet me upstairs," Saintcrow said. "I'll buy you a cup of coffee."

She knew an order when she heard one. She waited until he was gone, then swung her legs over the edge of the bed and stepped into her slippers. As she pulled on her robe, she wished fleetingly that she had something more fitting to wear.

She found Saintcrow in the living room, a large cup of takeout coffee on one of the end tables. Sitting on the sofa, she reached for the cup, hoping its warmth would chase away the chill of the room.

"Did you hear anyone prowling around outside last night?" he asked.

"I think someone tried to break in. Ethan said someone had definitely been here, but he didn't know who it was."

Saintcrow nodded. "Somebody was here all right."

"Do you know who it was?"

"Not who, but I know what."

"Not who, but what?" Sofia blinked at him. "I don't understand?"

"It was a black witch. And a damned powerful one, unless I miss my guess."

"Why would a witch come here?"

"I'm thinking Browning knew he couldn't defeat me on his own, so he hired a little help."

First vampires and now witches, Sofia thought. What next? Zombies? "Could a witch defeat you?"

"I have no idea. The few I've met never tried."

She wondered if the thought of facing a witch scared him, but she couldn't imagine anything in heaven or earth scaring Saintcrow. "So, what are you going to do?"

"Good question. I could restore the wards around the town, I guess, and see if they'd hold."

"Wards?"

"I guess you could call it vampire voodoo. Years ago, I warded the town so anyone who crossed the bridge couldn't leave. It also kept people from leaving by going over the mountains. I don't know if it'll fend off witches." It had kept Mahlon out, he thought, but he had no proof Braga's henchman had been a witch. If he warded the town again, he would have to tweak the spell a bit, so the workers and the mailman could come and go.

It seemed like a lot of trouble. Better to just face the threat, whatever it was, and be done with it.

He frowned as he watched Sofia sip her coffee. He could handle himself. Ethan was growing stronger and more confident every day. But Sofia . . . she was completely vulnerable. He had grown rather fond of her. And then there was Ethan, who was crazy in love with her, whether he knew it or not.

Black witches meant black magic. He hadn't lived as long as he had without learning a thing or three. Salt was a known defense against black magic. Some thought it had to be in the shape of a circle to protect you, but that wasn't true. And while he'd never had occasion to test it, he decided now might be a good time. He grinned inwardly, thinking he would need a buttload of salt to scatter around his lair and Sofia's office.

Blessed amulets—religious items, herb bags, crystals—were also supposed to be effective but, again, he had no experience with any of them.

Saintcrow slapped his hands on his thighs. "Come on;

I'll take you to the office," he said briskly. "And while you read the mail and pay the bills, I'll ward the town and we'll see how that works."

"I really need to go home," Sofia said. "If I'm going to stay here, I need to pack more clothes and put a stop on my mail and empty my fridge and . . ."

"All right. Are you ready?"

Before she could say ah, yes, or no, they were in the middle of her apartment. "Do what you've got to do," Saintcrow said. "I'll rest in the closet of your guest room for a couple of hours. Wake me when you're ready to go back."

"My closet?"

"It'll be dark in there." He sent her a wink and headed for the spare room.

Sofia shook her head. Could her life get any more bizarre?

She had showered and dressed, canceled her mail, emptied her refrigerator, and started packing a suitcase when her phone rang. It was Rosie.

"Hey, Sis, I haven't heard from you in a while, so I'm guessing things are going well with Holly's cousin."

"I guess you could say that," Sofia said.

"I sense some hesitation in your voice. Is everything okay?"

"Yes. And no."

"Uh-oh. What's wrong? Is he vamping out on you?"

"No," Sofia said, laughing. "It's just your normal human-girl-dating-vampire kind of problems. I'm really crazy about him, Rosie, but I don't want to be a vampire and I don't see any future for us otherwise." She decided not to mention the trouble at Morgan Creek.

"Well, if I were you, I'd end it now. The longer you wait, the harder it will be."

"I know. You're right."

"Mom and Dad are starting to wonder why you haven't come home. I told them you were probably pregnant."

"Rosa!"

"I'm kidding," Rosa said, hardly able to speak, she was laughing so hard. "But seriously, you should come home."

"I know. Did I tell you I lost my job? The company went out of business, but I got a new position that pays even better. How about you? Have you found another job? Or a new boyfriend?"

"Job, yes. I'm working as a receptionist in a dental office. Bor-ing. Boyfriend, no. Listen, I've gotta go. I'm meeting Mom for lunch. I wish you were coming with us."

"Me too. Hugs."

"Hugs."

Sofia sank down on the chair by the window. She really needed to see her family. Maybe being surrounded by her parents and siblings would help make up her mind about Ethan. She wondered when Micah and Holly were coming home.

She glanced over her shoulder toward the hallway. Was Saintcrow comfortable in her guest room? The thought had barely crossed her mind when she found herself tiptoeing into the bedroom and easing the closet door open.

He lay on his back, one arm at his side, the other folded over his waist.

"Are you ready to go?" he asked, eyes still closed.

"Just about. Sorry I bothered you."

"Curious?"

She nodded, even though he wasn't looking at her. "I'll be ready in about ten minutes."

He didn't answer, merely waved her away.

With a hmph, Sofia closed the door.

She had just tossed the last of her clothes into her suitcase when Saintcrow materialized in her bedroom.

"Is that it?" he asked, his voice laced with tension.

At her nod, he closed the lid. Picking up the bag, he wrapped his arm around her waist and hissed, "We're leaving."

Before she could ask what was wrong, they were back in his house in Morgan Creek. "Lock the doors. Don't leave the house. And when Ethan wakes up, tell him to stay put until I get back."

"What's wrong?"

"They've got Kadie! Dammit, I never should have left her alone." He dropped Sofia's bag on the floor. A wave of his hand and he was gone.

A tremor, cold as ice, slid down Sofia's spine. Kadie was helpless during the day. Would they kill her while she was at rest? Or was she bait to trap Saintcrow?

With her nerves drawn as tight as piano wires, Sofia paced the floor. Time lost all meaning as she tried to make sense of what was happening. Browning had come here to determine Saintcrow's whereabouts. A witch had come sniffing around. And now Kadie had been kidnapped.

Chilled to the marrow of her bones, Sofia wrapped her arms around her middle and sank down on the sofa, willing the hours to pass more quickly, wishing Ethan could be awake during the day like Saintcrow.

Saintcrow prowled the house he had rented in New Orleans. The wards he had erected were in place but hadn't been strong enough to repel the witch. The same black witch who had been in Morgan Creek. The stink of dark magic hung heavy in the air. It blocked his ability to track the witch. Worse, it somehow managed to hide Kadie's scent from him as well.

He swore long and loud as he prowled through the house, looking for a clue, for anything that would tell him the identity of the witch who had taken Kadie. He came up empty, which only added to his growing frustration. All he knew for sure was that Kadie was still alive. His only hope was that, once she woke from her daytime sleep, he would be able to find her through their blood bond.

Returning to the living room, he expanded his senses, filtering out older scents, separating human from inanimate. An oath escaped his lips and he whirled around, surprised that no one was there. If he hadn't killed the man with his own hands, he would have sworn Mahlon was in the room.

Saintcrow was about to leave the house when he saw the small slip of paper, half-hidden under the sofa. Apparently, it had blown off the coffee table when he opened the door.

He read it once, twice, his anger growing with every word.

> *We have your woman,*
> *but it's you we want.*
> *When we have you,*
> *we will let her go.*
> *We'll be in touch.*

It was signed *NB*.

"Nolan Browning." Saintcrow crushed the paper in his hand. "You're a dead man."

Chapter Twenty-Two

Ethan caught the scent of Sofia's distress as soon as he emerged from the dark sleep. He instantly willed himself to her side, his worry rising when he saw how pale she looked.

"What is it?" he asked.

"Someone's taken Kadie."

Someone with a death wish, he thought. "Where's Saintcrow?"

"I don't know. He's been gone for hours. He told me to stay inside and to tell you to do the same."

"Does he know who's got her?"

"Not that I know of. You don't think they'll hurt her, do you?"

"Not until they have what they want."

"Nolan can't be doing all this just to get the town back, can he?"

"I don't know, but I don't think so. I think someone wants Saintcrow dead."

"Browning?"

Ethan shrugged. "Maybe. Maybe not. Saintcrow's been around a long time. I'm sure he's made a lot of enemies. Maybe one of them just found out where he is. Maybe . . ."

His words trailed off as Saintcrow materialized in the room. "Did you find Kadie?"

"No. But I caught a scent that . . ." Saintcrow shook his head. "It can't be him, and yet I'd swear it was."

"Who?" Sofia asked.

Saintcrow paced the floor. "You remember Leticia Braga?"

A shiver ran down Sofia's spine. She had never met the crazy vampire who had terrorized some of her family, but what she'd heard had horrified her.

"And Mahlon?"

She frowned. "He was her bodyguard, right?"

"Yeah." Saintcrow paused in midstride. "I always wondered about him, about what he was. I knew he wasn't entirely human. Now I think he must have carried witch blood. Or maybe demon blood. Whatever. I think one of his kin has come seeking revenge." Hard to believe there was anyone on the planet who gave a damn about avenging Mahlon's death. The man had been a soulless monster.

"Are you talking about the witch who was sniffing around here?" Ethan asked.

"It's the only thing that makes sense. What I don't understand is the relationship between Browning and the witch," Saintcrow muttered. And then frowned. "Unless Browning agreed to lead the witch here. I guess he figured once I was out of the way, Morgan Creek would be up for grabs. Although how Browning and Mahlon's kin got together, I have no idea." He resumed his pacing, then stopped abruptly. Eyes narrowed, hands tightly clenched, he said, "Kadie should be awake by now."

Sofia and Ethan exchanged glances. From the taut expression on Saintcrow's face, it was obvious he still had no sense of her.

Saintcrow fixed his gaze on Ethan. "How brave are you?"

"What do you mean?"

"I want to try something I don't think has ever been done before. It could be dangerous for both of us, but more so for you."

"What are you trying to say?"

"I want a blood exchange between us."

Brow furrowed, Ethan muttered, "Didn't we already do that?"

"I want to do it again."

"I'm already a vampire, remember?"

"If I'm right, it might make you strong enough to walk in daylight."

The possibility was tempting. "And if you're wrong?"

"Hopefully, you won't be any worse off."

"Yeah, hopefully," Ethan said.

"I can compel you to do it," Saintcrow reminded him with a feral smile.

Ethan went still all over as he tried to decide whether his master was serious.

"The choice is yours, fledgling, but it would be a big help to have you here to back me up during the day."

Ethan glanced at Sofia, who stared back at him, eyes wide. She shook her head almost imperceptibly.

"I've gotta try it," Ethan said, giving her hand a squeeze. "It would be great to be able to be awake during the day." He might even be able to get his old job back if he could come up with a good enough excuse for his long unexplained absence.

She nodded unhappily.

"All right!" Ethan slapped his hands on his thighs. "Let's do it."

"Stretch out on the sofa," Saintcrow said, pulling a chair up to the couch. "Sofia, stay close. If something goes wrong, a little human blood might come in handy."

Hands damp, mouth dry, Sofia sat on the floor, hoping she wouldn't faint.

"You don't have to watch," Saintcrow said.

"Thank goodness," she murmured.

Saintcrow took hold of Ethan's forearm. "Ready?"

Ethan nodded, then flinched when the other vampire buried his fangs in one of the large arteries in his arm.

Sofia tried not to watch, but she couldn't seem to look away. She was repelled yet oddly attracted at the same time. Power thrummed through the air and skittered over her skin. Ethan didn't seem to be breathing; his face was deathly pale.

Just when she started to worry that Saintcrow was going to drain Ethan dry, the master vampire lifted his head and sealed the puncture wounds in his fledgling's arm.

"Your turn," Saintcrow said, and pressed his wrist to Ethan's lips. When he didn't respond, Saintcrow slapped him, hard. Twice. "You've got to drink! Now!"

And Ethan sank his fangs into Saintcrow's forearm.

Sofia held her breath as she glanced from one vampire to the other and back again. Both had their eyes closed. Saintcrow groaned once, the sound seeming to come from the very depths of his soul. Pain or pleasure, she couldn't tell.

She practically jumped out of her skin when Saintcrow growled, "Enough!" and jerked his arm out of Ethan's grasp.

Ethan's fangs carved a long bloody furrow in the master vampire's arm.

To Sofia's amazement, the wound healed almost instantly.

Ethan jerked upright, his eyes wild and blazing red, his fangs stained with crimson.

Pushing Sofia out of the way, Saintcrow stood in front of her.

Ethan didn't seem to notice. His nostrils flared as he took a deep breath.

"Ethan, look at me." Saintcrow's voice was low and

compelling. Staying between Ethan and Sofia, he asked, "How do you feel?"

"Strange."

"Do you need to feed?"

"Didn't I just do that?"

"Vampire blood isn't always satisfying to another vampire."

"I'm fine." Hands clenched, Ethan's gaze moved back and forth across the room before focusing on Sofia.

She scrambled to her feet and took an involuntary step backward, let out a huff of relief when the red faded from his eyes and his fangs retracted.

"I didn't mean to scare you," he said, his voice tight.

"I know. Are you sure you're okay?"

Rising, Ethan flexed his hands and shoulders. "I feel great." Better than great, he thought. All his senses seemed stronger, more intense, as if they were an inbred part of him and not a gift from his sire. As if he had been born a vampire. It was an amazing sensation. He tried to find words to describe it but failed. "I'm fine," he said again, then glanced at Saintcrow. "How do *you* feel?"

"Still able to whip your butt," Saintcrow said, grinning. "And don't you forget it."

Ethan nodded as the weight of his sire's ancient power crawled over him. "So, your experiment seems to be a success, so far. Now what?"

"I'm going to go scout around to see if I can find a clue as to Kadie's whereabouts."

"What do you want me to do?"

"Stay here and keep an eye on Sofia. If Browning shows up, do whatever you have to do to keep him here. Sofia, I'll stop at the store and pick up enough groceries to last you a couple of days."

"Thanks," she said automatically.

With a wave of his hand, Saintcrow vanished from their sight.

Now that they were alone, Sofia tried not to stare at Ethan, but she couldn't help it. He looked the same. And yet he didn't. Even though he was just standing there, she could feel the power radiating from him like heat from a blast furnace.

But it was more than that. Tilting her head to the side, she tried to figure out what was different. And then she knew. Drinking Saintcrow's blood hadn't just changed him on the inside—it had also transformed him on the outside. The changes were subtle. Was she only imagining them? But no, his hair *was* a bit thicker, his eyes a deeper shade of brown. And yet the difference went deeper than that. There was an air of self-confidence, of total acceptance of who and what he was, that was palpable. She shivered with the realization that Ethan now exuded the same powerful, scary aura as his master.

Without realizing what she was doing, she took several steps away from him.

It was a move not lost on Ethan. He glanced around, as if seeking the cause of her sudden anxiety. "What's wrong?"

Suddenly speechless, she shook her head.

"Sofie, talk to me."

"You . . . you're . . . different." She took a deep breath, and for some inexplicable reason, her fear turned to desire. He was beautiful and sexy and she wanted him. Needed him. Now.

Ethan sucked in a breath as the scent of her sexual hunger filled the room. *What the hell?*

"Ethan . . ." Hips swaying provocatively, she closed the

distance between them and slipped her arms around his neck. "Kiss me."

"Sofie . . ."

Rising on her tiptoes, her body flush with his, she kissed him deeply, passionately.

His first response was to carry her to bed and bury himself in her sweetness. But something wasn't right. Taking hold of her wrists, he gently drew her arms away from his neck. "Sofie?"

She blinked up at him, her lips slightly parted, her expression confused. "What's wrong?"

"I think you're reacting to . . ." Ethan frowned. *To what?*

"I thought you wanted me."

"I do." He squeezed her hands gently. "Believe me, I do. But this isn't like you."

Her gaze slid away from his and she took several deep breaths. Of course, she thought, Ethan's vampire allure must have spiked as a result of his blood exchange with Saintcrow. Not only had he become stronger and more powerful physically, but his sexual appeal was off the charts. How was she supposed to resist something like *that*?

"Sofie? What's going on in that pretty little head of yours?"

"Your stud quotient just went up about a thousandfold."

He stared at her, dumbfounded. "What the devil are you talking about?"

"I think Saintcrow's blood has made you even more irresistible to females."

Ethan frowned. She had mentioned something about some innate vampire allure before, but he hadn't really believed her.

"Maybe you could turn it down a notch?" she said, grinning.

He snorted. "Just tell me how."

"I just know you've got it," she said with a shrug. "I don't know how it works."

"Yeah? Well, me either." Taking her by the hand, he sat on the sofa and pulled her down on his lap. "I think we need to try out my new studly powers. How about you?"

"Just remember, I've got a sharp stake in my pocket and I know how to use it."

"Do your worst, darlin'," he murmured, and claimed her lips with his.

Chapter Twenty-Three

Saintcrow made a thorough sweep of the town. He checked every house, every building, every floor of the hotel, including the basement and the attic. He walked every street and path, tramped through the graveyard. The faint scent of the witch lingered in the air, but there was no physical trace of Mahlon's kin, if that's who it was. No sign of Browning. Or Kadie. Not that he expected whoever had kidnapped her from their place in New Orleans would have brought her here. Dammit! Where was she?

There was little in life that had scared him since he'd been turned, but not being able to connect with his mate made Saintcrow's gut churn with fear. He didn't know if they had drugged her or if the witch had put her under some kind of enchantment, but whatever they'd done, it effectively prevented him from finding her. But find her he would, sooner or later. And when he did, Browning and the witch would wish they had never been born.

He lingered in the graveyard. The ghosts had spoken to Kadie. They had warned Micah when Holly was in danger, whispered a similar warning to Ethan when Sofia was in trouble. But for him, they remained silent. He supposed he couldn't blame them. If not for him, none of them would be here.

Hands shoved into his pockets, he strolled toward the bridge. Browning's scent was fresher on the far side, which meant the vampire had been here recently. It also meant the new wards had kept Browning from returning to Morgan Creek, the first good news he'd had since Kadie had been abducted.

A thought took Saintcrow across the road. Lifting his head, he glanced right and left. Picking up the vampire's scent, he followed it until it disappeared.

Brow furrowed in thought, Saintcrow willed himself to the next town, where he picked up enough food and drink to last Sofia a week or more.

A thought took him back to the office in Morgan Creek. He put half the groceries he had bought in the kitchen, then went up the hill to his place, intending to put the other half in his own kitchen. Good thing he'd bought that stove and refrigerator for Kadie after all.

Kadie. This was the first time since he'd made her his wife that they had been separated for more than a few hours. The loss of her presence, the complete absence of the blood bond between them, was more painful than he would have thought possible. He tamped down his rage, knowing if he let it get out of control, people would die, perhaps the only two people besides Kadie that he cared for.

He paused, his hand on the front door, when he realized Sofia and Ethan were entwined in each other's arms on the floor in front of the fireplace.

Saintcrow grunted softly. Exchanging blood with Ethan had increased all the boy's powers. He laughed softly, wondering how the young lovers were handling Ethan's increased sexual appeal. From the sounds of it, neither Ethan nor Sofia seemed to be complaining.

He would have been amused if he hadn't been so worried about his woman. Where was she?

Darkness surrounded her. Kadie knew night had fallen, but this darkness was like nothing she had ever known before. It weighed her down, left her unable to move. She couldn't open her eyes, yet she knew she wasn't alone. She tried to call Saintcrow's name, tried to reach out to him through their bond, but she couldn't speak, couldn't concentrate enough to find the bond between them.

Was she dead? Had they buried her alive? Was she trapped deep in the earth? She told herself over and over again that Rylan would find her. But what if he didn't?

She wanted to scream, to cry out for help, but all she could do was lie there, helpless, mute.

And more afraid than she had ever been in her life.

Saintcrow materialized inside the office. Booting up Sofia's computer, he did an Internet search for Mahlon. With nothing but a name, which could have been the man's first name or last, he didn't really expect to find anything, but he needed to feel he was doing something to locate Kadie.

There were numerous links, all of them referring to Mahlon as one of two brothers mentioned in the Book of Ruth in the Bible.

Sitting back in the chair, he pinched the bridge of his nose, thinking it was a good thing vampires weren't subject to headaches, because if they were, he was sure he'd have one by now.

Returning to the Internet, he searched the Deep Web. He was about to call it quits when he stumbled onto a blog written by a vampire hunter who called himself Thornwood—a very old hunter, one who had once crossed paths with Leticia Braga and Mahlon and had escaped with his life by the skin of his teeth. But, while being held prisoner, Thornwood had overheard Mahlon and Braga whispering about someone named Shiloh.

"Another Biblical name," Saintcrow murmured.

The blog went on to say that the hunter had never discovered anything about Shiloh, other than overhearing something that made him believe Shiloh was related to Mahlon and that the two had been conceived by black magic.

"Conceived by witchcraft?" Saintcrow frowned. Did that mean Mahlon and his sibling were the progeny of witches? Or that they actually had been created by some sort of magical enchantment?

Saintcrow leaned back, elbows resting on the arms of the chair, his fingers steepled. He had always suspected Mahlon carried witch blood. What he had just read seemed to confirm that. But witch or mortal, ripping the man's heart from his chest had killed him.

But his brother—or sister—still lived.

Saintcrow fisted his right hand. The one that had ripped Mahlon's beating heart from his chest.

The same hand that would destroy whoever had dared lay hands on his woman.

Chapter Twenty-Four

Ethan stared up at the ceiling. One minute he had been trapped in the dark sleep of his kind, the next he was wide awake. He stared at the window. Even though blackout curtains shut out the light, he knew it was morning.

He glanced at Sofia, asleep at his side. He had carried her to her room last night, then stretched out on the bed. He had intended to stay only a little while, but he'd fallen into oblivion with the coming of dawn.

And now the sun was high in the sky and he was awake.

The blood exchange with Saintcrow had worked.

It took a moment for the enormity of that to sink in. It opened a whole new world of possibilities. If he could be out and about during the day, he might be able to talk his boss into giving him his old job back. He could renew acquaintance with his buddies, live a reasonably normal existence. He might even have a chance at a life with the woman he loved.

He ran his knuckles along her cheek. He didn't know what he would have done these past weeks without her. She had grounded him somehow, given him hope, made him laugh when he'd thought he would never laugh again.

She stirred at his touch but didn't wake.

Deciding to let her sleep, he slid out of bed. Eager to see if he could really endure the sun's light, he ran downstairs. At the front door, he took a deep breath before he pulled it open and took a wary step outside.

A thrill of excitement ran through him as he blinked against the sunlight he hadn't seen in what seemed like forever. Its heat warmed his skin, but there was no pain. He didn't burst into flame.

Grinning like an idiot, he went back inside and came face-to-face with Saintcrow.

"So, it worked."

Ethan nodded.

"How do you feel?"

"How do you think? I feel like I've got my life back!"

"Yeah, well, before you start making plans for your future, you might want to remember why we tried it in the first place."

"Right. To find Kadie."

Saintcrow pulled a crumpled envelope from his pants' pocket and handed it to Ethan. "One of the construction workers found this nailed to the bridge this morning."

"I figured with all this going on, you'd put a stop to the construction," Ethan remarked.

"That's got nothing to do with this."

Opening the envelope, Ethan pulled out a single sheet of plain white paper.

Meet me at midnight tonight at Palmer's.
Come alone.

It was signed *NB*.

Ethan tucked the note back into the envelope and returned it to Saintcrow. "What's Palmer's?"

"It's a deserted fun zone located about fifty miles from here. It was a popular attraction some thirty or forty years ago. J & A Palmer Developing Company tried to breathe some life into it a few years back, but they went belly-up. The city condemned the place, but it's still standing."

"You think Browning and the witch will be there?"

"I don't know." Saintcrow folded the envelope in half and shoved it in his back pocket.

"So, what's your next move?"

Saintcrow shook his head. "I went to Palmer's earlier. I walked every inch of that damn place twice, searched every building and concession stand. I can smell the witch. I can smell Browning." Impotent rage boiled like acid in his gut. "But I can't locate Kadie. I can't tell if she's even been there." He hated not knowing where she was, hated feeling helpless. "Dammit!" His hands clenched as he pictured them around the witch's throat. "I don't have any idea what Browning's next move will be. All we can do is wait. Damn, I hate waiting."

As his frustration grew, Saintcrow unleashed a torrent of profanity.

Ethan took a step back as the master vampire's power washed over him, grateful that all that pent-up rage and frustration were directed at someone else.

Gradually, the tension seeped out of Saintcrow. "I can't just wait around, doing nothing. There's no point in going back to Palmer's again. Browning can't do anything while the sun's up." Saintcrow took a deep breath, and then another. "We've got some time to kill before midnight. I'm going down to check on the progress they're making on the hotel. Wanna come along?"

"Sure."

Deciding the exercise would do him good, Saintcrow decided to walk to town. "You still feeling all right?" he asked. "You're not feeling weak? Or tired?"

"No." Ethan fell into step beside Saintcrow. Lifting his face to the sun, he reveled in its warmth. "Why?"

"As far as I know, nothing like this has ever been tried before. Pays to be careful. Don't overdo it."

Walking past the residential area, Ethan noticed several of the houses had already been repainted; some had new windows and doors. A couple of men were carrying a roll of new carpet into the house next to the office.

When they neared the hotel, Ethan saw dozens of men hard at work, accompanied by the sound of raucous laughter and the deep-throated buzz of power tools.

Ethan was amazed by the progress that had been made in such a short time. The outside of the hotel had been completely refurbished. The tavern had been repainted inside and out, but, like the hotel, it retained its 1920s charm. The exterior of the grocery store looked like something out of an old movie. Glancing in the window, he saw the interior had been outfitted with new flooring, shelves, and checkout counters.

He followed Saintcrow into the hotel. The lobby boasted new wallpaper with a cabbage-rose motif that complemented the large sage-green rug in the center of the new oak floor. The old reception area had been redone; a crystal chandelier sparkled from the ceiling. Several sofas and chairs covered in a floral print were scattered throughout the lobby. The old walnut banister had been replaced with one made of oak to match the floor.

"Not bad," Saintcrow remarked. "Maybe you should take up interior design."

"Sofia made most of the decisions about fabric and color. But you're right. It looks great, even better than I imagined."

A couple of workers, each carrying buckets of paint, nodded in their direction as they headed up the stairs.

"This isn't taking near as long as I thought it would," Ethan said.

"Well, we've got two crews working from sunup to sundown, seven days a week," Saintcrow remarked.

"Must be costing you a fortune."

Saintcrow grinned at him. "Good thing I've got one. Come on, let's go. We're in the way here."

"Still no sense of Kadie?" Ethan asked as they left the town behind.

"No." A muscle twitched in Saintcrow's jaw. When he got his hands on them, Browning and the witch would wish they'd never been born. "Sofia's awake. Tell her I left some due bills on her desk and there's food in the fridge."

"Where are you going?"

"I think I'm going to go check out Palmer's one more time."

"I thought you said there was no point in going back until tonight?"

Saintcrow shrugged. "It's probably a waste of time, but I don't know what else to do."

Ethan nodded. If Sofia went missing, he wouldn't rest until she'd been found. "Do you want me to come along?"

Saintcrow shook his head. "No. You stay here and keep an eye on Sofia. I won't be gone long."

Sofia had just stepped out of the shower and was reaching for a towel when Ethan entered the bathroom. She let out a shriek when she saw him. "You're awake!"

"Obviously."

"It worked," she murmured, sounding every bit as dazed as he had felt. "It really worked."

Ethan grinned at her, watched her cheeks turn scarlet when she remembered she was naked. Chuckling softly, he turned his back while she wrapped up in the towel. "I'll see you downstairs. Saintcrow said to tell you there's food in the kitchen." Still chuckling, he left the room.

Sofia stared after him. The sun was up and he was awake. It was a miracle, she thought as she dried her hair, then dressed. If something like that was possible, maybe there was a way for him to regain his humanity. Smiling at the thought of a life with Ethan, she went downstairs.

He was waiting for her in the living room. Determined to pretend his seeing her naked was no big deal, she said, "You must be excited."

"About seeing you in the altogether?" he asked with a wicked grin. "You bet!"

"You know that's not what I meant. The sun's up and you're awake!"

Ethan nodded. "I'm still trying to get used to the idea." He followed her into the kitchen, sat at the table while she put two slices of bread in the toaster.

Pouring herself a glass of orange juice, she said, "Maybe there's a way for you to be human again."

"I doubt it."

"Why?"

"I don't know. Maybe there is a way."

"You'd like that, wouldn't you?" She buttered the toast and put it on a plate, picked up her juice, and carried it all to the table.

"Well, sure. I guess."

Sitting across from him, she said, "You don't sound very positive."

"I don't, do I?" He raked his fingers through his hair, wondering why that was. Ever since Saintcrow had turned him, he had been regretting it. So why wasn't the idea of being human again more appealing?

"Do you *like* being a vampire?" she asked, frowning.

Did he? Would he really want to be mortal again if he had the chance?

"Ethan?" She stared at him, the toast in her hand forgotten as she waited for his answer.

"I don't know." He scrubbed a hand over his jaw. "I thought I hated it. Hated Saintcrow for turning me. But now . . ." He was stronger than he had ever been, his senses were sharper, he was more aware of the world around him. And now that he'd gotten the hang of it, he got a kick out of transporting himself wherever he wanted to go, being able to dissolve into mist. Even the blood thing wasn't so bad once you got used to it. He shook his head, surprised to hear himself say, "I think I'd miss it."

Sofia leaned back in her chair, unable to believe what she was hearing. "You'd miss it? Seriously?"

He nodded, wondering if he had just damaged their relationship. He was a vampire. She knew that. Did the fact that he liked it make a difference? Or was it his admission that he wouldn't give it up if he had a choice? Did that make him a monster in her eyes? No longer a victim but a willing participant?

Sofia dropped her toast on the plate and pushed away from the table. "I'm going for a walk."

He didn't have to ask if she wanted company. It was obvious she wanted to get away from him. The question was, for how long?

After leaving the house, Sofia walked down the long narrow path to the bottom of the hill. She stood there a moment, then turned left, toward the graveyard. It seemed apropos, somehow, though she wasn't sure why. Nor could she explain why she had felt so depressed when Ethan admitted he liked being a vampire. It hadn't changed anything. He'd been a vampire when she'd met him. He was still a vampire. So why was she so upset? It made no sense at all.

The path she followed twisted and turned, now meandering through tree-lined avenues, now bordered by lacy ferns, sometimes running between spiny bushes.

One last turn and she reached the cemetery. She paused a moment before opening the rickety wooden gate. She had never been fond of graveyards—and this one was supposed to be haunted. She stopped inside the entrance. Nothing but row after row of weathered wooden crosses. A few of them had names scratched into the wood.

One grave, marked by a tall marble cross, stood out from all the others. Curious, Sofia walked toward it.

She stopped when she reached the foot of the grave. The wording on the marker simply read,

SHIRLEY ELIZABETH HAGUE
GONE BUT NEVER FORGOTTEN

Shirley. The name sounded vaguely familiar. She must have been someone special, Sofia thought, judging by her memorial. And then she frowned. Was this the woman Saintcrow had mentioned? The woman Micah had been in love with? *That* Shirley? It seemed an odd combination, an older woman and a young vampire. Maybe one day she would ask Micah about his affair.

Leaving the graveyard, Sofia walked back to Saintcrow's house, but she wasn't ready to see Ethan yet. The Viper was parked out front. If the keys were in it, she could drive to the office. Fingers crossed, she hurried up the hill, smiled faintly when she saw the key fob in the cup holder.

* * *

Ethan stood at the front window, looking out. He knew a moment of hope when he saw Sofia coming up the hill, followed by a rush of disappointment when she slid behind the wheel and drove away.

Was she going to the office?

Or leaving Morgan Creek for good?

Chapter Twenty-Five

Sofia parked the car at the far end of the bridge, then sat with the engine idling while she tried to decide what to do. She was being foolish and she knew it. She had never heard of a cure for being a vampire. Of course, that didn't mean it wasn't possible. But whether it existed or not, she had fallen in love with Ethan just as he was. He was everything she had ever wanted in a man: tall, good-looking, easy to get along with. He made her laugh. He treated her with respect. And there was no doubt about the attraction between them, no doubt he would be a wonderful lover. So why was she letting the fact that he liked being a vampire bother her so much? Shouldn't she be glad he was happy? Everyone knew that a happy wife meant a happy life. Wouldn't the opposite also be true? Did she want him to be miserable?

Drumming her fingers on the steering wheel, she glanced over her shoulder. She couldn't just drive away with nothing settled between them. Putting the car in reverse, she backed off the bridge, made a U-turn, and drove to the office. After shutting off the engine, she stepped out of the car and almost bumped into Saintcrow when he materialized in front of her. "Geez, would you stop doing that!" she snapped.

"You should be used to it by now."

"Well, I'm not. What are you doing here anyway?" She took a step back as he turned the full force of his gaze on her.

"What's wrong?" he asked.

"Nothing." She closed the car door.

"You might be able to lie to Ethan," Saintcrow remarked, falling into step beside her as she climbed the porch stairs. "But you can't lie to me."

With the master vampire trailing behind her, she went into the kitchen. "It's nothing," she said, filling the coffeepot with water.

"In my experience, when a woman says it's nothing, it's something."

"Oh, all right. If you must know, I asked him whether he'd be human again if he had the chance and he said no. Satisfied?"

"Even if he said yes, it wouldn't change anything. Once a vampire, always a vampire. Even if he was able to do everything mortal men can do, he would still be a vampire. To survive, he would still need to consume human blood from time to time." Saintcrow cocked his head to the side. "Is that really what's bothering you?"

She plugged in the pot, then turned to face him, her back resting against the counter. "I don't know."

He lifted one brow.

"I love him," she confessed. "At least, I think I do. I just don't know if I want to spend the rest of my life with a vampire. How do I know he won't change, over time? That he won't turn into some kind of . . . of . . ."

"Monster?"

She nodded. "I overheard Micah talking about Leticia Braga, about how horrible she was. And her brother, too.

And how her brother nearly killed Holly. How do I know Ethan won't become like them?"

Saintcrow pulled a chair from the table and straddled it, his arms folded over the back. "Being a vampire doesn't usually change who you really are. Good people don't suddenly become evil. Monsters don't turn into saints. If something happened that prevented Ethan from feeding for a long time, he would likely lose control of his hunger. Being deprived of blood for an extended period is more excruciating than anything you can imagine. If that happens—and the chances are slim—all bets are off. If necessary, he'd kill to survive. And regret it for the rest of his life. But under ordinary circumstances, there's no reason to think he'll ever become like me. Or Braga. He'll always be Ethan."

Sofia nodded as she poured herself a cup of coffee. Carrying it to the table, she sat across from Saintcrow. "Do you regret the lives you've taken?"

"Ethan told you about my past, did he?"

"Yes."

"I've killed a lot of people over the centuries, mortals and vampires alike, but I don't have many regrets." He stared into the distance for a moment, then said, "There are two kinds of fledglings—those whose sires stay with them and show them the ropes and those who wake up as vampires with no idea of what's happened to them.

"The majority of people who are turned are basically decent people who aren't given to killing. With the guidance of their maker, most of them quickly learn to control their hunger and don't present much of a problem to humanity. Even without help, most of them don't turn into monsters, although their survival rate is slim.

"But there are some, though few in number, who would think becoming a vampire was a dream come true. It lets them indulge their lust for blood. They love the thrill of the hunt, the kill. Those are the ones who turn into savages, who take lives indiscriminately. I was like the second kind," Saintcrow admitted. "I'd been a soldier most of my life. Killing was what I did." He shook his head ruefully. "You wouldn't have liked me back then," he said, grinning. "I'm not sure you like me now."

Sofia knew she was blushing, but she couldn't help it. There *were* times when Saintcrow frightened the daylights out of her. All that barely leashed power and macho male ego was intimidating.

Rising, he said, "You're not going to like what I'm about to suggest either."

Alarm skittered down her spine as she waited for him to explain.

"I want you to drink a little of my blood."

"What? No way!"

"It's merely a precaution. If you drink from me, we'll be able to communicate mentally, the way I do with Kadie."

Sofia shook her head. The last thing she wanted was for Saintcrow to be able to read her thoughts. Or to read his.

"I can already read your thoughts," he said mildly. "I want you to be able to connect with me if the need arises."

"And if I refuse?"

He lifted one brow, as if to suggest that doing so would be foolish and futile. "I thought you'd see things my way." Dropping down on one knee in front of her, he bit into his wrist.

Sofia grimaced at the sight of the dark red blood that welled from two tiny punctures.

Looking amused, Saintcrow held out his arm. "Try it, you'll like it."

"I can't."

"You can and you will. It's for your own safety, Sofia."

With a sigh of resignation, and feeling a little embarrassed, she bent her head to his wrist. His blood was hot on her tongue and surprisingly pleasant. She had tasted her own on occasion. Who hadn't licked their own blood from a minor cut? But his tasted nothing like hers.

She looked up when he withdrew his arm.

"I want you to drink from Ethan, too."

She watched the tiny wounds in his arm disappear. "Does all vampire blood taste the same?"

"No."

"Does human blood?"

He shook his head. "Everyone's is a little different. Some are sweet. Some are bitter. Witch blood is supposed to be poisonous to vampires, although I don't know if that's true or just a rumor started by witches. Stop worrying about being with Ethan. You're safe with him."

Sofia nodded.

"Ah, young love," Saintcrow muttered, getting to his feet. "I've got to go check something out. You two kiss and make up while I'm gone."

"Wait!"

"What's wrong?"

"I was wondering about . . ." Her voice trailed off as his eyes filled with despair.

He shook his head. "Nothing's changed, but I'll find her." To think otherwise was out of the question.

"I know you will."

With a nod, he vanished from her sight.

Saintcrow had no sooner left the office than Ethan appeared in the doorway. Hands in his pockets, he leaned one shoulder against the jamb, his face impassive. "I was afraid you'd decided to leave."

"I thought about it."

"I didn't mean to upset you."

"I know. I'm glad you told me the truth, even if it wasn't what I wanted to hear."

He shifted from one foot to the other. "Being a vampire is very seductive, Sofie. I guess being human again would be kind of like being Superman, you know? Enjoying all those amazing powers and then being hit with kryptonite and just being ordinary again."

"I guess," she said dubiously.

"Don't knock it until you've tried it."

"But you can't just *try* it."

Pushing away from the doorjamb, he moved closer to the table, his gaze intent on her face. "So, where does that leave us?"

She swallowed hard, her stomach fluttering as he drew near.

Taking her hands in his, he pulled her to her feet. "Sofia?"

She swayed toward him, her heart overruling the little voice in the back of her head that reminded her that nothing had been settled. But when he was this close—when he was looking at her like that—it just didn't seem to matter.

"We okay?" he asked.

Going up on her tiptoes, she wrapped her arms around his neck. "What do you think?"

"I think I'm the luckiest guy on the face of the earth."

Grinning, she murmured, "I think so, too. Where was Saintcrow going?"

"Who the hell knows? My guess is that he's gone back to Palmer's to see if he can find a clue as to Kadie's whereabouts. I don't know how many times he's been there. I hope he finds her soon. I think he'll explode if this goes on much longer." Ethan dragged his hand over his jaw. "Do you want to do it now?"

"Do what?"

"You know, what Saintcrow said."

"Kiss and make up?"

"*He* said that?"

Sofia nodded.

"He's full of surprises, isn't he? But that's not what I meant."

Feeling suddenly queasy, she said, "Oh. You mean the blood thing."

"Yeah." Taking her by the hand, Ethan led her into the living room, then drew her down on the sofa beside him. "I know you don't want to do this, but he's right. I can't always rely on a ghost to warn me when you're in trouble."

"Fine, let's just get it over with."

Ethan bit into his wrist, thinking she was probably sorry she had ever answered his phone call. He had turned her whole life upside down, and now she was drinking the blood of vampires. Holding out his arm, he murmured, "I'm sorry, Sofie."

With a faint shrug, she licked his blood. It sizzled through her, warm and intoxicating, with a little kick that made her want more. Taking hold of his arm, she drank.

"Whoa, girl!" Ethan exclaimed.

She looked up, her expression filled with wonder. "I . . . I . . ." She shook her head. "What happened?"

"You tell me."

"I didn't want to stop." Funny, she hadn't felt this sense of euphoria when she tasted Saintcrow's blood.

Slipping his arm around her shoulders, he whispered, "I'm glad." And then he kissed her.

Sofia snuggled against him, feeling closer to him than she ever had before. It was because of the blood, she thought, as his tongue dueled with hers. It had formed some kind of bond between them, like an invisible wire connecting her mind to his. Not only that, but she felt stronger, too, as if nothing could hurt her.

Sighing, she looked up at him. No words were necessary. Whatever happened in the future, she was his.

And he was hers.

* * *

On the outskirts of the Palmer Fun Zone, Saintcrow dissolved into mist. There were disadvantages to being in an incorporeal state—all his preternatural senses were muted. But there were advantages, too. No one—not Browning or the witch—would know he was there.

The place was surrounded by a twelve-foot fence topped with razor wire to discourage vandals.

He drifted like smoke over the barrier, then floated through the premises. He thought it odd that the former owners hadn't liquidated the attractions. The Ferris wheel stood silhouetted against the sky, looking dejected somehow, as did the horses on the merry-go-round. There were a number of other rides—the tilt-a-whirl, the giant slide, a number of kiddie attractions.

The fun house and the house of mirrors were still intact, as were a number of empty game and food booths.

When he was certain he was alone, Saintcrow materialized near a hot dog stand. Lifting his head, he opened his preternatural senses. There was no trace of Kadie, but Browning's scent was stronger than it had been before. If the witch had been here since his last visit, she had managed to mask her presence. Where was she now?

He followed Browning's scent to the house of mirrors. The man had recently been in and out several times.

Dissolving into mist again, Saintcrow went inside, winding in and out, until he came to the middle of the maze. A pair of silver-coated handcuffs dangled from a long chain attached to a beam in the ceiling. They had not been there earlier. No doubt Kadie's captors intended to bring her here and attack him when he came to her rescue.

As if he had any other choice.

* * *

Sofia stood at the window of Saintcrow's living room, watching the sun go down. Ethan and Saintcrow sat at opposite ends of the sofa, each apparently lost in his own thoughts. Her nerves tightened with every passing minute. She told herself there was nothing to be afraid of. She would be safe down in Saintcrow's lair while the men went after Kadie.

She wasn't afraid of being alone in the lair. She was afraid that whatever wards and protections Saintcrow had placed on the town and around his house wouldn't be powerful enough to keep the witch out. She told herself there was nothing to worry about. Saintcrow and Ethan would destroy Browning and the witch and her life would return to normal. Or at least as normal as it could be for a girl dating a vampire.

She turned away from the window when Ethan slapped his hands on his knees.

"So, what's the plan?" he asked.

"I'll go in after Kadie," Saintcrow said. "If I run into trouble, you're my backup. Whatever happens, get Kadie to safety."

"So your plan is just to play it by ear?"

"Pretty much." Saintcrow shrugged. "Two of them. Two of us."

"Have you ever gone up against a witch before?"

"No."

"Do you have any idea what she's capable of, or which of you might be stronger?"

"No way to tell."

"Well, shit," Ethan muttered. "What could possibly go wrong?" He shook his head. "You know once they have you, they aren't going to let Kadie go."

"What do you want me to do?" Saintcrow snapped. "Just leave her there?"

Ethan rose to pace the floor in front of the hearth. "Of course not, but . . ."

Saintcrow's eyes narrowed ominously. "You changing your mind?"

"No. I just wanted to know what we're up against. I'd still like to know."

Saintcrow clapped him on the shoulder. "They can kill us, but they can't eat us."

"Yeah? Are you sure about that?"

"Right now, I'm not sure about anything, except that they've got my woman. If they take me, I'm counting on you to get Kadie safely away. Come on, it's time to go."

Kadie blinked at the woman bending over her. She would have recoiled, would have cried out in revulsion, if she had been able to move or speak. What had they done to her? And who was this angry woman with lank brown hair and eyes as yellow as a cat's? She looked like a creature out of a low-budget horror movie. But power radiated from her like heat from a forge. It wasn't the kind of preternatural power Rylan possessed, but it was hellishly strong and scary. The word *witch* rose in the back of her mind.

"It will all be over in a little while," the woman said, her voice like the echo of rocks falling into a well. "The vampire will die. I have not yet decided what to do with you." She raked a blood-red nail down Kadie's cheek. "Browning would like to have you for his own private stock when he takes over that dreary town." The witch woman circled her, then ran her fingers through Kadie's hair. "You're a pretty little thing. Men would probably be willing to pay a high price for an hour or two of your company, if you get my meaning." She nodded. "I'm always looking for a fresh face."

A silent scream rose in Kadie's throat. She took the

witch's meaning all too well. Her stomach knotted with fear as the witch waved her hand.

And then she knew nothing at all.

When awareness returned, Kadie found herself hanging by her wrists in the middle of a maze of mirrors. Stark naked. Her distorted reflection stared back at her from every direction. A thin ribbon of bright red blood trickled down her neck.

She glanced around, surprised to find herself alone. And even more surprised to discover she could move again. *Rylan.* She whispered his name in her mind. *Don't come after me. They're waiting for you.*

A mile from the fun zone, Saintcrow's head went up. "Kadie!"

Chapter Twenty-Six

Ethan darted a confused glance at Saintcrow. "What the hell? I just heard Kadie's voice in my mind. How the hell is that even possible?"

Saintcrow shrugged. "For the record, you heard it in *my* mind. Until tonight, I was blocking you. But for now, the three of us need to be aware of each other."

Ethan frowned. The last thing he wanted was to be able to read Saintcrow's mind. Or have his sire prowling around in his. Damn! There was no point in worrying about it now. Like the man said, at this moment, it was probably a good thing.

Ethan shifted restlessly from one foot to the other. He and Saintcrow had hunted earlier, taking as much as they dared from their prey. Now, it was almost midnight, and they were a mile from the fun zone. They had left Sofia in Saintcrow's lair with the door bolted and a dozen candles burning. The master vampire had assured Ethan that she would be safe, but he couldn't help worrying about her.

Were any of them really safe? He didn't know about Saintcrow, but if the witch was here, he couldn't detect her presence. Ethan had no idea what witches were capable of, but one thing he did know—this one was evil to the core.

The taint of black magic hung heavy in the air. Browning's scent lingered, but he knew the vampire was gone.

Ethan glanced at Saintcrow, who stood unmoving beside him. "What now?"

"You stay here. I'm going after Kadie. If I get into trouble, you'll know it."

"Great."

"Buck up, kid. Browning won't be a problem. You'll be able to take him with no trouble at all. The vampire who turned him was weak. If the witch takes me down, you do whatever you have to do to get Kadie out of here. Take her back to my place. I salted the grounds around the house. If you're worried, hole up in my lair with Sofia. Between the salt and my wards, the witch shouldn't be able to get in. And whatever you do, don't look into her eyes. Got it?"

"Yeah."

Saintcrow flashed Ethan a wry grin, then vanished from his sight.

Dissolving into mist, Saintcrow went over the fence. He hovered there for several moments, then materialized on the roof of the house of mirrors. Kadie was in there. She was alone, though the scents of the witch and Browning lingered in the air.

From his vantage point, he scanned the surrounding area, but there was no sign of witch or vampire. *Kadie?*

Rylan, go away. Hurry!

No chance, darlin'. Just sit tight.

Dissolving into mist again, he drifted into the house of mirrors through a crack in one of the windows. The silence in the building was thick, ominous. He moved stealthily forward, going deeper into the maze as he followed Kadie's scent. And suddenly her image was all around him.

Yet none of them were her.

Swearing softly, he swiftly made his way through another maze. And she was there, alive. Naked. Shivering.

Run! Her voice screamed in his mind.

And then she was gone, pulled up through a hole in the roof, while all around him the mirrors exploded. Jagged pieces of glass sliced into him from every angle. Before he could transport himself outside, the sprinklers came on, only it wasn't water that gushed from the faucets in the ceiling but liquid silver. It burned deep into the cuts, draining his strength, bringing him to his knees.

And then the witch was there, a maniacal gleam in her eyes as she stood over him.

Ethan! Get Kadie!

Gathering his strength, Saintcrow stared up at her, though he was careful not to look into her eyes. "Now what?"

"You die."

"Where's Kadie?"

"Browning fancies her." The witch licked her lips. "But I have other plans for your pretty little mate."

Stalling for time, Saintcrow said, "You were supposed to release Kadie when you had me."

The witch's cackle filled the air. "I changed my mind. Women are allowed to do that."

Saintcrow's command rang out in Ethan's mind. From his position behind the house of mirrors, he watched through narrowed eyes as Browning pulled Kadie through a hole in the roof, then slung her over his shoulder like a sack of potatoes and dropped, light as a cat, to the ground, only to trip and fall when Kadie began to thrash about as best she could with her hands bound. She managed to roll out of the vampire's grasp, then struggled in vain to get out of his reach.

With a burst of supernatural power, Ethan sprang at Browning. The other vampire darted sideways. He grabbed Kadie's ankle, but before he could transport them away from the fun zone, Ethan grabbed a handful of Browning's hair and jerked him off his feet.

Browning let out a roar of outrage as Kadie again slipped from his grasp. Lips peeled back to reveal his fangs, he lunged at Ethan.

Ethan set his feet wide as he waited for the vampire's attack, but it didn't come. With a snarl, Browning dissolved into a thick black mist and drifted away.

Muttering, "Coward," Ethan watched the mist fade into the distance, then, muscles still taut from the heat of battle, he went to help Kadie to her feet.

Slipping off his shirt, he draped it around her hunched shoulders. He kept his gaze carefully averted while he untied her wrists. "Come on," he said, tossing the rope aside. "I'm taking you home."

"No!" She shook her head defiantly. "I'm not leaving without Rylan!"

Ethan swore under his breath. "All right, but if he loses the fight, we're out of here. Got it?"

She nodded, looking suddenly shy as she shoved her arms into the sleeves of his shirt. "He's badly hurt," she whispered, her voice laced with anguish. "Maybe dying."

Saintcrow let his head droop, as though the pain lancing through him with every breath was overpowering, which it was. But he could stand it. He could endure anything to ensure Kadie's safety. Ethan should have her by now. The thought no sooner crossed his mind than he heard the boy's voice.

I've got her, but Browning got away.

Saintcrow smiled inwardly. Kadie was safe. That was all that mattered. He would deal with Browning later.

The witch began singing, an odd singsong chant that raised the hairs on Saintcrow's arms and along the back of his neck.

"You killed Mahlon, didn't you?" She screamed the words at him.

"What's it to you?" He groaned under his breath as the power of whatever spell she had invoked washed over him. Kadie was safe. He found the link that bound them together, pictured her in his mind, as he drew on that love, letting it strengthen him. He would not let the witch defeat him. Kadie loved him. She would be in danger as long as the witch lived. Anger churned in his gut and he called on that, too, felt it fire the ancient power that had sustained him for centuries.

Grabbing a handful of his hair, the witch jerked his head up. "He was my brother! My little brother! And you killed him!"

"Damn right. I ripped his beating heart right out of his chest," Saintcrow snarled. "Just like this!" He lunged up and forward, his right hand plunging into her breast, his fingers curling around her heart. It burned his skin like acid as he ripped the bloody organ from her body and hurled it across the room, where it hit a wall and burst into flame.

Bracing one hand against a wall support, he watched the witch's lifeless body spiral to the floor. Blood pooled around her. It scorched the wood beneath her, then, igniting the hem of her dress, the fire consumed her and went out.

Feeling as though his whole body had been sliced and diced, Saintcrow took several deep breaths before he staggered out of the house of mirrors, then dropped to his knees.

"Rylan!" Kadie ran to him, Ethan's shirttail flapping

against her legs. Tears welled in her eyes as she knelt on the ground and threw her arms around Saintcrow's shoulders.

He groaned at her touch.

Noticing the blood splattered on his face and arms for the first time, Kadie took a step back. "Oh, Rylan!" she exclaimed. "What did she do to you?"

"Nothing that won't heal." With an effort of will, he gained his feet. "Let's get the hell out of here."

Ethan had let Sofia know they were on their way home, so she was waiting for them in the living room when they appeared. She gasped when she saw Saintcrow. He looked like he'd been through a meat grinder. His clothing was shredded and drenched with blood from the numerous cuts and gashes on his arms, legs, face, and chest. "What happened?"

With a shake of his head, Saintcrow dropped down on the sofa and closed his eyes. Drops of dark crimson leaked from the wounds onto the cushions.

Sofia tugged on Ethan's hand. "Tell me." ·

She shifted from one foot to the other as Ethan explained what had happened, all the while trying not to stare at Saintcrow, who looked like death warmed over.

"He needs blood to heal," Kadie said, her gaze darting to Sofia. "Human blood."

Sofia grimaced. "And I'm the only game in town, right?"

Kadie nodded. "The witch used her magic to douse him in silver. It's slowing the healing process. Please, Sofia, he's in pain."

Sofia looked at Ethan, her expression filled with doubt.

"It'll be all right," Ethan said. "I won't let him take too much. Trust me."

Overcome with a sense of doom, Sofia forced herself to walk to the couch, sit on the edge of the cushion beside

Saintcrow. He looked awful, his cheeks sunken, his eyes like dark pools of agony. How much blood would he need? What if Ethan couldn't stop him from taking too much?

In spite of the pain he was feeling, Saintcrow managed a lopsided grin as he read her tumultuous thoughts. "Neck or wrist?"

"What?"

"Where do you want me to bite you?"

"Oh!" Sofia thrust out her arm, unnerved by the thought of Saintcrow nibbling at her throat. She closed her eyes when he took hold of her hand. Her heart thundered in her ears when he bit her. But there was no pain. Gradually, she relaxed.

When she opened her eyes, Ethan stood beside her, a glass of wine in his hand. "You should drink this." He handed her the glass, then stood there to make sure she downed all of it.

Wiping her mouth with the back of her hand, Sofia glanced at Saintcrow. His eyes were closed again, but she had to admit he looked a hundred percent better than he had only moments ago.

Kadie squeezed her hand. "Thank you."

Sofia nodded as she set her goblet on the table. She experienced a sense of relief when Kadie and Saintcrow went down to his lair.

Sitting beside Sofia, Ethan stretched his legs out in front of him. "Well, it's been a hell of a night."

She couldn't argue with that, she thought, snuggling against him. "I didn't think anything, or anyone, could beat him."

"She didn't beat him."

"How can you say that? I mean, didn't you see how he looked?"

"How can you think *he* lost when *she's* dead? Sure, he's a little beat up, but he's still breathing."

* * *

Kadie undressed Saintcrow, led him into the shower and washed him from head to foot, muttering under her breath all the while.

He stood with one hand braced against the wall, his eyes closed, enjoying the touch of her hands on his skin, amused by her nattering about stupid males who had to prove their manhood. When he'd heard enough, he pulled her into his arms and kissed her until she was breathless.

"Did you think I was just going to leave you there, at her mercy?" he asked, running his tongue along the side of her neck.

"She could have killed you."

He snorted. "She wasn't half as tough as I thought she'd be." His hands slid up and down her sides. "Are we going to stand here and argue all night?"

"You don't look like you're capable of anything else," Kadie said, stifling a grin.

"Really? I guess I'll have to prove otherwise." And with that goal in mind, he carried her to bed, both of them heedless of the trail of soapy water they left along the way.

Chapter Twenty-Seven

Nolan Browning materialized in his favorite vampire nightclub. Taking a seat at the bar, he ordered a glass of the house special: red wine mixed with fresh blood. He downed it in a single swallow and asked for another. He couldn't believe Saintcrow had defeated his witch. Sure, Saintcrow was ancient, a master vampire, practically older than dirt, but Shiloh had been almost as old and rumored to be as powerful. Browning shook his head. One thing was certain. She hadn't been strong enough to do the job he'd hired her for.

He scowled into his empty glass. If she hadn't been able to destroy Saintcrow, he sure as hell didn't stand a chance. Not on his own. And if a witch couldn't destroy Saintcrow, he'd just have to keep looking until he found someone—or something—that could.

Because he was determined to have Morgan Creek for his own, one way or another.

And the tasty-looking, raven-haired young woman, too.

Chapter Twenty-Eight

For Sofia, life gradually returned to normal as the days following Kadie's rescue passed without further incident. Even so, Ethan and Saintcrow didn't relax their guard. One or the other patrolled the town several times a day and through the night, but there was no sign of Browning. No suspicious-looking strangers wandered into town.

To Sofia's surprise, Saintcrow's wounds healed practically overnight, leaving no telltale scars. Work continued on the hotel. The pool was repaired and filled. Restorations on the tavern were completed.

She was amazed by how quickly the renovations had been accomplished. Most of the houses had been spruced up with new paint, curtains, and carpet. She had ordered new appliances for all the residences and the office. Delivery had been promised for the following week.

Best of all, she had overcome all her doubts about Ethan. Sure, there were bound to be problems in their relationship, but every couple had differences to resolve, and she had no doubt they could find a way to make things work.

She was sitting at her desk, going over the books, when he came up behind her.

Bending down, he brushed a kiss across the top of her

head. "It's a beautiful day. Why don't you take a break and we can go try out the pool?"

She swiveled her chair around so she could see his face. "That would be a terrific idea except for one thing. I don't have a bathing suit."

"Not to worry. I've already taken care of that," he said, and dropped a department store sack into her lap.

"Really? I can't wait to see what you bought." She shook her head when she opened the sack and pulled out a bright red-and-white bikini. "Seriously? You expect me to wear *this* with all those construction workers running around?"

"I thought you'd say that, so I brought this along as backup." He handed her another bag. This one held a black one-piece.

"Much better," she said. "Why don't you grab a couple of towels while I shut down my computer?"

Sofia hadn't been to the pool since it had been replastered, and it was a sight to behold. Sunshine sparkled on the water. A swath of bright green grass surrounded the deck. Wrought-iron benches were placed at intervals. Tall trees offered shade.

"It's beautiful," she said.

"Yeah," Ethan agreed. "And so are you." He whistled softly as she shed her cover-up. The modest black bathing suit outlined every delicious curve.

"You're not so bad yourself," she replied. And it was true. He was gorgeous in a pair of navy trunks. His arms, legs, and chest seemed to be made of solid muscle.

He grinned at her, thinking his life had never been better than it was now. He could walk in daylight again. And Sofia loved him.

Swinging her up into his arms, he jumped into the pool.

Sofia let out a shriek as the cold water closed over them. She surfaced, sputtering, but feeling young and carefree in a way she hadn't for weeks.

"Beat you to the other side!" she challenged.

"Are you kidding? No way!"

"Chicken?"

He laughed. "Honey, I'll give you a head start and you still won't win."

"You're on!"

Ethan watched her, admiring the way the sun's light glinted in her hair. He waited until she was halfway across before he struck out after her. Tempting as it was to let her win, he just couldn't do it.

"You cheated!" she said, coming up beside him.

"What?"

"You used all that vampire power. Not fair!"

"Hey, I can't help it."

"Can't you?"

"Do you want a rematch? I'll swim with one arm behind my back."

She looked up at him, her expression so solemn, he felt a twinge of unease. Her next words threw him for a loop. "Will you marry me, Ethan?"

"What is this, a trick question?"

"No. Will you?"

He pushed a lock of wet hair behind her ear, nipped her lobe, and then kissed her lightly. "I was going to ask you."

"Really?"

He nodded. "I love you, Sofia Ravenwood. I'd be honored to have you as my wife."

* * *

"Married?" Saintcrow glanced from Ethan to Sofia and back again. "Well, hell, congratulations."

Ethan nodded. The four of them had gathered in the living room at Saintcrow's place after Sofia closed the office for the night. Saintcrow kept his arm around Kadie, who seemed to have recovered from her ordeal.

"I think it's wonderful!" Kadie exclaimed. "When's the big day?"

Ethan glanced at Sofia.

"Well, not until I tell my parents," she said, "which is something I'm definitely not looking forward to. And not until Micah and Holly get home. After all, Holly's the one who brought us together."

"They've been gone a long time," Kadie said. "They must be having a great time."

"Last I heard, they were on their way to Graceland."

Kadie elbowed Saintcrow. "I've always wanted to go there."

"I know. And since the work on the town will be finished soon, and Ethan will be taking over, you and I can take off for Elvis country. Maybe you'll meet his ghost."

"Very funny," Kadie muttered. "Rylan's just jealous because the ghosts talk to me, but not to him."

"They talk to Ethan, too," Saintcrow remarked.

"I think it's amazing," Sofia said, "but also kind of creepy."

"Hey," Ethan said. "If that ghost hadn't whispered in my ear, I might not have known you were in trouble."

She smiled up at him. "True, but . . ." She paused when her cell phone rang. A quick look at the display told her it was Rosa. Excusing herself, Sofia went into the other room to take the call. "Hey, Rosie; what's up?"

"You need to come home right away," her sister said,

tears evident in her voice. "They've just rushed Dad to the hospital. I'm on my way there now."

Sofia's hand clenched around the phone. "What happened?"

"He took a bad fall."

"Oh no! From where?"

"The roof."

"What on earth was he doing on the roof?"

"Some of the tiles were loose, and he decided to fix them. I don't know why he didn't ask one of the boys. Anyway, right after it happened, he said he was fine and then, a little while later, he just collapsed. He was unconscious when the ambulance came."

"Tell the family I'll be there as soon as I can."

"Hurry!" Rosa said, and disconnected the call.

Feeling suddenly numb, Sofia stared at her phone, a silent prayer on her lips. *Please. Please don't let him die.*

Before she could return to the living room, Ethan was at her side.

"I heard everything," he said, wrapping his arms around her. "Are you ready?"

Sofia nodded, more grateful than ever for the vampire powers that carried them from Wyoming to Arizona in minutes instead of hours.

When the world stopped spinning, they were standing outside the hospital.

"I'll wait for you out here," he said.

"That's not necessary."

"Just worry about your dad right now. I don't want to be in the way."

"But . . ."

"Don't argue with me," he said, giving her hand a squeeze. "Go see your family."

She kissed his cheek, then turned and ran toward the emergency room entrance.

The nurse at the desk directed Sofia to the waiting room. Her mother was there, her cheeks wet with tears, along with the rest of the family, save for Micah and Holly.

"Sofia, how did you get here so fast?" her oldest sister, Angela, asked.

"Ethan brought me. He . . . he ah, flew me here. Has anyone called Micah?" she asked, hoping to change the subject.

"We haven't been able to get in touch with him. Delia left a message on his phone."

After hugging everyone, Sofia took the chair next to Rosa's. "Any news?"

"Not yet. I don't know if that's good or bad."

Sofia nodded, then tugged on Rosa's hand. "You haven't told anyone about Ethan, have you?"

"No," Rosa said, crossing her heart. "Not a word. So, how are things with the two of you?"

"Let's not talk about that now. I can't think straight."

The next hour dragged by. Every time Sofia heard footsteps approach the door, she looked up with a sense of dread, afraid it was a doctor coming to tell them that her father had passed away.

Her brothers, Paolo and Enzo, went down to the cafeteria and bought coffee and doughnuts for everyone.

Finally, two hours later, a doctor came in with the news. Her father had suffered severe head trauma from the fall and was still unconscious. Preliminary tests had been done, but they were still waiting for the results.

"We'll keep him under close observation, of course," the doctor assured them. "He's still in recovery, Mrs.

Ravenwood. You may go see him now. The rest of you can visit in pairs, if you wish, but only for a few moments."

Sofia's mother broke into tears after the doctor took his leave. Sergio put his arms around her. "I'll take Mom to see Dad," he said.

"It doesn't sound good, his being unconscious after so long," Sofia's brother Enzo remarked after their mother left the room.

Paolo shook his head. "He's gonna be fine," he said, wiping his eyes. "The old man's too tough to let a little thing like a fall slow him down."

Sofia hoped he was right, but thoughts of her father slipping into a coma and then quietly slipping away tore at her heart.

"How long are you going to stay?" Rosa asked while she and Sofia were waiting their turn.

"I don't know. At least until I'm sure Dad's going to be all right."

By the time Sofia was able to spend a few minutes with her father, it was quite late. It hurt to see him looking so pale, so fragile. A wide bandage swathed his head; tubes attached him to several machines.

She looked across the bed at Rosa, who looked as stricken as she felt. "He was always so strong," Sofia murmured, blinking back her tears. Now he just looked old and worn out.

"He'll be all right," Rosa said, sniffling. "I know he will."

Sofia nodded because she couldn't bear to think of the alternative. Like all little girls, she had idolized her father. He had been her hero. No matter what problems had beset her, he had been there, a shoulder to cry on when she needed comfort, a cheerleader when she needed a boost.

When they rejoined the rest of the family, Lena insisted

Sofia come and stay at the house with her and Rosa. Sofia had planned to meet Ethan at her apartment later, but she didn't have the heart to refuse her mother's request.

At home, Lena wandered aimlessly through the house for a few minutes before deciding to go up to bed. She hugged Rosa, then turned to Sofia. "Thank you for staying."

"He'll be all right, Mama," Sofia said, hugging her mother. "Try not to worry."

Nodding, Lena went upstairs, her steps slow and heavy.

"Do you want some hot chocolate?" Rosa asked, tossing her sweater over the back of the sofa.

"Sounds good." Sofia kicked off her shoes.

While Rosa was busy in the kitchen, Sofia took a moment to call Ethan and bring him up-to-date.

He readily agreed with her decision to stay with her mother. "She needs you," he said. "Keep in touch, okay? I'll be nearby if you need me for anything. I love you, Sofie."

"Love you more. Good night."

In the kitchen, Sofia sat across the table from Rosa. "Remember how we always had cocoa after our dates?" she mused, adding a few marshmallows to her cup.

Rosa nodded. "And how Dad always waited up for us, even though he pretended he'd fallen asleep in his chair?"

Sofia nodded. "Remember when he caught Micah smoking out behind the garage?"

Rosa laughed. "And how he made him smoke a whole pack of cigarettes?"

"I never knew you could actually *turn* green," Sofia said. "And how about the time . . ." Her words trailed off as Micah and Holly materialized in the doorway.

"Speak of the devil," Rosa muttered.

"And he appears," Sofia finished.

"Very funny," Micah said, flashing a grin.

After shared hugs all around, he beckoned for Sofia to join him in the living room for, as he put it, a little private chat.

"All right," he said, one arm resting on the mantel, "tell me what's going on with you and this Ethan guy."

"Nothing is *going on*," she retorted, perching on the edge of the coffee table. "We're dating."

"That's all?" Micah asked skeptically. "*Just* dating?"

Sofia shook her head in exasperation. "Whatever I'm doing is none of your business. I'm a big girl now."

"When you're fifty, you'll still be my little sister and I'll still be worrying about you."

"Do we have to talk about this now? Aren't you worried about Dad?"

"Of course I am, but he's not likely to run off and do something stupid."

"And I am?"

"You're dating a vampire."

"You're a vampire!"

"That's not a good argument, Sofie, and you know it. It wasn't my idea."

"Let me ask you the same thing I asked Ethan. If you could be human again, would you?"

Micah stared at her. "What kind of a question is that?"

"A yes-or-no question. So, what's your answer? Would you be human again if you had the choice?"

"Well, sure, I guess so."

She shook her head. It was basically the same answer Ethan had given her. "You'd miss it, wouldn't you? All those vampire powers. The strength. Being able to just think yourself wherever you want to go."

Brow furrowed, Micah dropped into the easy chair catty-corner to the coffee table. "What's this all about? You're not thinking of asking Ethan to turn you?"

"No. But I asked Ethan the same question, and he said

no. And I think, if you were honest with me, that would be your answer, too."

"It can't be undone, Sofie. Once it's a fact, the only thing you can do is make the best of it. If you don't . . ." He shrugged. "You're gonna be miserable for a hell of a long time."

"Does Holly have any regrets?"

"Not that I know of, but you'd have to ask her."

"Do you?"

"Well sure, one or two. I always liked being part of a big family, and I'd hoped to have one of my own someday. I guess that's my biggest regret." He leaned forward, hands braced on his knees. "You're thinking about it, aren't you? Asking him to turn you?"

"I've considered it once or twice," she admitted. "I love him, Micah. We're going to be married."

"Dammit, Sofie, you just met the man! At least wait a while before . . ." He bit off his words when he saw the mutiny in her eyes. "Do whatever you want. As you've told me so often, you're all grown up."

"You'll like him, Micah," she said, smiling. "He's a lot like you."

"Are you trying to butter me up?"

"Maybe a little."

"So, when do we get to meet Mr. Wonderful?"

"I don't know. I wasn't sure now was the right time, what with Dad being in the hospital and everything."

"But he's here, isn't he?"

Sofia nodded. "Do you know a vampire named Browning?"

"I know *of* him. Why?"

"He's been snooping around Morgan Creek. Saintcrow thinks he wants to take over the town and make it what it was before." As succinctly as possible, she told him about the witch.

Micah hissed an oath. "But Kadie's all right?"

"She seems to be. Ethan convinced Saintcrow to renovate the town. Ethan hopes to turn it into a resort."

"No kidding?"

"Yeah. Saintcrow's financing the work. Ethan's going to manage the place."

"Did they tear down the graveyard?"

"No. Ethan wanted to spruce it up a little, but Kadie said to leave it alone. You're thinking about that woman, aren't you? Shirley?"

"Saintcrow's got a big mouth."

"He said you loved her."

"Did he?"

"And that she was older than you."

Micah sighed. "Her age didn't matter. I owed her a great deal."

"Did she love you, too?"

"Not enough." Micah stared into the distance a moment, obviously thinking about the past. With a shake of his head, he took her hands in his. "We're here to talk about your love life, Sofie, not mine. I want you to promise me you won't make any rash decisions." Rising, he pulled her into his embrace. "If you ever need help or advice or just a shoulder to cry on, you know you can always count on me."

She smiled up at him. "I love you, too."

"Why don't you call this guy and tell him to come over now?"

"Why?"

"Why do you think? I want to meet him."

"You want to give him the third degree."

"That too." He dropped a kiss on the top of her head. "I've got to meet him sooner or later. Might as well get it over with."

With an exasperated sigh, Sofia called Ethan, hoping

that introducing the two men she loved wouldn't bring about the end of the world as she knew it.

He answered on the first ring. "Hey, Sofie, what's up?"

"Micah wants to meet you."

"You sure that's a good idea?"

"Well, as much as I hate to admit it, he's right," she said with an exaggerated sigh. "You two have to meet sometime. Might as well be now."

"All right. I'll be at your parents' place by the time you say good-bye."

Sofia ended the call and opened the front door. Ethan stood there, his hands shoved in his pants' pockets. For a moment, she drank in the sight of him—so tall and handsome in blue jeans and a leather jacket over a black shirt. "You look just like a rebel from the fifties," she said, grinning. "All you need is a cigarette behind your ear."

Ignoring her remark, he gave her a look that clearly said he'd rather be anywhere else.

"I know," she said. "Come on in."

As with all houses, Ethan experienced a shimmer of preternatural power as he crossed the Ravenwoods' threshold and followed Sofia into the living room.

From her place on the love seat, Holly smiled a welcome.

Ethan lifted his chin in acknowledgment. "Hey, Cuz."

Making introductions, Sofia said, "Ethan, this is my sister Rosa."

He nodded at the dark-haired young woman sitting in a chair beside the fireplace. There was no mistaking the family resemblance.

"Nice to finally meet you, Ethan," Rosa said.

He nodded again.

"And this is my nosy brother, Micah. Micah, Ethan."

Sofia held her breath as the two men shook hands,

thinking they looked for all the world like two stags poised to fight over territory.

Sofia resumed her seat on the couch and beckoned for Ethan to join her.

"Sofie tells me you're doing some remodeling in Morgan Creek," Micah remarked, settling on the love seat beside Holly.

"We're about done," Ethan replied easily. "I think we can make a go of it."

"What about Browning?" Micah asked.

Ethan glanced at Sofia, who shrugged. "She told you about that, huh?"

"Yeah, but I'm more interested in your intentions toward my baby sister."

"She asked me to marry her and I said yes."

"She proposed to you? Interesting." Micah sent an accusing glance in Sofia's direction. "She forgot to mention that."

"With good reason," Sofia retorted. "Are you two through now? You're both Saintcrow's prodigies, so to speak, and we're all going to be family soon, so maybe the two of you could make an effort to get along."

Micah and Ethan glared at each other.

Holly jabbed her elbow into Micah's side. "Enough of this foolishness. I'm drowning in testosterone. Either you play nice with my cousin or you'll be spending a lot of time on the sofa, if you know what I mean."

"We're still on our honeymoon!" Micah protested.

"Are we?" Holly asked.

"Fine," Micah said. "Welcome to the family, Parrish."

Sofia nudged Ethan.

"Thanks," he muttered. "I'm happy to be here."

Sofia looked at Holly, then at Rosa, and the three of them burst out laughing.

* * *

"Well, that was a night I could have done without," Ethan remarked later, when he and Sofia were alone in the living room. Rosa had gone to bed. Micah and Holly had gone back to the hospital to check on the old man.

Sofia rested her head on Ethan's shoulder. "It wasn't so bad."

Ethan snorted. "Not so bad? Your brother looked at me like I was going to steal the family silver as soon as he turned his back. Or worse."

"He's my big brother. Well, one of many. But Micah's always been more protective of me than the others."

"I don't think he's going to be too thrilled to have me in the family."

"Do you care?"

"Not really," he said, pulling her into his arms. "You never told me how your dad's doing."

"Hopefully, we'll know something by tomorrow." Sofia worried her lower lip. "If we get bad news . . . I mean, if things look hopeless . . . I saw how your blood helped that woman Mateo attacked. Would it make my father well?"

"I don't know if it would fix what ails him, but it would likely help him recover his strength. Don't you think you should be discussing this with Micah? He is family."

"I know, but your blood is stronger, don't you think?"

"Maybe."

"You wouldn't have to turn him, would you?"

"Not unless he's on the brink of death. But that would have to be his decision, if he's conscious. Or your mother's, I guess. In any case, you should be discussing this with her and with your brothers and sisters, not me."

"I can't imagine any of them would object. I mean, they all know about vampires now."

"That doesn't mean they want another one in the family," he said with a wry grin. "But I'll do whatever you want. For now, you should probably get some sleep."

She nodded. "I can hardly keep my eyes open."

"Go on up to bed. I'll see you in the morning."

"Micah's going to be green with envy when he finds out you can be awake during the day and he can't."

"Good." He kissed her, long and slow, savoring the taste of her, the scent of her hair, the softness of her skin, loving the way she always melted against him. Soon, he thought, soon she would be his in every way that mattered.

Chapter Twenty-Nine

Nolan Browning stood on the bridge at the entrance to Morgan Creek. It galled him that Saintcrow had killed Shiloh so easily. He had been told she was a powerful witch—but not, it seemed, powerful enough to defeat Saintcrow.

So, now he was on his own again.

Curious, he walked across the bridge, only to be stopped in his tracks when he reached the other side. Damn Saintcrow! He had warded the town again, only this time it was against his own kind instead of humans.

He gazed at the buildings beyond. The darkness hid nothing from his preternatural vision. The work was going faster than he had expected.

Perhaps he would bide his time, wait until the renovations were complete, before he tried to get rid of Saintcrow again. Or maybe he would just wait until Saintcrow or Kadie got tired of the place and decided to leave. New as he was, the fledgling, Ethan, wouldn't be much of a challenge. With Saintcrow gone and the fledgling destroyed, it would be no trouble at all to take over Morgan Creek. He had spoken with Felix, Quinn, Lonigan, and Vaughn. All had expressed interest in returning to Morgan Creek.

Nodding, he walked back to the highway, where he had left his car parked.

Waiting was the smart thing to do.

After all, he had all the time in the world.

Chapter Thirty

In the morning, Sofia and Rosa accompanied their mother to the hospital. It was all Sofia could do to keep from crying when she saw her father. He looked much the same as he had the night before: pale, fragile. Vulnerable.

"He looks better, don't you think?" Lena murmured, stroking her husband's brow.

Sofia and Rosa exchanged looks.

"Sure, Mom," Sofia said.

The doctor came in a short time later, his expression grave as he explained the patient's condition. The only thing Sofia really understood was that there had been no change and that the longer he remained unconscious, the more unlikely his recovery would be.

Lena collapsed in a chair, sobbing. She sat there for several minutes, her face buried in her hands. "I'm going to the chapel to pray," she declared, blinking back her tears. "Only the good Lord can help him now."

"Rosie, why don't you go with her?" Sofia suggested. "I'll be there as soon as I check in with Ethan."

Nodding, Rosa led their mother out of the room.

When she was alone, Sofia took her father's hand in hers. "I don't know if you can hear me, Dad, but I'm not going to let you go, not like this. Not when I might be able to help." Leaning down, she kissed his cheek, then whispered, "I love you, Daddy. Please don't leave us."

"I'm staying here, at the hospital," Lena said. "He might wake up and need me."

Instead of arguing with her mother, Sofia sent a group text to her brothers and sisters, and they decided to take turns staying with Mom, each one taking a shift, with the women going during the day and the men scheduled for a few hours after work at night. Sofia volunteered for the nine-to-midnight shift. Micah and Holly were the logical choice for midnight until three a.m.

Rosa decided to stay and take the first shift. "I might as well," she said, "since I'm already here."

Sergio nodded. "Sounds good. I'll relieve you at noon."

When Sofia returned home, Ethan was waiting for her on the front porch.

"I'm so glad you're here," she said, unlocking the door. "Bad news?"

"He's still unconscious." Sitting on the edge of the sofa, she peeled off her sweater and kicked off her shoes. "Mom's staying at the hospital, afraid to leave for fear that . . . you know. My sisters and brothers are all going to take turns staying with her."

Nodding, he sat beside her, his hand massaging her back.

"That feels so good." She closed her eyes. "You'd probably rather be at Morgan Creek overseeing the finishing touches on the renovation than stuck here with me."

"I'm not *stuck here* with you. I'm here because this is

where I want to be. Saintcrow can look after things while I'm away. It's his town after all."

Sofia smiled up at him, then laughed softly when her stomach growled. "I haven't eaten since breakfast."

"Do you want me to make you a sandwich?"

"Seriously?"

"Hey, I might not be able to eat it, but I haven't forgotten how to make one."

"That would be nice, thanks." Settling back on the sofa, she closed her eyes again, thinking what a sweet guy he was. She couldn't ever remember having a boyfriend who offered to fix her anything to eat. Sure, they had taken her out for dinner, sometimes to lunch, but there was nothing personal about that. She grinned as she listened to Ethan moving about in the kitchen, amused by the thought of a vampire fixing her a sandwich.

"Hey," he called from the kitchen. "Do you want something to drink? Milk? Soda? Water?"

"Soda sounds good."

A few minutes later, he returned, carrying a plate in one hand and a glass of root beer with ice in the other. "Here you go."

"Looks perfect," she said as he placed it on the coffee table. And it was. The sandwich was thick with roast beef, Swiss cheese, tomato, onion, and pickles, light on the mustard and mayonnaise. Just the way she liked it. She frowned as she took a bite. "Did you read my mind? Is that how you knew what I like?"

"Guilty as charged." He dropped into the chair next to the couch. "Are you mad?"

"Not a bit." She sipped her drink, took another bite of her sandwich. "Do you miss eating?"

"Not as much as I thought I would. I remember what

things taste like, but . . ." He shrugged. "I don't really have a desire for any of it."

"And the . . . blood?"

"Do you really want to talk about that while you're eating?"

She shrugged.

"I never really thought about liking it or not. It's necessary." He paused a moment, thinking about it. "If you want the truth, I guess I do like it. When I prey on someone, I get a glimpse of their whole life—who they are, what they want, if they're happy or miserable. It's a kind of high that's hard to explain."

"Do you get all that when you drink from me?"

"I don't take enough of your blood for that."

"When you exchanged blood with Saintcrow, did you see his past?"

"More of it than I wanted."

"What did you see?"

"Just bits and pieces, some longer than others. I got a glimpse of his life before he was turned. And after—years of savagery and killing until he learned to control his hunger and his power. I caught snatches of life in Morgan Creek. And a sense of the peace he found when he met Kadie." His gaze met hers. "Sort of the way I feel with you."

Whether it was because they could read each other's thoughts or because they both had a sudden need to touch, she didn't know, but they stood at the same time, each reaching for the other.

"Sofie." Her name was a groan on his lips as he stroked her back.

She rested her cheek against his chest, utterly content to stand there with his arms tight around her.

"Marry me now. Tonight. I can't wait any longer."

It was tempting. Oh so tempting. "My family," she

murmured. "It would break my mother's heart if she wasn't there. My . . . my dad's, too."

"We could keep it a secret for now and have a big wedding later."

"We don't have a license. And I don't want to leave here, even for a few minutes, you know, in case my dad takes a turn for the worse, or . . ." She couldn't finish the sentence, afraid if she said it out loud, it might happen.

He nodded. "You're right. I was only thinking of myself. Sorry."

"I love you, too. As soon as my dad's out of danger, we'll get married, I promise."

Later that afternoon, Sofia decided to take a nap, since she had chosen to take one of the late-night shifts at the hospital.

"I think I'll go check on things at Morgan Creek," Ethan said. "I'll be back before it's time for you to go keep your mom company."

"Okay. Be careful."

"Right." A hug and a kiss, and he was gone.

Workers were swarming over the residences when Ethan arrived. A couple of men were painting the outside trim on the hotel. Two others were pouring a section of new concrete in front of the tavern.

He was checking out the freshly planted shrubbery at the park when Saintcrow fell into step beside him.

"I was beginning to think you'd found another interest."

"Sofia's dad's in the hospital. It's not looking real good."

"You can fix that."

"Yeah, she asked me to, but I told her she needed to talk

it over with her family, especially Micah. He's not too keen on having another vampire in the family."

"It's a territorial thing," Saintcrow remarked. "He can't help it. None of us can."

"Territorial? What the hell does that mean?"

"Just what it sounds like. It's unusual for more than one or two vampires to occupy the same city, and when they do, one is usually a master vampire who keeps the others in line."

"Is that how it was when you and your fanged friends all lived here?"

Saintcrow nodded. "I was the boss. I laid down the rules. I disposed of anybody who broke the law."

"Are you saying Micah's a master vampire?"

"Hardly. But it's his hometown, and that gives him priority."

Ethan grunted softly. *Live and learn.* "Are there a lot of vampires in the world?"

"No. Like I said, we're territorial. Old vampires tend to get rid of new ones in their territory. Those who go rogue are destroyed. The fewer of us there are, the better for everyone." He paused at the edge of town, nostrils flared, eyes narrowing as his gaze swept the area. Satisfied there was no danger lurking in the shadows, he resumed walking. "Reed says his crew should be finished here by the end of the month. You'd better start hiring people if you want to open this place."

"Right. I'll put an ad in the paper on Monday." They needed someone to man the front desk in the hotel, a couple of maids, cooks, and waitresses for the hotel dining room and the tavern, someone to sell tickets in the movie theater and work the concession counter, maybe a lifeguard or two for the pool, maids to clean the rentals, a couple of guys to run the gas station. Damn, it was going to be one heck of a long ad!

"When are you and Sofia gonna tie the knot?"

"Not until her old man recovers."

"Is that likely?"

"How should I know? I'm not a doctor." They walked in silence for a moment. "Where do you think Browning's gone off to?"

"I don't know. He was here the other night. I caught his scent on the bridge."

"You don't think he'll go looking for another witch, do you?"

"I doubt it. They're not that easy to find. And most of them don't want anything to do with vampires. Alone, he's no threat."

Ethan nodded. "I hope you're right."

Saintcrow huffed a sigh of exasperation. "When have I ever been wrong?"

Ethan might have taken exception to that if he hadn't heard Sofia's voice in his mind, begging him to hurry back. Ethan bid a quick farewell to his sire and returned to the Ravenwood home as fast as preternatural power could take him.

He found Sofia pacing the living-room floor, her eyes red from crying.

"Rosa called," she said, blinking back her tears. "My dad is . . . is . . . Oh, Ethan, you have to do something!"

"All right, let's go." Wrapping his arm securely around her waist, he transported her to a back entrance where their sudden appearance would, hopefully, go unobserved.

Luck was with them. A little vampire magic unlocked the door, and they hurried toward the elevator. There were times, Ethan mused, when having enhanced senses was more of a curse than a blessing. Now was one of those times. He wrinkled his nose against the strong scents of blood, death, and disinfectant that permeated the air, along with other, even less pleasant smells.

Sofia was surprised to find Rosa standing on one side of the bed and their mother on the other, each holding one of her father's hands. His breathing was shallow, labored, his heartbeat slow.

"Isn't this Angela's shift?" Sofia asked.

"One of her kids was sent home from school. He's got a high fever."

"How's Dad?"

Rosa shook her head imperceptibly.

Sofia beckoned for her sister to come away from the bed.

Frowning, Rosa joined Sofia and Ethan near the door. "I'm glad you're here. I've called everyone. They're on their way. Well," she said, sniffling, "everyone except Micah and Holly."

"Rosie, Ethan thinks some of his blood might help Dad recover. There's no guarantee, but at this point, it can't hurt."

"I'm willing to try anything, but we should ask Mom first."

Sofia nodded. "Of course."

Ethan stayed by the door while Sofia and Rosa went to talk to their mother. He had no trouble overhearing what was said, or reading the shock in Lena's eyes as Sofia explained what Ethan proposed to do. For a moment, he thought she would refuse, and in some ways, he hoped she would. He was pretty sure a little of his blood would, at the least, strengthen Ravenwood and give him a fighting chance. But if he was wrong, it might make the old man feel worse.

In the end, Lena agreed.

Taking a deep breath, Ethan approached the bed. "Mrs. Ravenwood, you might not want to watch."

"I'm staying."

Ethan glanced at Sofia, who nodded.

Praying this would work, Ethan bit into his wrist.

Lena Ravenwood's face paled when she saw the dark red blood welling from the twin puncture wounds. Vampire blood was a lot darker than its human equivalent. In the dim light of the room, it looked almost black.

Lena looked as if she was about to faint as she watched drops of that dark red blood dripping into her husband's mouth.

Rosa gagged and looked away.

Sofia's gaze moved from Ethan's face to her father's and back again. Would it help or hurt? How long before they knew?

After what seemed like forever, but was only a minute or two, Ethan withdrew his arm.

Sofia glanced over her shoulder as Sergio and Paolo arrived. They glanced at their father, then at Ethan.

Paolo frowned.

"What the hell's going on?" Sergio asked.

Sofia forced a smile. "Nothing; why?"

Before her brother could say anything else, her sisters, Angela and Delia, arrived, closely followed by her two other brothers, Enzo and Mario.

Rosa looked at Sofia, her expression clearly saying, *what now?* as the tension in the room grew thick enough to cut with a knife.

Sofia moved closer to Ethan, her hand finding his. Hoping to distract her siblings, she said, "I'm not sure this is the right time or place to tell you this, but Ethan and I are getting married and . . ."

"And what?" Sergio demanded. He glared at Ethan, then looked back at Sofia, his eyes narrowed ominously. "Are you in trouble?"

"No. No! I didn't want to say anything with Dad so sick, but . . ."

"Luciano!" All eyes swung toward Lena, who was openly weeping tears of joy. "Luciano, you've come back to us!"

Sofia looked at Ethan, mouthing the words *thank you*, as the rest of the family congregated around her father's bed.

"Where'd this blood on the sheet come from?" Sergio asked. "There's blood on Dad's chin, too."

"It's nothing," Lena said, quickly wiping the blood from her husband's face with a corner of the sheet. "Luciano, can you hear me? How do you feel?"

Sofia held her breath as she waited for her dad's answer.

"I feel . . . good," he said slowly. "Kind of strange, but good. Enzo, raise the bed." He frowned when he was sitting up. "I had the strangest dream," he said, taking Lena's hand in his.

Sofia looked at Ethan again, her expression worried. *Can he possibly know what happened?*

Ethan shrugged. *I don't know.*

"What kind of dream?" Rosa asked, darting a glance at Sofia.

"Is Micah here?" Luciano asked, looking around.

"He should be here soon, Dad," Delia said. "The sun's going down."

Luciano nodded, his brow furrowing. "Of course."

"The blood," Paolo murmured. "Vampire."

"Why did you think Micah was here?" Mario asked.

Somewhat sheepishly, Luciano said, "I dreamed he was beside me, giving me his blood."

Silence fell over the room and then, as if pulled by the same string, all heads turned toward Ethan.

Chapter Thirty-One

Feeling like an alien invader, Ethan faced Sofia's increasingly suspicious siblings as they murmured among themselves. He was wondering whether to stand his ground or get the hell out of Dodge when Micah and Holly burst through the door.

"What's going on?" Micah asked, his gaze sweeping the faces of his parents and siblings. "I could feel the tension in this room a mile away."

"That's what we're trying to find out," Sergio said.

Micah's nostrils flared, and then he turned all his attention to Ethan. "What have you done?"

"Saved your father's life," Ethan retorted. "Why didn't you?"

Micah took a step forward, his rage a palpable thing.

"Stop!" Lena exclaimed. "You will not fight in here! Instead of being angry, you should be thanking Ethan . . ." Her voice trailed off.

"Vampire," Paolo said. "I knew it."

There was little point in denying it, so Ethan nodded.

Lena looked at Micah, accusation in her eyes. "Would *your* blood have saved your father?"

"I don't know. I guess so. I would have given it to him

if I'd been here." Micah frowned as he again focused his attention on Ethan. "How long have *you* been here? The sun just went down."

"The sun's not a problem for me anymore."

"How is that possible? You're still a fledgling."

"Maybe you should talk to Saintcrow."

"I'm asking you."

"Children, enough." Luciano's voice cut through the tension. "Micah, could you get me something to eat? I'm starving."

Keeping his gaze on Ethan, Micah said, "Send Sergio."

"Micah, shame on you!" Lena chided. "Do as your father asks."

"He's just trying to get me out of here!"

"Then go."

Eyes blazing red with anger, Micah stalked out of the room. Holly sent Lena an apologetic glance, then followed him.

"Mrs. Ravenwood, I think I should go, too," Ethan said as the door closed behind Holly.

"That's not necessary," she said quietly. "You saved my husband's life. You are welcome here and in my home."

One by one, the Ravenwood sons and daughters nodded in agreement.

Luciano cleared his throat. "Excuse me, but who is this man who is causing such a fuss?"

"His name is Ethan Parrish," Sofia said, tugging Ethan toward her father's bedside. "He's Holly's cousin."

Luciano's gaze moved over Ethan. "And you are a vampire, like Micah?"

"Yes, sir."

Ravenwood glanced from Ethan to Sofia. "You two are together?"

Sofia squeezed Ethan's hand. "Yes."

"Why have we not met him before?"

Sofia gave her father a why-do-you-think look that brought a faint smile to his face. "I would not have approved."

"I hope you will now," she said, "because we're going to be married as soon as you're well."

"With your permission, Mr. Ravenwood," Ethan added.

"How can I refuse?" Luciano replied with a wry grin. "I owe you my life."

Sofia blinked back tears of happiness as her father and Ethan shook hands.

"I was happy to help," Ethan said. "But I think I'll say good night for now. I'd rather not be here when Micah gets back."

Luciano nodded. "As my Lena said, you are always welcome in our home."

"Thank you, sir. Good night."

Sofia kissed her father on the cheek. "I don't want to be here when Micah gets back either," she said. "I'll see you tomorrow." She gave her mother and siblings quick hugs, then took Ethan's hand. "Let's get out of here while the getting's good."

Ethan wasn't keen on going back to the Ravenwood home and mingling with the family, and he didn't feel safe staying at Sofia's place, so he transported them to the warehouse he had once intended to use as his lair. There was still no electricity, but he'd bought some candles, which turned away the night.

Muttering, "Well, all the cats are out of the bag now," he sat on the couch and pulled Sofia down on his lap.

"Not exactly the way I planned to tell the family we're getting married—or that you're a vampire," she remarked, "but I'm glad it's all out in the open. No more sneaking around."

"Micah's never gonna forgive me for doing what he feels he should have done."

She couldn't argue with that. "Do you think he'll ask Saintcrow to do that blood exchange thing?"

"I don't know."

"I wonder if Saintcrow would do it?"

Ethan shook his head. "I don't know that either, but somehow, I doubt it."

"Why?"

"If Kadie's life hadn't been in danger, he wouldn't have suggested it. I'm sure of that. One of the perks of being a master vampire is being able to walk in daylight. It gives them an edge over those less powerful. I don't know about Saintcrow, but if I was a master vampire, I'd want to keep that particular talent to myself."

After days of searching, Nolan Browning finally found another witch.

She lived in Newport Beach and called herself Madame Zola. She agreed to meet him at the bar in a lavish club near her house an hour before midnight.

He had no trouble picking her out. She wore a low-cut white blouse, a colorful skirt, and two-inch heels. A mass of long red hair fell over her shoulders. She looked to be in her mid-twenties, but his vampire senses told him she was far older.

Her unblinking gaze ran over him as he took the stool beside her. It was like being watched and weighed by a hungry lioness.

"What do you want, vampire?" Her voice was like sandpaper sliding over silk.

"I'm looking for someone to help me destroy an enemy of mine."

"Why come to me?"

"I need a witch."

Her nostrils flared. "What happened to the last witch you employed?"

Her question took him aback. How did she know about Shiloh? He considered lying, but decided against it. "She was killed."

"Indeed. Think I am foolish enough to pit my powers against those of Rylan Saintcrow?"

Browning couldn't subdue his look of surprise. "You know him?"

"I know *of* him. He is a vampire without equal. I have no desire to make him *my* enemy."

Browning drummed his fingers on the table. "You make potions, right?"

She nodded.

"Can you create one that would make it impossible for him to sense my presence?"

"Yes."

"Can you also make it possible for me to get past the wards he's set around the town?"

She looked thoughtful, then nodded again. "There might be a way to disguise your true nature so the wards will be ineffective. Of course, it all depends on whether or not the price is right."

Chapter Thirty-Two

Two days later, Luciano's doctor declared him 100 percent recovered. Lena and Sergio drove to the hospital to bring him home.

The whole family—save for Micah and Holly—were there to greet the patriarch when he arrived.

Lena had prepared all his favorite foods for lunch: homemade pasta with marinara sauce, antipasto, rolls fresh from the oven, and cannoli for dessert. A huge "Welcome Home" sign—painted by Rosa and Sofia—hung on the dining-room wall.

Ethan had tried to avoid showing up, but Sofia wouldn't hear of it. "You're family now. You saved Dad's life. You have to be there."

Now, he stood in a corner of the living room, watching while the Ravenwood children and grandchildren gathered around the patriarch, all talking at once.

He couldn't help envying Sofia her family. The love and concern they felt for one another was a beautiful thing to see, something he had never experienced in his own home. He had no idea why his parents were still married, or why they had married in the first place.

Luciano insisted Ethan sit at his left hand at the table.

It was a little awkward, sitting there while the family passed food and drink back and forth. And yet it gave him an opportunity to see how a loving family interacted. One after another, Sofia's brothers and sisters told their favorite stories about their dad. Some were funny, some were serious, but the love was real. So was the laughter.

For a moment, he hated Saintcrow for turning him. He would never have a family like this. Of course, there was no guarantee any family he might have had would be as full of love and laughter as this one. But it might have been. Now, he would never know. How could he marry Sofia and rob her of the chance to enjoy life fully, to watch her own children grow up? Would she come to despise him for what he had stolen from her: a normal life with a mortal man who could give her children and grow old at her side?

He couldn't ask her to make a sacrifice like that. He loved her too much to yoke her life with his.

Hating Saintcrow, hating himself for what he was, Ethan stood abruptly and left the table. Once out of sight of the family, he dissolved into mist and fled the city.

He prowled the streets of another town, feeling more lost and alone than he had since he'd been turned. He blocked Sofia's thoughts, afraid hearing her voice would weaken his resolve to do the right thing. Leaving was for the best. At least for her.

He was a vampire. Being able to walk in daylight didn't change that. He would never be able to fully trust himself not to hurt her, either by accident or in a fit of anger. He didn't want to watch her grow old. Didn't want her to hate him because he didn't age. Didn't want her to decide to give up her humanity just so they could be together. True, she had once thought she wanted to be a vampire, but he'd been in her mind often enough to know she no longer felt that way. He knew he was hurting her now, by leaving, but better now than later, when she had given him her youth. He could have taken her aside and told her good-bye, but he couldn't bear to see her tears, couldn't take a chance she would change his mind. Better to do it this way, so her hurt would turn to anger. They had only been together a short time. She would forget him soon enough.

But in the deepest part of his soul, he knew he would never forget her.

Sofia refused to cry, but it was difficult to hold back her tears when everyone wanted to know why Ethan had left so abruptly and whether he was coming back.

He wasn't. Before he'd shut her out of his mind, she had read enough of his thoughts to know why he'd left. But it didn't ease the pain. It was as if he had ripped her heart from her chest, leaving nothing but a great, empty hole she would never be able to fill.

With a shake of her head, she kissed her father's cheek and excused herself from the table.

In her room, she stood in the center of the floor, her mind in turmoil, her throat burning with unshed tears. She would not cry for him. If he could walk away without so much as a good-bye, if he didn't have the guts to try to make a life with her, if he didn't think she was strong enough to be his woman, the hell with him.

The tears came then, slowly at first, then faster and faster. She sank to the floor, her face buried in her hands, and wept until she had no tears left.

She was still sitting there when someone knocked on her door.

"Sofia?" It was Rosa.

Wiping her eyes, she called, "Come in."

"Sofie, what happened?" Closing the door behind her, Rosa dropped down on the floor and reached for her sister's hand.

"He left me."

"Just like that? Why?"

"He thinks he's ruining my chance to have a normal life and a family of my own."

Rosa nodded slowly. "Don't get mad, but maybe he's right."

Sofia glared at her. "Shouldn't what I do with *my* life be *my* decision?"

"Well, yes, but . . . you're in love and not exactly thinking straight. I mean, have you ever seriously stopped to think about what it would mean to be married to a vampire?"

"Of course I have."

"Really? You'll age and he won't. You can't have kids."

"We could adopt."

"Suppose you do. But what about those kids? Are you going to spend your whole life lying about their father? Or burden them with the truth? And then there's that age thing again. You'll have to move every fifteen or twenty years because your neighbors will notice that you're growing older and he isn't. Or do you want to spend your whole life hiding in Morgan Creek? Or, worse, have him bring you across? I know you're miserable right now, but honestly, Sofie, I really believe he did you a favor, and he did it because he loves you."

"He has a funny way of showing it," Sofia muttered. "I hope he's miserable for the rest of his life when he realizes what he's thrown away."

* * *

During the next week, Ethan focused on helping Reed's men finish up the renovations on the last of the houses. He started early in the morning, took shelter in his lair when the sun was at its hottest, then went back to work with the second shift. But physical labor didn't make him stop thinking about Sofia, didn't make him miss her less.

He hunted nightly, but there was no solace to be found in the women he preyed on, no pleasure to be had in easing his hellish thirst.

Saintcrow remained oddly quiet, limiting his conversation to topics that pertained to Morgan Creek and nothing else. His reticence ended after two weeks. They were sitting in the newly refurbished tavern splitting a bottle of cabernet when he asked Ethan how much longer he was going to go on moping.

"I'm not moping," Ethan replied flatly.

"Mourning?" Saintcrow suggested. "Grieving? Acting like a damn fool?"

"Why don't you mind your own business?"

"I am. If you don't start thinking straight, you're gonna do something stupid. I poured a ton of cash into this place. I don't want to have to destroy my partner."

"It won't come to that," Ethan retorted sullenly.

"No? One of these nights you're gonna lose that control you're barely holding on to. You're gonna sink your fangs into some woman and drain her dry. And I'll have to kill you."

"I don't think I care."

"We've been down this road before," Saintcrow said, his patience growing thin. "I don't want to have to destroy you. I don't have that many friends or people I trust. I'd like to hang on to the ones I have. So either go and patch things up with Sofia, or forget about her."

"I can't," Ethan said quietly. "As much as I'd like to, I can't."

"I can make you forget."

Ethan shook his head. "She's the only good thing in my life. I did what was right."

"That's not going to keep you warm on cold nights."

"Vampires don't feel the cold."

"Have it your way." Saintcrow looked up as Kadie stepped into the tavern.

"Lecture over?" she asked, dropping onto Rylan's lap.

"It is as far as I'm concerned," Ethan muttered.

Kadie kissed her husband on the cheek. "He's stubborn, isn't he?"

"You have no idea," Saintcrow said.

"Listen, you two," Ethan said irritably. "You don't understand. Yes, Kadie, you and Holly and even Micah seem perfectly happy as vampires, but it wasn't a decision any of you had to make. Saintcrow turned you to save your life. Micah did the same for Holly. Sofia's not in any danger, and I intend to keep it that way. I don't want to have to make her a vampire and I don't want her to have to decide between me and living a normal life. She's a big girl. She's young. She'll forget about me."

"Like you'll forget about her?" Kadie asked.

"Okay, that's enough. I'm outta here." Ethan stood, then froze. "What is that?" he asked, his nostrils flaring.

"Fresh blood," Saintcrow said. "Out on the bridge."

It took only moments for the three of them to reach the end of the bridge. The scent of freshly spilled blood was unmistakable, as was the cause of death of the woman sprawled on her back, eyes wide and staring but seeing nothing. The blood pooled in the hollow of her throat glistened like black ink in the light of the full moon.

Saintcrow walked around the body, then swore softly. "I don't detect any scent but the woman's. Do either of you?"

"I don't," Ethan said.

"Me either," Kadie agreed. "How is that possible?"

"It's a new one on me. Every corpse I've ever found carried the scent of the vampire responsible for their death. This body smells of cheap perfume overlaid with blood and death and a faint odor I can't identify."

Ethan drew a deep breath. And frowned. "What *is* that smell?"

Saintcrow shook his head. "I don't know, but if we can figure it out, we might be able to find out who killed her and why."

"Maybe someone wanted to draw us out of town," Kadie suggested.

"There's no one else here," Ethan said. "And no way anyone could get by the three of us."

"Are you sure about that?" she asked, moving closer to her husband.

"Something's not right," Saintcrow said. "But damned if I know what it is."

Lurking in the shadows across the highway from the bridge, Nolan Browning watched Saintcrow and the other two vampires return to town. He had drained his bank account to pay for the witch's potion, but by damn, it had been worth every cent because, in addition to the magical elixir that disguised his true nature, she had given him a charm that would render him invisible for short periods of time. He had yet to try crossing the bridge. If there was one thing being a vampire had taught him, it was the value of patience. All he had to do now was bide his time until he caught Saintcrow alone.

Browning smiled into the darkness. The master vampire might be the most powerful of their kind, but even he couldn't fight an enemy he couldn't track or see.

Chapter Thirty-Three

Sofia allowed herself a two-day pity party; then she washed her face, combed her hair, put on her best dress, and went looking for a new job. She hadn't really expected to find one, but, to her surprise, she found an opening for a hostess in a five-star restaurant. As luck would have it, the owner, Carlo Russo, played bocce ball with her father, and he gave her the job on the spot.

She had to laugh, though without much humor, when she found herself keeping vampire hours—sleeping days and working nights.

Her father had recovered fully. His doctors were calling it a miracle, which, in a way, she supposed it was.

Micah and Holly were house hunting. Micah was still in a snit, not because his father was better but because Ethan had been the hero of the day.

So, except for the fact that Ethan was out of her life, things had pretty much returned to normal. She couldn't help feeling a little thrill of expectation every time her phone rang, and a sharp stab of disappointment when it never was Ethan, though if he did call, she had no idea what she would say.

Antonio, the manager of the restaurant, had asked her

out several times. So far, she had declined, even though she told herself she was being foolish. Tony was a nice guy, good-looking, with curly black hair, blue eyes, and a wry sense of humor. Rosa urged her to go out with him. Sofia knew she would eventually. But not now. It was too soon, her heart still too raw.

Ethan and Saintcrow accompanied Reed on a walk-through of the renovated buildings, with Ethan taking notes. He had to admit, Reed and his crew had done a hell of a job in a remarkably short time. Ethan was especially pleased with the tavern, which, though modernized, retained its roaring twenties' atmosphere. The theater's sound system had been updated, the screen and projector replaced. Several boxes of new books had been added to the library. The pool sparkled like a diamond in the middle of an emerald sea of grass.

Returning to the office, Saintcrow wrote out a check for the final payment. He and Ethan thanked Reed for a job well done, promised to call him if they decided on any new construction, and watched him drive away, a good deal richer for his labors.

"Well, your town's done," Saintcrow remarked, one shoulder propped against the office door. "And you still haven't hired anyone."

"I know. I'll get on it first thing in the morning."

"Why don't you call Sofia?"

Just hearing her name made Ethan ache deep inside. "She's getting on with her life. She's got a new job in a fancy restaurant and the manager is panting after her."

Saintcrow grunted softly, but said nothing.

"They've got two vampires in the family. They don't need another one."

His sire nodded, but again refrained from commenting.

"You've got nothing to say?" Ethan asked.

"Call her. You won't be happy until you do. And neither will she."

"Where do you think Browning is?"

"I wish I knew."

"Do you think he killed the woman at the bridge?"

"That would have been my first guess, but we would have caught his scent."

"What if he found a way to hide it?"

Saintcrow stared at him. "Shit!"

"Hey, I was kidding."

"Witches," Saintcrow muttered. "I'd bet the rest of my fortune that he's found another black witch."

"You think a witch could conjure something strong enough to keep us from scenting him?"

"I think it's very possible."

"Crap."

"Exactly."

Ethan nodded. Just one more reason to stay as far away from Sofia as he could.

"Dinner tonight?" Antonio asked. "A movie? A walk? Ice cream at the mall?"

Sofia laughed, charmed and amused by his persistence.

"Is that a yes?"

"Antonio, I—"

"Tony. My friends call me Tony."

"Tony, I really like you, but I'm just not ready."

"I guess there's someone else."

"There was."

"Ah. How about if I take you out for a hot fudge sundae? That always works for my sister when she's feeling blue."

Sofia started to say no, then bit back the word. Why not go out with Antonio? She hadn't been out in weeks. Smiling, she grabbed her handbag and her coat. "Let's go."

It was a weeknight, so the mall wasn't as crowded as usual. Sofia ordered a sundae with chocolate ice cream, double hot fudge, and marshmallow. Tony opted for a strawberry malt.

They carried their orders to a small table near the front window.

"Do you want to talk about it?" he asked, peeling the paper from a straw.

"Not really."

He nodded. "So, tell me about yourself."

"Not much to tell. I'm the youngest girl in a very large family."

"How large?"

"Three sisters and five brothers."

He whistled softly. "You're lucky you survived."

She laughed, thinking it was the second time in one day. It felt good.

Later, he drove her back to her car. When she was settled behind the wheel, he leaned in the window. "Any chance of taking you out on a real date Friday night?"

"I'd like that."

"Great. See you at work tomorrow."

She smiled all the way home.

Ethan was surprised that it took less than a week to fill all the positions at the new resort. Apparently, jobs in the surrounding towns were scarce, and they had more applicants than jobs. Two of his new employees—the bartender and the guy doing hotel security—didn't have homes of their own, so Ethan offered to rent each of them one of the houses in town.

He advertised the Morgan Creek Campground and Hotel in all the major newspapers and a dozen websites, and in less than two weeks, all the houses had been reserved and they had a growing waiting list.

"I really didn't think people would come here," Saint-crow remarked as the first guests drove across the bridge three weeks later.

"Seriously? You loaned me a small fortune and you expected to lose it?"

"It's only money," Saintcrow said with a negligent shrug.

"I'll pay you back."

"No hurry. Now that you've got the place staffed and running, Kadie and I are leaving as soon as she rises."

"What? Why?"

"This place has a lot of memories for both of us. Not all of them are good. Don't worry; we'll come back from time to time."

"What about Browning?"

"It's been over a month since he was here. He's probably long gone. Just don't forget to set the wards when the sun goes down and you should be fine. If you run into any trouble, call me." He slapped Ethan on the back. "Keep a light burning in the window."

"Right. Listen, I really appreciate everything you've done."

"You want to do something for me? Call Sofia." And with that last piece of advice, his sire was gone.

Nolan Browning prowled the outskirts of Morgan Creek from the bridge to the surrounding mountains, but he detected neither scent nor sight of Saintcrow or his mate to indicate either one of them was still in the town. Was it possible the master vampire had gone, leaving only his fledgling behind?

Browning surveyed the town every night for the next week with the same result. If Saintcrow had indeed left, taking control of the place was going to be a hell of a lot easier. All he needed was the right bait to draw Parrish away from Morgan Creek.

Parrish's woman might make a handy lure if he couldn't find another way to get the fledgling alone, Nolan thought absently. If he remembered correctly, her name was Sofia Ravenwood. She no longer resided in Morgan Creek either, but it shouldn't be too hard to find her if necessary. He knew her name and her scent. That should be enough.

Ethan sat in the tavern, an untouched glass of wine on the bar in front of him. He stared out the window while Saintcrow's words repeated themselves over and over again in his mind: *Call Sofia. Call Sofia.*

Questions plagued him. What was she doing now? Was she happy? Did she miss him? Did she ever think of calling him? Why hadn't she? Stupid question. *He* had left *her.* If there was any calling to be done, he needed to do it. A dozen times in the last hour, he had reached for his phone, but he had never made the call.

He checked the time. It was a little after nine in Arizona.

And suddenly, talking on the phone wasn't enough. He had to see her.

A thought carried him to the front door of her apartment. He took a deep breath, raised his hand to knock, and froze when he heard a man's voice. Ethan's eyes narrowed as he listened to a stranger professing his growing affection for Sofia.

Anger and jealousy exploded within him, and before he

knew what he was doing, Ethan slammed his fist against the door. The force broke the lock. The jamb splintered with a horrendous screech and the door swung open, revealing Sofia and a dark-haired man locked in each other's arms on the love seat.

The man lunged to his feet and put himself between Ethan and Sofia. A brave move, but not a very smart one.

"Ethan, no!"

Her harsh cry was the only thing that stopped him from tossing the other man out the window.

"What the hell?" the stranger exclaimed. "Sofia, do you know this barbarian?"

"Yes. We were once engaged."

"Do you want me to throw him out?"

Ethan snorted. "I'd like to see you try."

"Tony, I think you'd better leave. I'll be fine," she said when he started to protest. "Please."

With a curt nod, he grabbed his jacket, glared briefly at Ethan, and stalked out of the apartment.

"You owe me a new door," Sofia said, her voice arctic cool.

"Who the hell is that?"

"He's the manager of the restaurant where I work, not that it's any of your business. What are you doing here?"

"You serious about that jerk?"

"I might be. You still haven't told me why you're here."

"Can't you guess?"

"No." She folded her arms across her chest, her expression and mind closed to him. "I think you should go."

She could shut him out of her thoughts. She could shutter her expression. But he could scent her yearning for him, hear the rapid beat of her heart. "I miss you, Sofie. I'm sorry if I hurt you. I told myself you were better off without me, that I couldn't give you the kind of life you deserve, and that you'd always be in danger if you were with me. I guess what I need to know is how you feel. Are you happier here, without me? If so, I'll leave, and you'll never see me again."

Tears surfaced in her eyes as she opened her heart and her mind to him, letting him feel the pain and sadness she had suffered without him.

"Sofie." Her name whispered past his lips as he drew her gently into his arms. "I'm so sorry."

She buried her face in the hollow of his shoulder, her tears wetting his shirt.

He brushed a kiss across the top of her head, then, tugging her gently toward the love seat, he pulled her down on his lap. "I'm sorry," he said again. "Sofie, I don't want to live without you in my life."

"Me either, without you," she said, sniffling.

"I love you, Sofia. I'll never leave you again."

"You promise?"

"I swear it."

Her gaze probed his while her mind searched his thoughts. He did love her. He had missed her, been as miserable without her as she had been without him.

"Can you ever forgive me?" Using his thumbs, he wiped the tears from her cheeks.

"You owe me a wedding."

"Name the day, darlin', and I'm yours. What's wrong?" he asked when she frowned.

"My family."

"What about them?"

"My mom will want a big wedding. That takes time, and I don't want to wait."

"So, let's elope and not tell anyone. What do you say?"

She looked up at him, her brow furrowed as she considered his suggestion, and then she nodded. "All right, but only if we have a big wedding later."

"Fine by me," he said, kissing the tip of her nose. "Two weddings, two wedding nights. So, how about tomorrow for the first one? We can go anywhere you want."

"Not so fast. We need a license and . . . and I really don't know what else. I've never been married before."

"All we need is a license and someone authorized to perform the ceremony. According to the Internet, there's no waiting period here. We can go to the county clerk's office tomorrow afternoon. I'll mesmerize him so he puts it through right away. We can be married tomorrow night."

"You've thought this out, haven't you?"

"I might have looked into it. So, what do you say?"

"All right." She hesitated. This was a big decision, perhaps the biggest one she would ever make. Was she rushing into something she might regret later? Was she ready to tie her life to Ethan's? But then she thought of how empty her life had been without him. Did she want to feel like that for the rest of her life? She loved Ethan with all her heart, for better or worse. So why was she hesitating?

"Sofia?"

Shaking aside her doubts, she said, "Where will we go on our honeymoon?"

"Anywhere you want."

"How about that new hotel in Morgan Creek this time, Italy next time?"

"Morgan Creek? Seriously?"

"I haven't seen the town since the work was finished. Are there any rooms available?"

"I know the owner. I'm pretty sure I can find something." Ethan smiled inwardly. As part of the renovation, he had used his own money and hired a separate crew to remodel and redecorate Blair House—new paint, new carpets, new drapes. He'd had the furniture in the warehouse in Arizona sent to Morgan Creek and ordered appliances for the kitchen, as well as some additional furniture. And done a major remodel of the lair. He had done it all on the sly when he and Sofia were still engaged. The house had been vacant since he'd decided Sofia would be better off without him. Now, he couldn't wait to carry her over the threshold and show her what he'd done.

"Are you happy with the way the town turned out?"

"Yeah. It looks great. I can't wait for you to see it."

"What about Saintcrow?"

"He seemed satisfied before he left."

"Where did he go?" Sofia asked.

"Kadie wanted to go to see Graceland."

"He really loves her, doesn't he?"

Ethan frowned. "Well, sure. Why do you sound so surprised?"

"I don't know. He doesn't seem like the kind of guy to fall head over heels in love with anyone."

"The way I heard it, he wanted her the minute he laid eyes on her."

"Did he make her fall in love with him?"

"No. For a while, she hated him. Or at least she said she did."

"Will we be as happy as they are, Ethan?"

"I hope so. I won't be able to whisk you away to far-off countries, at least not until I make a dent in what I owe Saintcrow, but I'll do everything in my power to make you happy."

Sighing, she snuggled against him. "You already make me happy."

"I should let you get some sleep," Ethan said. "I'll come by for you tomorrow around noon and we'll go to the county clerk's office for a license." He kissed her lightly. "Tomorrow night, we'll be married."

"Tomorrow night," she murmured, and closed her eyes as he claimed her lips again. This kiss was deeper, longer, and filled with promise.

* * *

After Ethan left, Sofia couldn't sit still. Excitement thrummed through her at the thought of being his wife. And marrying in secret made it all the more exciting.

Going to her closet, she went through every dress she owned. None seemed appropriate for a wedding and she discarded them one by one. Nothing for it but to buy something new.

Sofia woke early. After showering, she dressed, then headed into the kitchen for a cup of coffee. She came up short when she saw the front door. The damaged lock had been replaced. Two shiny new keys sat on the table in the foyer.

Frowning, she went into the kitchen. Ethan must have come back and repaired the damage last night after she went to bed. She smiled as she poured a cup of coffee, thinking how sweet it was of him to do so.

After finishing the coffee and rinsing the cup, she dropped one of the keys in her handbag, then drove downtown. She found exactly what she wanted in Sally Ann's Bridal Shoppe—a white tea-length gown with fitted sleeves and a scoop neck adorned with brilliants. She also bought a darling little hat with a fingertip veil, new underwear, and a sheer black nightgown.

She was back home in less than an hour.

After a quick sandwich, she packed a suitcase, then checked the time. She had thirty minutes to spare.

At eleven-forty, her phone rang. She groaned softly when she saw Tony's name.

Taking a deep breath, she answered. "Hi."

"How are you?" he asked. "I've been worrying about you since I left your place last night."

"I'm fine, really. But thanks for worrying."

"I hope you don't mind, but I replaced the lock and repaired the frame. I hope you found the new keys okay."

"*You* replaced the lock?"

"You're not mad, are you?"

"No, of course not. Thank you. How much do I owe you?"

He made a dismissive sound. "I'm glad you're all right. Would you mind if I dropped by tomorrow night, say around seven?"

Sofia glanced at her watch. It was five to twelve. Ethan would be here any minute.

"Sofia?"

"I'm sorry, but I'm busy Saturday night." She couldn't help smiling. Busy indeed. She would be on her honeymoon.

There was a long pause. "Any point in my asking about Sunday night?"

Sofia glanced at the door when the bell rang. "Tony, I really have to go. Someone's here."

"I'll bet I can guess who that someone is," he said, his voice tinged with bitterness. "I'll see you at work tonight."

"Oh! I was going to call you. I can't make it tonight. I'm sorry for the short notice, but something's come up and I won't be able to work for you anymore. I'm so sorry, but I really have to go."

"What's going on? Does this have anything to do with that guy who busted into your place last night?"

"Yes. I thought Ethan and I were through, but . . . we're getting married. I'm so sorry if I led you to believe . . ." Sofia bit down on her lower lip. What more was there to say?

After a long pause, Tony said, "Good-bye, Sofia."

Before she could say anything else, he disconnected the call. She stared at the phone. She hadn't meant to end things so abruptly. True, they'd only been going out for a few weeks. It wasn't as if they were dating exclusively or anything. But she couldn't help feeling guilty at the way she'd ended things between them, and for quitting on such short notice. But it couldn't be helped.

She smiled as she ran to answer the door.

Chapter Thirty-Four

"Ethan!" She gasped his name as he swept her into his arms.

"How's my bride this afternoon?"

"Wonderful. Nervous. Excited. How's my groom?"

"Wonderful. Nervous. Excited." He grinned at her. "Are you ready?"

She nodded.

"All right. Grab your suitcase and let's go see the county clerk. I made an appointment for twelve-thirty."

Trembling with anticipation, she grabbed her suitcase and handbag, then closed her eyes as Ethan wrapped his arm around her waist.

When she opened her eyes, they were standing behind the courthouse. "I can't believe we're doing this," she said as they rounded the building and climbed the steps.

"Me either."

The clerk's office was at the end of a long corridor. She knew it was silly, but Sofia kept glancing over her shoulder, expecting to find her father bearing down on her, waving a wooden stake in one hand and a bottle of holy water in the other.

It didn't take long to show their identification and fill

out the forms. The clerk informed them that blood tests weren't required and there was no longer any waiting period. He also pointed them in the direction of a nonde-nominational church where they could be married that day.

Sofia felt as though she was floating on air as they left the courthouse. "We need to find a hotel."

Ethan grinned at her. "Are we having the honeymoon before the wedding?"

"No, you idiot. I'm not getting married in jeans and a sweater."

"Ah." He glanced around. "How about that one?" he asked, pointing at a place down the block—The Traveler's Rest.

She nodded. Made of red brick and fronted by a low wall lined with trees, it looked clean and well cared for.

Ethan paid for a room, kissed Sofia on the cheek, and told her he'd be back in an hour.

She glanced around the room, then opened her suitcase and laid out her wedding dress. She was getting married. To Ethan. A vampire.

She sat on the edge of the bed, waiting for some sense of unease, some dire portent that she was making the biggest mistake of her life. Instead, butterflies took wing in the pit of her stomach, and all she could do was smile as she pictured herself as Ethan's wife.

Humming softly, she took a quick shower, applied fresh makeup, and brushed out her hair.

When she was dressed, she stood in front of the mirror, turning this way and that. She was reaching for her shoes when her cell phone rang.

It was Rosa.

Sofia let it ring a couple of times, then, thinking it might be news about her father, she scooped it up. "Hi, Rosie. What's up?"

"Nothing much. I stopped by your apartment, but you weren't home."

"Oh.. Did you need something?"

"No, I was just in the neighborhood and thought maybe you'd like to go to a movie or something. So, are you out with Tony?"

"No. We . . . uh . . . broke up."

"Why?" she exclaimed. "He was so hot!"

Sofia scrambled to find a good answer, but nothing came to mind. She was still trying to think of something when Rosa said, "It's Ethan, isn't it? You're still in love with that vampire."

"Rosie . . ."

"I knew it! You're with him right now, aren't you?"

"You should have been a detective," Sofia muttered. "Listen, Rosie, I have to go. We're on a . . . a date."

"Something special?"

"You could say that."

"All right, but I want to hear all about it. Call me later."

Sofia had just slipped on her heels when the door opened, and Ethan stepped inside. But it was an Ethan she had never seen before. All she could say was, "Wow!"

"Like it?" he asked, grinning from ear to ear.

She nodded. All men looked good in a tux, but he looked like he had been born to wear one.

"You're the most beautiful bride I've ever seen," he said, reaching for her hand.

"How many have you seen?"

"One or two. But none have been mine. Are you ready? The minister is waiting for us."

* * *

The church, built of white stone and topped off with a large wooden cross, was two blocks away from the hotel. One of the oak doors stood open in welcome. Sunlight glinted off the stained-glass windows.

"It's lovely," Sofia murmured. Pausing, she pulled her phone from her handbag. "Go stand on the stairs."

"Seriously?"

"Oh! Can you . . . I mean, do vampires photograph?"

"I don't know."

"Well, let's find out. Go on, get up there. I want to remember this."

"Let me take your picture."

"You first."

At that moment, an older woman walking a dog passed by. She paused when she overheard their conversation. "Here now, you two," she said. "Let me take that photo."

"Thank you." Sofia handed her the phone. "Just press here."

The woman nodded. "I know what to do. My grandkids showed me. Smile now." She took a picture, then took a second one. "Just in case, although the first one is lovely. Such a handsome couple," she said, returning Sofia's phone.

Sofia glanced at the images, relieved to see Ethan standing beside her in the photos.

"I married my Henry in this very church fifty years ago," the woman remarked with a wistful sigh. "I hope your marriage will last as long and be as happy."

Ethan smiled at Sofia as the woman tugged on the dog's leash and continued on her way. If Sofia ever agreed to let him bring her across, they would be together a lot longer than half a century.

* * *

The inside of the church was as impressive as the outside. Vaulted ceilings. Dark pews and an altar polished to a high shine. A lovely parquet floor. Sunlight came through the most beautiful stained-glass windows Sofia had ever seen.

The minister, wearing a long black robe, smiled a greeting as they walked down the aisle. Ethan introduced his bride to the cleric, who introduced the two of them to the middle-aged couple who would stand as their witnesses. Ethan shook their hands; then he and Sofia took their places in front of the altar.

"Please, join hands," the minister said. "Sofia Ravenwood, do you take Ethan Parrish to be your lawfully wedded husband? Will you love him in sickness and in health, through good times and bad, and give yourself only to him as long as you both shall live?"

"I do." Sofia gazed into Ethan's eyes, thinking he would never be sick, never grow old.

"Ethan Parrish, do you take Sofia Ravenwood to be your lawfully wedded wife? Will you love her in sickness and in health, through good times and bad, and give yourself only to her as long as you both shall live?"

"I do."

"I understand you have a ring for your bride."

Nodding, Ethan reached into his pocket, then took Sofia's hand in his. "I love you, Sofie," he said fervently, and slipped an engagement ring on her finger. Leaning forward, he whispered, "You get the wedding ring next time."

"By the power vested in me, I now pronounce you husband and wife. Ethan, you may kiss your bride."

Sofia's eyelids fluttered down as he took her in his arms. His first husbandly kiss was achingly tender, so filled with love it brought tears to her eyes. She could feel the tumult of emotions within him—his need, his hunger, but most of all, the intensity of his love for her.

She blinked away her tears when he stepped back.

"I wish you all the happiness in the world," the minister said, handing them an embossed certificate certifying their marriage had been lawfully and legally performed. "Go with God."

Sofia couldn't stop smiling as they left the church.

Outside, Ethan pulled her into his arms and kissed her again, his tongue ravishing her mouth. She melted against him, her heart pounding with happiness and anticipation. He was hers. All hers.

He kissed her cheek. "What do you say we go back to the hotel and warm up that bed?"

"I'd say, let's hurry!"

If there hadn't been so many people on the street, Ethan would have used a little vampire magic and whisked her back to the hotel. Fortunately, it was only two blocks away. Any farther than that and he was afraid he might have dragged her behind a bush.

"Walk faster," she said, tugging on his hand.

Ethan laughed, delighted to know she was as eager as he.

Some of Sofia's eagerness waned when they were alone in their room. The bed suddenly seemed enormous. She had never been intimate with a man. She knew her friends thought there was something wrong with her, but she had never met anyone she liked enough, wanted enough, to go all the way.

And now the time was here.

She kicked off her shoes, shivered as Ethan came up behind her, his arms sliding around her waist as he nuzzled her neck.

Sofia closed her eyes, then opened them again. Did vampires make love like everyone else?

Behind her, she heard Ethan laugh.

"Not to worry," he said, his hands sliding up to cup her breasts. "You'll find everything where it should be. And it all works."

"Well," she murmured, pressing herself against him. "There's good news!"

Turning her in his arms, he said, "I won't hurt you, Sofie."

"I know."

Hoping the pounding of her heart was anticipation and not fear, he unfastened her gown, revealing a lacy white bra and matching bikini panties. He whispered, "Sofie, you're beautiful," as he dropped her gown on the foot of the bed.

She flushed under his admiring gaze, shivered as his fingers stroked her bare skin. With hands that trembled, she reached for his belt. "I've never been intimate with a man before." Her voice was barely audible as she tossed his belt aside.

"Sofie."

"I just thought you should know."

He didn't know what to say. In lieu of words, he shrugged out of his jacket and shirt and tossed them on a chair, then pulled her into his arms again, his lips trailing fire as he rained kisses along her neck and breasts.

She moaned softly as he lifted her into his arms and lowered her onto the bed, then slid in beside her to draw her close.

He had kissed her before, but never like this. Always before, she had sensed he was holding something back, but not tonight. Her underwear and the rest of his clothing disappeared as if by magic, and she was lost in the thrill of skin against skin, the exhilaration of his caresses, the excitement of knowing he was hers, that she could touch him and taste him—everywhere.

Most amazing of all, she knew his thoughts, felt his

excitement, his arousal, and knew, in the same way, that he was keenly aware of what she was thinking, feeling. What she wanted that she was too embarrassed to ask for.

She had never made love to a man before, had no one to compare Ethan with, yet she knew that no mortal man could have loved her so completely. Or so deeply.

Or been so ready to do it over again as quickly.

Pleasantly tired and aching in places that had never ached before, Sofia lay curled in Ethan's arms, her finger drawing lazy figure eights on his chest. She had never felt so contented, so happy, or so loved.

Had she been a cat, she thought she might have purred when he began lightly stroking her back. "Mrs. Ethan Parrish," she murmured. "Mrs. Sofia Parrish." She smiled at him. "Isn't *Mrs.* a beautiful word?"

"Not nearly as beautiful as *wife*." His gaze searched hers. "No regrets?"

"Ethan!"

"It's a big step for you, tying your life to mine."

"I know, but someone had to do it," she said with mock despair.

"Very funny," he muttered, nipping her earlobe.

"Can I ask you something?"

"Today you can ask me anything."

"Do you think we might be able to adopt a baby?"

"I don't see why not."

"Not right away," she said, her fingers playing over his flat belly. "Right now, I want you all to myself."

"Believe me, honey, I'm all yours."

"Does it hurt to become a vampire?"

"You want to talk about that now?"

She nodded. "Did it?"

"It hurt like hell," he said, frowning at the memory. "But it doesn't have to."

"What do you mean?"

"It all depends on the vampire who's turning you," Ethan explained. "They can take their time and do it gently, like I'm sure Saintcrow did with Kadie. And part of it depends on the one being turned. It's easier when both parties are willing."

"That's good to know."

He raised himself up on one elbow. "Why?"

"Well, when we start to look the same age, I mean, well . . . I don't want to look older than you."

He cocked one brow. "Are you saying what I think you are?"

"I've always been really close to Micah, and now that you and I are married, I'd like to spend more time with him and Holly. I don't want to be the odd girl out in the group forever. So, after we've been married a while and we've adopted a baby or two, I want you to make me what you are."

"Sure, Sofie. As long as you're certain it's what you want when the time comes."

She smiled at him. "But right now, I just want you to make love to me again."

"Anytime," he said, cupping her face in his hands. "All you have to do is ask."

Chapter Thirty-Five

Sofia was duly impressed with what she saw when they returned to Morgan Creek that night. The town looked great, from the refurbished hotel to the remodeled tavern and everything in between.

Most surprising of all was seeing ordinary people doing ordinary things—strolling down the streets, grocery shopping at the store, buying drinks in the tavern, sitting on the library steps, pumping gas, taking pictures. In the distance, she could hear laughter, something she was sure had been scarce when the vampires lived here.

She shook her head as they reached the residential area. "Wow, the houses all look great. Which one will be ours?"

"None of them." Ethan glanced around to make sure no one was watching them, then transported her to his new lair.

Sofia's eyes widened. Blair House had been painted pale yellow, trimmed in white. The old iron bars had been replaced with fancy wrought iron. Only the door remained the same.

Ethan waved his hand, and the massive door opened on silent hinges. Sofia gasped as Ethan swung her up into his arms.

"Welcome home, Mrs. Parrish," he said as he carried her over the threshold.

The door closed behind them.

Ethan kissed her, then set her on her feet.

"This doesn't look like the same place."

"Do you like it?"

"It's beautiful," she remarked, moving into the living room. "Your furniture looks wonderful here."

"Anything you don't like, anything you want to change, just let me know."

Sofia shook her head, touched that the rooms reflected the same colors she had used in her apartment.

Ethan followed her from room to room, pleased with her reaction to the changes he had made. The bedrooms had been painted, the floors carpeted, but he hadn't furnished any of them, thinking she might prefer to do that. Wondering if the time would come when children would run through the halls.

Sofie clapped her hands when she saw the kitchen, which was equipped with the latest appliances. A round table and two chairs stood in one corner.

"Come on." Taking her hand, Ethan led her down to the basement lair.

"Oh, Ethan," she murmured when he opened the door. "This must have cost a fortune."

"Only a small one."

A king-size bed with a carved cherrywood headboard dominated the room. Matching nightstands stood on either side. A gilt-edged mirror hung over a cherrywood dresser. The walls were pale blue, the carpet a darker shade, both of which were picked up in the quilt and throw pillows on the bed. A wide-screen TV took up a portion of one wall. It was flanked by a pair of bookcases.

"If you don't want to sleep down here, we can furnish one of the bedrooms upstairs."

"No, this is perfect," she said, wrapping her arms around him. "And so are you."

"I'm glad you think so."

She made a gesture, encompassing the room. "Did you do all this yourself?"

"I had a little help from a designer."

Sofia nodded. He had done this for her. She glanced at the bed, then looked up at him. "Is that bed as comfortable as it looks?"

"Only one way to find out."

"Last one under the sheets has to give the loser a back rub. And no fair using your vampire powers either."

"You're on!"

Sofia blew out a sigh of perfect contentment. Never in all her life had she felt this wonderful, this happy. She rolled onto her side, her gaze moving slowly over the man lying naked beside her. Men weren't supposed to be beautiful, but this one was.

He opened one eye. "Beautiful?"

"Yes."

"I can live with that." He grinned when her stomach growled. "I guess I'd better feed you."

"I guess you'd better."

"The chef at the hotel is supposed to be pretty good. Let's get cleaned up and I'll take you to dinner."

"And a movie?"

"If you like."

"You're so good to me," she said, straddling his hips.

"You keep wriggling around like that and it'll be a long time until dinner."

She batted his hands away when he reached for her, then scrambled off the bed. "Food first!" she exclaimed, and ran out of the room.

With a shake of his head, Ethan sat up, then grinned as he heard the shower come on upstairs. Maybe he'd better call Reed and have him install a shower down here. Be a heck of a lot more convenient than having to go upstairs. Funny, he hadn't thought of it before.

Swinging his legs over the side of the bed, he took the stairs two at a time. Maybe, if he caught Sofia in the shower, he could sweet-talk her into making love one more time before dinner.

Nolan Browning paid in advance for a rental house in Morgan Creek. He arrived on a Friday night as soon after sunset as he could, hoping to blend in with other tourists checking in at the same time.

To his surprise, he'd had no trouble at all crossing the bridge. He hadn't been sure the witch's potion would disguise his true nature, but either it had worked or the town was no longer warded against vampires.

As he had suspected from his earlier surveillance, Saintcrow was no longer in residence.

He signed the register with a false name, collected a key, and drove toward the residential area. He was amazed at the changes in the town, and, considering the place had been open such a short time, even more amazed at the number of tourists. He had managed to get the last available house.

He parked the car in front of the residence that had once belonged to Rosemary. Like all the other houses, it had been repainted. Pulling his suitcase from the backseat, he unlocked the front door. The inside had also been repainted. He hardly recognized the place.

He had hoped to kidnap the Ravenwood woman and use her to get to Parrish, but no opportunity had presented itself. He couldn't go after her when the sun was up, and he had never managed to find her alone after dark. But that no longer mattered.

He smiled inwardly. Once he got rid of Parrish, he would set new wards around the town so no one could leave, and voilà! He'd have an impregnable lair and prey aplenty.

Ethan leaned back, arms crossed, while Sofia attacked the biggest lobster he had ever seen. Watching her eat didn't spark his appetite—at least not for food. He barely remembered what mortal fare tasted like, though he had once been particularly fond of seafood. Reaching for his glass, he sipped his wine, thinking how lovely his bride looked by candlelight, and how eager he was to make love to her again.

Looking up, she caught him watching her. "It's really good. Too bad you can't have a bite."

His gaze moved to her throat. "I'll get a bite later."

"It won't be the same."

"It'll be better," he said with a wink.

"I can't believe you don't miss eating." Head tilted to one side, she frowned at him. "You said you don't really miss it, but I don't believe you. How could you *not* miss this?"

"Being a . . ." He glanced around the hotel dining room. "Being what I am changes how you think about a lot of things. Which is why you need to be really sure before you decide to . . . you know."

"I'm sure I'd miss eating." She took a bite of wild rice and chewed thoughtfully. "I can't imagine a world without bread or chocolate or pasta or my mom's homemade cannoli."

"Like I said, think it over."

One more bite and she pushed her plate aside. "I'm stuffed."

"No dessert?"

"I don't think . . . oh! Maybe a slice of that decadent chocolate cake," she remarked when a waitress delivered a piece to the next table. "Could we get it to go?"

"I don't see why not."

Ethan signed the check, added a generous tip, and gave it to the waitress, who tucked it into the pocket of her apron, then handed Sofia a carry-out box.

"Do you feel like taking a walk?" she asked as they left the hotel.

He shrugged. "I can think of a couple of other things I'd rather do."

"I'll just bet you can."

The Viper was parked in front of the hotel. Ethan put the cake box on the front seat, then took her hand in his. "Let's walk."

"I'm really impressed with what you've done," Sofia remarked. "Everything looks amazing."

"What's amazing is that we're making money. The houses are all rented or reserved through next year."

"You don't suppose Saintcrow worked some kind of vampire magic to make people come here, do you?"

"I don't think so, but I wouldn't put it past him. I . . ."

"What?"

"Shh."

Sofia glanced around, wondering what had him looking so worried. "What's wrong?"

"I don't know. I feel like we're being watched." Dropping her hand, Ethan made a slow 360-degree turn. "I could have sworn . . ." He shrugged as he reached for her hand again. "I guess I'm just imagining things."

"Do you often do that?"

"Never."

She glanced sharply to the left and then the right. "Now you've got me doing it." Tugging on his arm, she said, "Let's get the car and go home."

* * *

Browning felt a rush of satisfaction as Ethan and Sofia turned and headed back to the hotel. Next time, he mused, rubbing his hands together. Next time he caught the fledgling out in the open, he would drive a stake into the vampire's heart; then the girl and the town—which was profitable beyond expectation, according to Parrish—would be his. But for now, it was time to take cover before the witch's spells wore off. He could already feel them fading. Another few minutes and he would no longer be invisible, his scent no longer masked.

A thought took him to the safety of Rosemary's old house.

Ethan experienced that same sense of being watched several times in the next few nights, whether he was chatting with one of the tourists, taking a turn behind the hotel desk, or sitting on a bench in the park with Sofia after sundown, the way he was now. He didn't mention it to her again, partly because he was beginning to think he was imagining it, but mostly because he didn't want to worry her needlessly. He might have thought Browning was behind it, but that was impossible. Wasn't it? Sure, vampires could be invisible, but another vampire could always sense their presence. Was it a witch? Or was he just going quietly insane?

A witch. Ethan frowned. Was it possible for a witch to concoct a spell that would shield one vampire from another? Damn.

"Ethan? Hello? Earth to Ethan."

"I'm sorry; I was elsewhere."

"Are you bored with me already?"

"No, love, not even close."

"Good, because now that the town is up and running and my dad is feeling better, we really should start thinking about wedding number two."

Ethan nodded. He didn't really think a second ceremony was necessary, but if it would make Sofia and her family happy, he was willing to go along with it. "Call your folks and get the ball rolling."

"You mean it?"

Nodding, he pulled her into his arms and kissed her, until the sound of childish laughter had him looking over his shoulder.

A little girl with long blond ringlets and bright blue eyes stared back at him.

Muttering, "I'll give you something to stare at," he willed himself and Sofia into the living room in the house on the hill.

"Ethan, shame on you! She's going to go tell her parents she saw us disappear and no one will believe her."

"Morgan Creek is known for ghosts. Maybe her folks will think she saw one."

"You're incorrigible."

"What I am is hot as hell." Letting her body slide against his, he lowered Sofia to her feet.

"So I see," she said, smirking. "I'm sure I can think of a way to cool you off."

"I've got an idea or two of my own," he said with a leer.

"Oh, I've no doubt of that."

He was undressing her as she spoke.

They never made it to the bedroom.

Chapter Thirty-Six

Sofia leaned back in her chair and stretched her arms over her head. She had decided to get caught up on the bookkeeping while Ethan was off hunting in some distant town.

What was it like, stalking human prey? Did he feed on men, too, or just women? Did he always bite them in the neck? When Ethan had drunk from Saintcrow, he'd fed from his wrist. Did it make a difference in the taste? Or did he just prefer to feed from one site over another? Biting someone on the neck seemed far more intimate.

She glanced around the office, thinking she would like to make some changes. Because this house wasn't going to be used as a rental in the foreseeable future, she thought she'd like to move her desk and filing cabinet into the living room, which provided a nice view of the mountains, as opposed to the dining room, which looked out on the backyard.

She frowned when she heard a knock at the door. Ethan wouldn't knock; neither would any of the town's employees.

Curious, she went to the door, let out a gasp when she saw Nolan Browning standing on the porch. She started to slam the door, but a wave of his hand drove her back into the entryway.

Before she recovered her balance, he was inside the house, with the door closed behind him.

"What are you doing here?" she demanded, forcing as much righteous anger into her voice as possible.

"I've decided to take over the town. Make it like it was before. You know, a smorgasbord for vampires."

"Ethan will kill you for this."

"I don't think so." He moved toward her, his eyes darkening, taking on a faint reddish glow.

She tried to dart past him, but he caught her easily, one hand grasping her arm, the other curling around her throat.

He smiled wolfishly, revealing his fangs. "You smell good."

Sofia stared at him, her heart pounding with terror as he lowered his head to her neck. She winced as his fangs pierced her skin. Ethan's bite had never hurt. Nolan Browning's bite was extremely painful. She tried to call Ethan's name, tried to send her thoughts to him, but the horror of what was happening was too great. Did Browning intend to drain her dry? Frightening as that thought was, the idea of being a vampire, with him as her sire, was more terrifying than death itself. She remembered Micah telling her that a fledgling was compelled to do whatever his sire demanded.

She was weak with relief when, at last, he released her.

"You'll be mine exclusively," Browning said, dragging his hand across his mouth.

When he reached for her again, the world went thankfully black.

* * *

Ethan lifted his head, the woman in his arms forgotten, as a sense of unease enveloped him. He tried to open the link between himself and Sofia, but there was no response.

Releasing his prey from his thrall, he willed himself back to Morgan Creek, but it was like trying to penetrate a cinder-block wall. Fighting down a sudden, nameless fear, he materialized on the bridge outside the town, unable to cross.

What the hell was going on?

Sofia groaned softly. Her head ached. Her neck hurt. When she opened her eyes, it was to darkness.

Where was she? Why was she on the floor? And why did her neck hurt so much?

And then she remembered. Nolan Browning had bitten her. Had he turned her into a vampire? Was that why she was in darkness?

Scrambling to her feet, she moved slowly forward, one hand outstretched. After a few steps, she bumped into a bed. She continued walking, her fingers searching for a light switch. Finally, she found one, but when she flicked it on, nothing happened.

Fighting down the panic rising inside her, she made her way to the window, drew back the curtains, and lifted the sash. But when she tried to climb out, she couldn't do it. It was like trying to fight her way through an invisible barrier.

Moonlight filtered through the window, lighting her way back to the bed. She climbed on the mattress and wrapped her arms around her knees. Ethan would find her.

Ethan! Her mind screamed his name. When she felt their connection, relief poured through her.

Sofia! What's going on?

Browning is here.

Where?

In Morgan Creek. Ethan, he drank from me. It was terrible. Did he turn me?

Did you drink from him?

I don't think so. He said he's taking over the town. He wants it to be like it was before, when the vampires lived here.

Ethan swore softly. He had walked through the town every night. How the hell had Browning managed to get inside without anyone being the wiser? How had he gotten past the wards that surrounded the town after sundown?

Not that it mattered now, he thought ruefully. What mattered was that Browning had erected wards of his own, effectively shutting Ethan out.

Ethan?

I'm here. Just sit tight.

It was time to call in the cavalry.

Saintcrow paced the floor, saying little as Ethan spoke to his mind. Why was it that every time he left Morgan Creek, something drew him back? He was tempted to tell Parrish to handle the problem himself, but in this case, a master vampire was the only one who could help.

Sit tight, he told Ethan, his voice curt. *I'm on my way.*

"You're doing the right thing," Kadie remarked when Rylan's mental conversation with Ethan ended. "He doesn't have the experience to deal with Browning alone."

"Yeah. I should have known Browning would show up sooner or later. I'm just surprised it wasn't sooner."

"You don't think he'll hurt Sofia, do you?"

"I sure as hell hope not. I've got to go."

"Be careful."

"Right." He kissed her as if he had all the time in the world, and then he was gone.

He found Ethan pacing back and forth on the bridge.

"I'm sorry about this," Ethan said.

Saintcrow waved his apology aside. "I thought I told you to put the wards up before sundown."

"I did."

Saintcrow looked thoughtful a moment, then muttered, "Gotta be witchcraft."

"So how do we dismantle Browning's wards and get across the bridge?"

"This town is mine. I own every square foot of it. My blood is here. Browning might think he can just waltz in and claim the place as his, but it doesn't work like that. The only way to take over a master vampire's territory is to kill him. Come on."

Saintcrow strolled across the bridge, chanting softly as he went.

Ethan followed close behind. A ripple of magical power filled the air as they stepped onto the paved road that led into town. It moved over Ethan's skin like thousands of tiny sparks as they breached Browning's wards.

Pausing, Saintcrow turned to face the bridge. Ethan felt his sire's power coalesce as he set new wards in place.

"Browning is mine," Ethan said as they made their way to the residential area.

Saintcrow nodded. "You kill him and I'll take his head."

Sofia's heart skipped a beat when the door opened. She scrambled off the bed and retreated into a far corner when a dark shape filled the entrance. Her blood ran cold as she recognized Browning's hulking form.

"Dinnertime," he crooned, shutting the door behind him.

"You'd better leave me alone." She glanced at Browning and then the door, wondering what the odds were of darting past him.

He laughed. "Why would I do that?"

"Because Ethan's here."

"Nice try, but I put up new wards." He backed her toward the bed. "The town is mine now. And so is this house. He can't come in."

She recoiled when his hand slid around her neck, let out a cry of dismay when his fangs pierced her skin. Even knowing it was useless to fight him, she kicked and scratched for all she was worth, felt herself growing weaker as he continued to drink. And drink.

Ethan. Lights danced behind her eyes as darkness swallowed her whole.

Ethan kicked in the bedroom door, his fury growing when he caught the scent of fresh blood. Sofia's blood.

Browning whirled around as Ethan lunged toward him. Then, seeing Saintcrow in the doorway, he vanished from the room.

Uttering a wordless cry of frustration, Ethan slid to a stop. Dammit!

The rage inside him turned to concern when he saw Sofia crumpled on the floor, her face as pale as death, her neck and chest splattered with blood. Kneeling beside her, he drew her into his arms. "Sofie? Sofie, can you hear me?"

Her eyelids fluttered open. "Ethan?"

"I'm here."

"Am I dying?"

"I don't think so." He looked over her head at Saintcrow for confirmation.

The master vampire shook his head.

"I'm going to give you some of my blood," Ethan said.

Recalling how it had saved her father's life, she nodded, then closed her eyes.

Ethan bit into his wrist, held the bleeding wound to her lips.

She had forgotten how wonderful it was to drink from him, forgotten how his blood sizzled through her, making her feel as if her veins were filled with sparkling champagne. Clasping his arm in her hands, she drank greedily.

"You should just turn her," Saintcrow said. "You're gonna do it sooner or later. Might as well be now. She's halfway there already."

Ethan shook his head. "We talked it over. She wants to wait a little while, until she's older."

"That's Micah talking. As long as she's human, she's helpless against our kind."

"Wasn't it Kadie, your *vampire* wife, we rescued not long ago? She seemed pretty helpless then."

"Witchcraft is something else entirely," his sire remarked with a dismissive wave of his hand.

Sofia pushed Ethan's arm away. "Saintcrow's right. We should just do it now."

"Are you sure?" Ethan asked. "You told me you wanted to wait."

"I know, but I was wrong. I let Micah talk me out of it because I wasn't really sure it was what I wanted, but I'm sure now."

"What about having to sleep during the day?"

"I guess I'll get used to it. After a while."

Saintcrow cleared his throat. "I might be able to help with that. Last time I was with Kadie, I did a blood exchange with her, like I did with Ethan. She's been able to be awake during the day for the last week or so. It might work for Sofia, too, once she's turned, although there's no guarantee, since I won't be her sire."

"Are you sure this is what you want, Sofie?" Ethan asked. "I don't want you to regret it, or hate me for turning you somewhere down the road."

"Are you sure it won't hurt?"

"As sure as I can be."

"All right. Just do it," she murmured, and closed her eyes, eager to taste him again.

Chapter Thirty-Seven

"He's done it!" Micah exclaimed, his eyes burning red with anger. "He's turned her!"

Holly stared at him, eyes wide. "Are you sure?"

"Damn right I am. I can feel it happening." Rising, he paced the floor, his hands clenched. "I'll kill him for this."

"Micah, calm down."

"I am calm!"

"Sure you are. If you were any calmer, you'd be breathing fire and farting smoke."

He might have laughed if he hadn't been so outraged. "I'm going to Morgan Creek."

"I'm going with you."

"I'd rather you didn't."

"I know. That's why I'm going."

When it was done, Ethan transported Sofia into their room at Blair House and lowered her onto their bed. She didn't move, was barely breathing. He removed her shoes and clothing, pulled a nightgown over her head, then tucked her under the covers. She would sleep the sleep of the Undead until sundown tomorrow.

He stood beside the bed, thinking how much he loved her, how beautiful she was, wondering if she would still love him when she woke tomorrow night.

Leaning down, he brushed a kiss across her lips.

"We've got company," Saintcrow announced from the doorway. "You'll never guess who it is."

Ethan blew out a sigh. "Micah," Ethan said. "And Holly."

"Right the first time."

"This isn't a conversation I'm looking forward to," Ethan remarked. Closing the bedroom door, he followed Saintcrow up the stairs into the living room, stood by the fireplace while his sire opened the door.

Micah stormed into the room, his face dark with anger. Holly trailed behind him. She looked at Ethan with an expression that clearly said *I tried to stop him.*

Ethan shrugged, then spun away as Micah lunged at him, fangs bared, hands reaching for his throat.

"Micah, stop it!" Saintcrow's voice cut through the room like a scythe.

Micah came to an abrupt halt, his expression mutinous as he glared at the master vampire.

Holly curled up in the chair by the fireplace, her gaze moving from one man to the other.

"He turned my sister." Micah fired his words like bullets. "My baby sister."

"She asked him to do it," Saintcrow said, his voice mild. "As you well know, it was inevitable."

"She's too young, too inexperienced to make that decision and *you* know it. What if she breaks up with Ethan?"

"That's not likely to happen," Ethan said quietly. "We're married."

"You're what?" Micah roared.

Holly stared at Ethan, wide-eyed. "When did *that* happen?"

"Recently. Sofie knew her mother would want a big wedding, but we didn't want to wait. We planned to tell her family in a few weeks and then get married again."

"You've ruined her life," Micah said, his voice thick with loathing. "I'll never forgive you for this." He turned toward Saintcrow. "Or you either." Taking Holly's hand, he sent a last, fulminating glare at Ethan, and vanished from their sight.

Ethan blew out a sigh, then, sinking down on the edge of the sofa, he cradled his head in his hands.

"He'll get over it," Saintcrow remarked.

Ethan shook his head. "I don't think so. What if he's right? What if Sofia hates being a vampire and hates me for turning her? I really will have ruined her life. I should have waited until we knew each other better, until she was older."

"What's done is done," Saintcrow said, clapping him on the shoulder. "There's no going back. She'll be hungry when she wakes tomorrow night. You can give her a little of your blood to ease the pain, but she'll need to feed. Hey, are you listening to me?"

"Yeah."

"She's got my blood in her and so do you, so she'll be strong. Make sure she doesn't kill her prey. She'll want to take it all the first few times. Don't let her."

Ethan nodded.

"Other than learning how to hunt, I don't think she's got much more to discover about being a vampire."

Ethan grunted. That was true enough. Maybe it would make her transition easier.

* * *

Sofia woke feeling stranger—and better—than she ever had in her life. For a moment, she lay there wondering why she felt as if someone had just given her a super dose of adrenaline.

She jackknifed into a sitting position, her hand searching the bed beside her. There was no one there. Frowning, she wondered where Ethan had gone. Since their marriage, she had quickly grown accustomed to waking up beside him.

Swinging her legs over the edge of the bed, she stood up. Why did the rug feel so different? Wiggling her toes, she glanced at the carpet, thinking she could feel each individual strand of fiber. But, of course, that was ridiculous.

Gradually, she realized she was seeing everything around her in sharp focus, even though there was no light at all in the room.

She doubled over as a sudden cramp knifed through her, cried out as the pain drove her to her knees. What was happening to her?

She looked up at the sound of footsteps, scrambled to her feet as the door to the lair swung open.

"Ethan!" She groaned as her stomach clenched. "Ethan, something's wrong."

Hurrying toward her, he lifted her into his arms, then sat on the edge of the bed, cradling her to his chest. "There's nothing wrong, love."

"There is. The pain . . ."

"It's normal."

She drew back a little so she could see his face. And frowned. He looked the same and yet . . . different somehow. She took a shaky breath, and his scent flooded her nostrils.

"Sofia. Listen to me."

"Hmm." She traced his lower lip with her fingers, then, leaning forward, she bit him lightly, gasped with surprise when her bite drew blood. The sight of it, the smell of it, went through her like chain lightning. Cupping his face in her palms, she licked the dark red drops, then stared at him, her eyes widening with comprehension.

"I . . . I'm . . ." She blinked at him. "A vampire."

He nodded, his expression wary.

"You turned me last night." *Vampire. I'm a vampire.* She searched her feelings, but she felt numb, empty, as if she was living inside someone else's body, seeing the world through a stranger's eyes. Colors were brighter, sounds more pronounced, her sense of touch more sensitive. She nodded slowly. "I remember now." She recalled the taste of his blood, the sense of euphoria, and then falling, tumbling helplessly into an endless black void. A low groan rose in her throat. "You said it wouldn't hurt."

"You need to feed."

Her breath caught in her throat. Feed. Prey. People. "No." She shook her head. "I can't do that. Why can't I just drink from you?"

"Because vampires don't feed on each other."

"You fed on Saintcrow."

"I wasn't feeding. It was like an exchange of energy, of power. I couldn't survive on his blood. And you can't survive on mine." He stroked her hair. "You knew this was part of it."

"Yes, but knowing and doing . . ." She shook her head again. "Can't I just visit the local blood bank or something?"

"You could. You can feed on animals, too. But not indefinitely. Like it or not, eventually you have to feed on the living. Otherwise, you'll weaken. I'm told the longer you wait, the more painful it gets."

"Did Saintcrow tell you that?"

"Yeah."

"Was it hard for you, the first time?"

"Not really. Saintcrow took me to some little town in

Southern Wyoming. The first lesson he taught me was that it's never a good idea to feed where you live." Ethan shook his head. "At the time, I remember thinking that feeding used to mean meat and potatoes, but from then on, it would mean blood."

He remembered it all as if it had been yesterday. "He picked a woman for me. Without even knowing how I was doing it, I imposed my will on hers. I thought I'd be disgusted by the whole thing, but it was all so easy. 'Take what you want, but gently' was Saintcrow's advice. 'You're a lot stronger now than you were before.' He showed me where to bite her. 'Not too deep,' he'd warned. 'You don't want to kill her.'

"I'd expected to feel revulsion for what I was about to do, but it seemed like the most natural thing in the world to sink my fangs into her throat." He laughed softly. "I remember wondering where those fangs came from. There's no way to describe it, Sofie. Saintcrow had to practically drag me away from her. That's when he told me his other rules."

"There are rules?"

"There are according to Saintcrow. You already know rule number one—don't feed where you live. Number two, you don't kill your prey. Number three, you don't wait until the pain is excruciating before you feed."

"Is that the last one?"

"No. His final directive was that if I killed anyone, he would destroy me."

"Even if it was an accident?"

"There were no exceptions."

Sofia shivered.

"Well, that's not entirely true. He said my sense of self-preservation would kick in if I was in desperate need of blood to survive or badly wounded. I had the feeling the rules didn't apply then."

She didn't look reassured.

"Nothing like that's going to happen to you," Ethan said. "I'll be with you until you get the hang of things."

She smiled faintly.

"You can drink a little from me, if you want. Saintcrow said it would ease the pain." He turned his head to the side. "Just take a little."

She stared at his throat. Always before, he had bitten his wrist and offered it to her. But the pulse beating in the hollow of his throat called to her. He groaned softly when she bit him, just below his ear. At first, she thought she'd hurt him; then she realized it wasn't pain but pleasure. His blood was hotter than she remembered, and quickly dulled her pain.

Lifting her head, she licked her lips.

"Better?" he asked.

"Much."

"So, are you ready to embrace the new you?"

"I guess there's only one way to find out," she said, sliding off his lap. "Let's go hunting."

"Okay by me," he said. "But you might want to change out of your nightgown first."

For all her apparent eagerness to embrace her new lifestyle, Sofia dug her heels in when it came time to actually bite the young man Ethan had chosen. It was one thing to drink from the man she loved and quite another to bite a complete stranger. She tried to picture it in her mind—pulling him to her, biting him, drinking his blood. What if he tasted bad? What if he had some horrible illness?

"You're immune to disease," Ethan said. "Nothing can hurt you."

She nodded, remembering how Mateo had added ground oleander to Ethan's wine to no effect.

"There's nothing to it," Ethan said. "Stop thinking like Sofia, the woman, and let your vampire nature take over. Like this." He folded his hands over the young man's shoulders and lowered his head to his neck.

The scent of warm, hot, fresh blood filled Sofia's nostrils. And with it, the undeniable urge to feed. When her fangs descended, she pushed Ethan aside and took her first taste of human prey.

It was like nothing she had ever known. Better than the finest wine, more satisfying than a glass of ice water on a blistering summer day.

She growled—actually growled—at Ethan when he laid his hand on her shoulder. "Enough, Sofia."

She knew she should stop, but she couldn't.

"If you kill him," Ethan warned, "you'll bring Saint-crow's wrath down on us."

That threat alone was enough to make Sofia back off, albeit reluctantly. She licked the blood from her lips, watched with regret as Ethan erased the memory of what had happened from the young man's mind and sent him on his way.

"Well?"

She turned to find Ethan watching her, his eyes narrowed. "What?"

"Was it as bad as you expected?"

"You know it wasn't. And I feel great. Why was Micah so worried?"

"He's your brother. It's what brothers do, I'm told."

"I know." She blew out a sigh, and then smiled. "It's just because he loves me."

"I worry about the same things he does, you know?"

"What things?"

"That in a year or two you might regret it, and hate me for turning you."

"How could I hate you? I asked for this."

"Sofie." He drew her into his arms and kissed her, ever so gently. "People change. Even vampires. I know there are no guarantees in life, but . . ."

Cupping his face in her palms, she said, "Stop worrying. I think I've been around enough vampires to know what I was getting into. And yes, I know actually being one is different, but if I ever regret it, I'll have no one but myself to blame. Okay?"

"Okay." He tapped the tip of her nose with his finger. "So, what do you say we go do what people on their honeymoons usually do?"

"Sounds good to me. I'd race you back to Morgan Creek, if I knew how to unleash my brand-new vampire powers."

Ethan caught Sofia's arm when they reached the outskirts of Morgan Creek. She was a quick study, he thought, pleased. She had almost beaten him.

"What's wrong?" she asked. "Why are we stopping?"

"Micah's waiting on the bridge."

"Oh."

Slowing, they walked the rest of the way.

Sofia experienced a sudden wave of uncertainty when she saw her brother's face. What if he hated her now?

For a moment, brother and sister regarded each other. Then Micah said, "I'd like to talk to Sofia alone, if that's all right with you, Parrish."

"You're welcome to go up to the house," Ethan said. "I've got a few things to take care of in the office."

Micah nodded curtly.

Ethan squeezed Sofia's hand. "I'll see you at home."

"Come on," Sofia said.

"Don't you want to exert your new powers? Or don't you know how?"

"I know how, but it's a nice night for a walk. What are you doing here, Micah?" she asked, starting across the bridge.

"I just wanted to make sure you were okay."

"I'm fine."

"You promised you'd wait until you were older."

"I intended to, but . . ." She took a deep breath, then told him about Browning and why she had decided not to wait.

"I see your point."

"How's Dad?"

"He's doing great. Mom and Dad are wondering where you are, why you haven't come around. You can't put it off forever."

"Look who's talking!" Sofia exclaimed. "You waited a good long time before you told any of us the truth."

"Are you happy with him?"

"Don't change the subject."

"All right, I know where you're coming from. But the family already knows about vampires now, so the rest should be easy. And you didn't answer my question."

"Yes, I'm happy. Blissfully, totally, wonderfully happy. He didn't force me, Micah. It was my choice and mine alone. Maybe someday I'll regret it, but I don't think so. And like I told Ethan, if I do, I've got only myself to blame."

"Do you want me to tell Mom and Dad for you?"

Sofia chewed on her lower lip, thinking it over. Then shook her head. "No, I should tell them." She took his arm, then stopped walking. "Please don't hate Ethan. I love you both. I can't have my two favorite guys always at each other's throats."

Micah snorted. "Bad choice of words, little sister."

She made a face at him, then said, "You know, Ethan wouldn't be a vampire in the first place if he hadn't gone to your wedding."

Micah threw up his hands in self-defense. "Hey, you can't blame that on me. Saintcrow's the one who turned him."

"Maybe we should just turn the whole family." Grinning, she tugged on his arm. "Come on; wait until you see our lair!"

Ethan looked up from the mail-order catalog he'd been perusing when Sofia entered the office. "Where's your brother?"

"He went back home. We've decided to turn the whole family."

"What?"

"I'm kidding. He just wanted to make sure I'm okay."

"Are you?"

Sitting on his lap, she wrapped her arms around his neck. "What do you think?"

"I think you're perfect."

"Thanks, I like you, too. I need to go home and talk to my folks. Do you want to go with me?"

"What do you think?"

She slipped her hands inside his shirt. "I think we should do what you suggested earlier, and go do what people on their honeymoons do."

He waggled his eyebrows at her. "No need to ask me twice."

A thought carried them into the bedroom, where they did what honeymooners do.

* * *

Later, after a quick shower, Sofia went through her closet, considering and discarding one outfit after another.

Reclining on the bed, Ethan shook his head as she threw off a light green sweater and pulled on a frilly pink blouse. "We're just going to see your mom and dad," he remarked. "Why all the fuss?"

"I want to look like me."

"You look pretty much the same as always." Which wasn't exactly true. Being a vampire had added a certain thickness and luster to her hair, made her skin a little more translucent. And then there was that vampire allure that came in handy when hunting prey.

She pulled on a pair of black pants, stepped into her shoes. "I'm a nervous wreck!"

Rising, he took her in his arms. "Relax. I'm sure it will come as a surprise, but your folks won't be totally freaked out, not the way they would be if you were the first kid in the family to become a vampire."

"I know. I keep telling myself that."

"So, are you ready?"

"I guess."

"All right, then. Let's get it over with."

Sofia took a deep breath when they arrived on the front porch. She could hear the TV playing in the living room, smell the chicken her family had had for dinner. She knew her mom and dad were in the living room, and that Rosie was upstairs.

Another deep breath, and she opened the door.

"Sofia!" Lena Ravenwood flew across the room to embrace her daughter. "Come in! Come in! This is a wonderful surprise!"

Luciano's smile spread from ear to ear. "Sofia!"

She hugged her dad and then Rosa, who had come downstairs to see who was at the door.

"Sit, sit." Lena gestured at the love seat. "Ethan, welcome."

"Thank you, Mrs. Ravenwood."

"Please, you must call me Lena."

"Lena." He shook hands with Luciano, then nodded in Rosa's direction, rolled his eyes when she winked at him.

"Have you had dinner?" Lena asked.

"We already . . . ate," Sofia said. She perched on the edge of the love seat, laid her hand on Ethan's arm for reassurance when he sat beside her.

"Dessert, then?" Lena asked. "I made cannoli."

Sofia forced a smile. "Maybe later," she said, glancing at Ethan.

With a sigh of resignation, Lena sat on the sofa with her husband and Rosa.

"So, how've you been?" Rosa asked.

"Good." Sofia twisted her hands together. "Ethan and I have decided to get married."

Rosa grinned.

Lena clapped her hands together. "That's wonderful!"

"Aren't you rushing things a bit?" Luciano asked. "I mean, you haven't known each other very long."

"Long enough," Sofia said.

Rosa leaned forward, her eyes shining with excitement. "Have you set a date?"

"Not yet, but the sooner the better."

Lena frowned. "You're not . . . ?"

"No, Mom, I'm not."

Her mother sighed with relief. "A wedding! So much to do. Have you thought about colors and flowers? You'll be married at St. John's, of course. I'll call Father Ralph to see about reserving the church. A Saturday morning would probably work best."

"About that . . . I'm afraid it will have to be an evening wedding because . . ." Sofia grabbed Ethan's hand.

"Because Ethan's a vampire?" Lena cut in to fill the awkward silence.

Sofia took a deep breath. "And so am I."

Chapter Thirty-Eight

After a lengthy silence, Rosa asked, "Does Micah know?"

Sofia nodded.

Her mother stared at her through grief-stricken eyes.

Her father glared at Ethan, his hands tightly clenched.

Rosa winked at her.

Sofia bit down on her lower lip, waiting for her parents to say something. Anything. "Mom, Dad, it was my choice. I wanted this. I hope you can accept it." Fighting back tears, she said, "I hope you'll still love me."

Tears welled in Lena's eyes. Rising, she held out her arms. "Of course we still love you, *mia figlia*," she said, her voice thick with emotion. "You're our baby girl."

Feeling as if she had been reborn, Sofia went into her mother's arms. "I love you, too, Mama. I didn't do it to hurt you or Daddy."

Luciano's gaze speared Ethan. "I don't know if I can ever forgive you for this, but I'll try. But know this: If you ever hurt my little girl, I will hunt you down."

"Yessir."

Rising, Luciano pulled Sofia into his arms for a bear hug; then, after a long pause, he approached Ethan and stuck out his hand. "Welcome to our family."

"Thank you, sir."

When Lena and Luciano went into the kitchen, ostensibly for wine, Rosa took Sofia aside. "So, what's it like, being a vampire? Did it hurt? Do you feel, like, radically different?"

"It's hard to describe. It's like I'm still me, but in a Supergirl kind of way. All my senses are enhanced and I'm never tired."

"But what about . . . ?" Rosa grimaced. "The blood thing?"

Sofia shrugged. "That's hard to explain, too," she said, relieved when her mother returned from the kitchen carrying a silver tray with five glasses of wine.

Luciano passed the drinks around, then lifted his goblet. "To the bride and groom. May they find as much happiness in their marriage as Lena and I have found in ours."

"I'm glad that's over," Sofia remarked. They had decided to take a walk when they left her parents' house. Now, she paused at a corner to let a car pass by.

"I thought your mom and dad handled it pretty well, all things considered, but you'd better look out for Rosa."

"What do you mean?"

"She asked me a lot of questions while you and your mom were talking about the wedding," Ethan said with a shrug.

"She talked to me, too, but you can hardly blame her for being curious. She's got two siblings, a sister-in-law, and a future brother-in-law who are vampires."

"Yeah. Wouldn't surprise me if she asked you to turn her one of these days."

"Seriously?"

"If you'd heard some of the questions she asked me,

you'd think so, too. Has she ever expressed any interest in vampires before?"

"Not to me."

"I just wanted to give you a heads-up."

Sofia nodded. "Thanks for telling me. I asked her to let the rest of the family know."

"Chicken."

"Yep. Are you sure you're okay with the extravaganza my mom is planning?"

"Right now, I'm willing to do just about anything to keep your family happy."

"I know," she said, smiling. "You're being really sweet about the whole thing."

"Maybe because I'm feeling a little guilty."

Punching him on the arm, she said, "Well, stop it! I asked for this, remember?"

"Yeah, I . . ." Ethan came to a dead stop, every instinct he possessed going on high alert.

Sofia glanced up at him. "What's wrong?"

"Do you feel that?"

"What?" She glanced around, but didn't see anything out of the ordinary. Most of the houses were dark, the sidewalks deserted.

"Unless I'm mistaken, Browning was here."

"Browning!" she exclaimed. "Are you sure?"

"Yeah."

"What's he doing here?" She peered into the shadows. He could be anywhere—hiding behind the bushes at the Sanders' house, lurking behind the Buckmans' pine tree, or the van parked in the driveway. "How did he find us?"

"He knows your name. Easy enough to find out where you live. I'm pretty sure it's me he's after, and because he knows we're together . . ." He shrugged. "Makes sense this is the first place he'd look."

"Oh, Ethan!" Sofia's heart sank. "You don't think he'll go after my family, the way Braga did?"

"I don't know, but I doubt it. It wouldn't gain him anything. Even if he got rid of me, he'd still have to destroy Saintcrow to get Morgan Creek, and I don't see that happening."

"So, why would he try again?"

"Beats me. Maybe he's pursuing some kind of personal vendetta against me now."

"He's not still here, is he?"

"No, he's long gone."

"I think we should be long gone, too," she said, tugging on his hand. "Let's go home."

For Sofia, the next few nights passed in a flurry of looking at pictures of wedding cakes, as well as flowers for the bride and the bridesmaids, corsages for the mothers of the bride and groom, and for the altar. They would be married in the church her family attended; the reception would be in the same venue Holly and Micah had used.

Ethan grimaced when Sofia told him the location.

She looked puzzled, until she remembered Leandro Braga had attacked him there. "We can find another place if you want."

"No, your mother's already arranged for it. Anyway, I don't think Braga has any more relatives."

"I had no idea planning a wedding was so involved," Sofia lamented. "The guest list is long enough with just my brothers and sisters and their families. And speaking of family, when am I going to meet your parents? You are going to invite them to the wedding, aren't you?"

"I guess so."

"You guess?"

"You don't understand." He shook his head. "I love my parents and they love me. But they're not a prime example of happily ever after. I mean, they can barely tolerate being in the same house."

"Then why are they still together?"

"I don't know. Both too stubborn to admit they made a mistake, I suppose."

"Maybe they're still in love?"

"If they are, they don't want anybody to know it."

"Well, we need to invite them. I think you should call them."

"Now?"

Sofia nodded.

With a sigh of resignation, he pulled his phone out of his pocket and made the call.

After nights of rehearsals, dress fittings for the ladies, trips to a tuxedo shop for the men, and 101 other errands, the big night arrived.

Sofia had never been so nervous in her entire life. As with Micah's wedding, most of the guests were friends of the family. She had felt a little sorry for Ethan when she learned the only attendees from his side of the family would be his parents. Neither his mom or dad had siblings, he was an only child, and his grandparents had passed away years ago.

She had met his parents at the rehearsal dinner. Lynn and Roger Parrish were a handsome couple. His mother looked like a movie star, with her long auburn hair and remarkable deep green eyes. She wore a tea-length dress that matched her eyes and outlined a perfect hourglass figure. Ethan looked very much like his father: tall, blond, and handsome. His parents had been extremely quiet at dinner, but Sofia could hardly blame them. With all her brothers and sisters in attendance, as well as her mom and dad, she figured Ethan's mom and dad had been overwhelmed by sheer numbers alone. He hadn't seen fit to tell them that he was a vampire.

Sofia's heart skipped a beat when one of her cousins popped his head in to tell her it was time. She took one last look in the mirror. The gown she had chosen was the first one she had tried on. It had a fitted bodice, a round neck, and a skirt that flared from the hips. Her veil fell to the floor in graceful folds. She had chosen to carry white roses. Her bridesmaids wore floor-length mauve gowns with pale pink sashes and carried pink and white bouquets.

Sofia let out a deep breath as she followed her sisters out of the dressing room and down a short hallway that opened into the foyer.

Her father winked at her as he came forward to meet her. "You look lovely, *mia figlia*," he remarked as Rosa started down the aisle.

"Thanks, Daddy."

His gaze searched hers. "Are you sure about this?"

"Very sure."

"Then you have my love and my blessing," he said, kissing her cheek. "Here's our cue."

Nodding, Sofia laid her hand on his arm, then whispered, "Don't let me fall down."

Ethan and her brothers stood with Father Ralph in front of the flower-bedecked altar, but as soon as Sofia saw Ethan, she forgot everything else. She had always thought him the handsomest man she had ever met, but tonight, clad in a tuxedo that fit as though it had been made for him, he looked absolutely mouthwatering.

He smiled when he saw her, but it was the love shining in his deep brown eyes that melted her heart.

Sofia scarcely heard the words the priest spoke, but she

didn't miss the slight change in Ethan's vow when, instead of vowing to love her "until death do you part," he promised to love her for all eternity.

A thrill of excitement ran through her when the priest pronounced them man and wife. True, they were already husband and wife, but somehow, being married in front of her family made it all the more meaningful.

Butterflies took wing in the pit of her stomach when he drew her into his arms and kissed her, long and leisurely, as if there weren't hundreds of people watching. She was breathless when he released her.

Sofia felt as if she was floating six feet off the ground when they walked down the aisle hand in hand.

Outside, Ethan pulled her into his arms and kissed her again.

All too soon, they were surrounded by her family, who showered them with good wishes, hugs, and kisses.

If Sofia had had her way, they would have skipped the reception/dinner altogether, but, of course, that was impossible.

Ethan handed her into the waiting limo, slid in beside her, and took her into his arms again the minute the driver closed the door. "Let's sneak away as early as we can," he murmured, raining kisses along her cheeks, her brow, the tip of her nose.

"Okay with me."

"Maybe we could take the long way to the reception?"

Sofia laughed softly. "You flatter me."

"What do you mean?"

"You'd think this was our first wedding."

"Must be the dress."

"You look very nice, too."

"Sofie . . ." His tongue stroked the side of her neck, sending frissons of desire racing through her.

"Ethan . . . you're not playing fair."

"I never do when I see something I want."

"But . . . the driver . . ."

"He can't see us. The partition is up." He eased her onto her back, his hand sliding up and down her calf. "All the windows are tinted. No one else can see us either."

Reaching for his belt, she said, "Tell him to drive slow."

Sofia straightened her dress and replaced her veil as the limo pulled up in front of the reception venue, certain everyone inside would take one look at her and know she and Ethan had indulged in a quickie on the way to their reception. Even without looking in a mirror, she knew her hair was mussed, her cheeks flushed, her gown wrinkled.

Sure enough, as soon as they walked in the door, Micah winked at her, then nudged Ethan. "Couldn't wait, huh?"

Ethan shrugged. "Perfectly legal, you know."

Before things escalated, Sofia grabbed Ethan's arm and hurried him across the floor to where the reception line was forming.

The next half hour passed in a blur of good wishes, handshakes, and more hugs.

She grinned inwardly as Ethan repeatedly glanced at his watch. Several times she heard his voice in her mind, always asking the same question: *Can we go now?*

Finally, all the rituals had been taken care of: their first dance as husband and wife, the throwing of her bouquet, numerous toasts and tears, the cutting of the cake.

They were dancing again when Ethan guided her toward the exit. "No one's looking," he whispered. "Can we go now?"

"Let's."

They ducked out the back door and ran around the corner of the building.

Ethan kissed her hungrily, then wrapped his arm around her waist. "Ready to go home, Mrs. Parrish?"

"More than ready, Mr. Parrish."

Grinning, he transported them to their lair in Morgan Creek.

Sofia's eyes widened with surprise. Someone had decorated their bedroom. A banner with the words "Congratulations, Mr. and Mrs. Parrish" had been tacked to the wall above the bed. There were vases of sweet-smelling flowers everywhere and perhaps a hundred white rose petals spread across the quilt. A bottle of red wine and two crystal goblets waited for them on the bedside table.

"Did Kadie tell you she was going to do this?" Sofia asked, stepping out of her heels.

Ethan shook his head.

"It had to be her, don't you think? I don't know of anyone else who could get in here."

"Well, she's the likely culprit; it doesn't look like Saint-crow's handiwork." He drew his bride into his arms. "We should have taken the limo to your apartment," he murmured, nuzzling her neck.

"I think I'd like to do it in a bed this time, if it's all the same to you."

"In a car, in a bed, on the floor." Ethan shrugged. "Where doesn't matter." He was undressing her as he spoke, his nimble fingers removing her gown and underwear with practiced ease. He whistled softly as she stood beautifully naked in front of him.

"My turn." After he'd obligingly removed his shoes and socks, her equally nimble hands divested him of his tuxedo.

They almost made it to the bed.

Chapter Thirty-Nine

Sofia blew out a sigh as she slipped a check into an envelope and sealed it, then filled out a bank deposit slip. Banking online would be so much easier and faster, but Saintcrow insisted on doing things the old-fashioned way. The town had only been open to the public for a short time and they were already turning a nice profit. Ethan had decided to pour concrete pads and rent spaces for motor homes and campers. He was also thinking of adding a section for tents.

The check she had just written was Ethan's first payment on the loan Saintcrow had given him. She stamped the envelope and dropped it in the out-box for tomorrow's mail pickup.

Pushing her chair away from the desk, she stood. To her surprise, Ethan had gone to spend the day with his parents. He hadn't told her why, but she couldn't help wondering if he was finally going to tell them he was a vampire. He had paid the day shift before he left, leaving her to see that the employees who worked nights received their wages. She scooped up the envelopes sitting on the corner of her desk and went outside. Standing on the porch, she could see the faint glow of the town's lights in the distance.

Hard to believe she had been married for over a month already. Vampire or mortal, time flew on by.

She considered willing herself to the hotel, but it was such a lovely evening, she decided to walk. Nearing the residential area, she waved to a middle-aged couple who were also out for a leisurely stroll.

She was nearing the hotel when Nolan Browning's scent was carried to her on the breeze.

Sofia came to an abrupt halt when she realized she had forgotten to set the wards around the town when she'd woken from the dark sleep this evening. Fear coiled in her belly. How could she have forgotten that? Had Browning been lurking on the outskirts of town all this time, just waiting for such an opportunity?

She took several deep breaths. Maybe she was wrong. But what if she was right? What if he was here?

Filled with a sudden sense of doom, Sofia followed his scent to the hotel's back entrance. When she opened the door, the coppery scent of freshly spilled blood was overpowering.

She tiptoed down the narrow hallway into the kitchen. The cook lay on his stomach, a meat cleaver buried in his back. His assistant lay beside him. In pieces.

Frozen with horror, Sofia stood in the doorway until a scream pierced the stillness. Galvanized to action, she skirted the pool of blood and peeked into the dining room.

Several bodies littered the floor. None were moving. Were they all dead? A little girl, perhaps three years old, screamed again. It was a bone-chilling sound, coming from one so young.

Rage engulfed her when Browning lifted the child, then made as if to throw her against the wall. Heedless of any danger to herself, Sofia grabbed a knife and launched herself at Browning's back.

He dropped the little girl, his roar of pained surprise

shattering windows as Sofia buried the knife between his shoulder blades.

It didn't kill him, of course.

Cursing, he clawed the knife from his flesh, turned on his heel, and threw it at her.

She sidestepped easily. The knife embedded itself in the wall behind her with a solid thud.

Poised on the balls of her feet, Sofia waited for his next move. And all the while, the little girl wailed in terror.

Ignoring the child, Sofia focused all her attention on Browning. He stared back at her as if he wasn't quite sure what to do next. Had he been surprised by her attack? She had been a little astonished by it herself. Once, she would have been horrified at the thought of sticking a butcher knife in someone's back. Now, she was ready to do it again if she got the chance.

She read Browning's intention in his eyes before he hurled himself at her, his arms wide-spread. If he thought to catch her, he had another think coming. She waited until the last moment, then ducked under his right arm, jerked the knife from the wall, whirled around, and drove the blade into the side of his neck.

Blood spurted from his severed jugular. It was a nasty wound but not fatal. Still, it slowed him down for a moment, giving her time to send a mental SOS to Ethan while she grabbed the sobbing child.

She was gathering her power, intending to transport herself and the little girl home, when Browning grabbed her by the hair and flung her across the room.

Sofia held tight to the little girl, turning in midair so that when she crashed into a table, the child wasn't hurt. She couldn't say the same for herself. Blood leaked from a cut in her head.

Ignoring the pain, she scrambled to her feet, thrust the

child behind her, then braced her feet, ready to defend the little girl to the death.

Covered in blood, not all of it his own, Browning scowled at her. "I'm going to rip out your heart," he snarled. "And then I'm going to drain that brat dry."

"I don't think so." Ethan's voice, darker, more dangerous, and more welcome than anything Sofia had ever heard.

There were no preliminaries. Ethan and Browning came together like two wild animals, claws and teeth viciously ripping and slashing, tearing through flesh and muscle. Dark red blood spurted from dozens of wounds. The shallow cuts healed almost instantly.

Breathing hard and splattered with blood, they parted.

"Sofie," Ethan said, "get the child out of here."

She didn't want to leave, but he was her sire, and when he exerted his influence on her, she had no choice but to obey. She didn't go far, though, just outside, where she could look in the window.

Eyes narrowed, Ethan glared at Browning. "You're dead."

Browning snorted his disdain. It was the last sound he ever made.

Drawing on the ancient power that flowed in his veins, Ethan sprang toward the other vampire, the urge to destroy the man who had dared to threaten his woman overwhelming every other thought as he plunged his hand into Browning's chest and ripped the vampire's beating heart from his body.

Browning stared at him a moment, the life fading from his eyes, before he collapsed.

Ethan glanced over his shoulder when he sensed a familiar presence. "What are you doing here?" he asked when Saintcrow materialized beside him.

"We had a deal, remember?" the master vampire said cheerfully. "You'd kill him and I'd take his head."

Sofia turned away from the window when Saintcrow bent down to fulfill his part of the bargain. Satisfied that Ethan would be all right, she willed herself and the child to the house on the hill.

"Mama," the little girl wailed through her tears. "I want my mama."

"I know, honey, but she can't be here now." Sofia stroked the girl's hair. "What's your name?"

"Jenny. Jenny O'Neal."

"I'm Sofie."

"Where's my daddy?"

"He had to go away with your mama. You're going to stay with me for a little while, okay?"

Lower lip quivering, the child stared at her through tear-bright blue eyes. "I want my mama!"

"I know." Taking a seat in one of the chairs by the fireplace, Sofia lifted Jenny onto her lap. "I know." She had expected the girl to pull away; instead, Jenny curled up in her arms. In minutes, she had cried herself to sleep.

Sofia wasn't sure how long she sat there before Ethan materialized in the room. She was glad to see he had washed up before coming home. "Where's Saintcrow?"

"He's cleaning up the mess in the hotel."

"How are we going to explain all those dead people?"

"We aren't."

"What do you mean?"

"There were only three couples in the dining room. That little girl was the only child. The other couples didn't have kids."

"But surely those people have family members who will wonder what happened to them."

"Saintcrow said he'd take care of it." Ethan lifted a hand to silence her next question. "I don't know what he's going to do, and I didn't ask."

She had a feeling no one would ever know what had

happened to those poor people. They would just disappear, along with their vehicles, more names added to the world's list of unsolved mysteries.

"Are you all right?" Ethan asked, his voice thick with concern.

"I think so."

"Why didn't you call me sooner?"

"I was too busy."

"He could have killed you."

She shrugged, then glanced at the child sleeping in her arms. "I was more afraid of what he'd do to Jenny."

"Uh-huh." Ethan rocked back on his heels. "You can't keep her."

"I know."

"But you want to."

Sofia nodded. "Maybe she doesn't have any other family."

"And if she does?"

Her arm tightened around Jenny.

"I'll ask Saintcrow to see what he can find out about her family."

Sofia nodded again. As much as she wanted to keep Jenny, she knew it was impossible. Jenny needed someone who could watch her day and night, something Sofia couldn't do.

Reading her mind, Ethan said, "You're forgetting I can be awake during the day," he remarked. "And there are always nannies."

Sofia's smile was like dawn breaking over the mountains. "Nannies!" she exclaimed. "Of course! Why didn't I think of that?"

Ethan scrubbed his hand over his jaw. "Remember what Saintcrow said about Kadie? He did a blood exchange with her, and now she's able to be awake for a few hours a day."

Sofia nodded. "I forgot about that." Maybe there was hope after all.

"Why don't you go get cleaned up?" he suggested. "There's blood in your hair and on your shirt."

Sofia glanced at Jenny, who was sleeping soundly, her thumb in her mouth.

Ethan jerked his chin at the little girl. "I'll hold her while you shower."

"All right." She felt bereft when Ethan lifted Jenny from her arms. How could she feel attached to the child so soon?

"A strong maternal instinct?" Ethan suggested. "Plus, vampire emotions run stronger and deeper than mortal ones." He stroked Jenny's cheek with his finger, only vaguely aware of Sofia leaving the room. He had never given much thought to being a father, but he suddenly found the idea appealing.

He couldn't seem to stop looking at the little girl. Her skin was soft and her blood smelled so sweet. . . . Shit! What kind of a monster was he?

Afraid of what he might do, he laid the child on the sofa, covered her with the blanket folded over the back of the couch. He had never fed on children. Would he be able to say that if one lived in his house? Would the day come when temptation overcame his resistance? What if he killed her? He would never forgive himself, and neither would Sofia.

Suddenly, the idea of having a kid in the house lost its appeal.

He was standing in front of the fireplace, his back to the little girl, his hands tightly clenched, when Sofia emerged from the bathroom wearing a robe, her hair damp and curling around her shoulders.

Her gaze moved from Ethan to Jenny and back again. Something was wrong. The tension in the room was thick enough to slice. "What is it? What's happened?"

"We can't keep her here," he said, his voice tight.

She started to ask why, but it wasn't necessary. She could sense the bloodlust emanating from him, knew he was fighting the urge to take the little girl's blood.

"I'm going out," he growled, and vanished from the room.

Sofia stared after him. As much as she wanted to keep Jenny as her own, maybe it wasn't such a good idea. And then she frowned. Ethan had been a vampire longer than she had. Why was he tempted to do something so despicable when the thought had never crossed her mind? Was it because of her innate instinct to mother the helpless child, as he had suggested?

Lost in thought, she carried Jenny down to their bedroom and tucked her under the covers. She could keep her safe tonight, but what about tomorrow?

Chapter Forty

Ethan strolled the dark streets of an unknown city, his stomach in knots, the sweet scent of Jenny's blood lingering in his nostrils. He told himself he was worrying for nothing. The kid probably had relatives somewhere. Saintcrow had connections everywhere. Surely someone his sire knew could find the girl's next of kin.

He swore under his breath when Saintcrow materialized beside him. "Speak of the devil and he appears."

"Sounds like the devil is just what you need. I could sense your distress all the way in New Orleans. What's wrong?" He took a deep breath. "Is that a *baby* I smell?"

"Not quite. It's some little girl from the slaughter in the hotel. Sofie wants to keep her."

"Ah." There was a wealth of understanding in that single word.

"I can't have a kid in the house," Ethan said flatly. "I won't be responsible for what happens to her. Can you find out if she's got kin somewhere?"

"Sure, no problem."

"Are we going to have trouble with the police over that massacre in the dining room?"

"No. The cook and his assistant were both single. The waitresses and the hostess managed to get away." Saintcrow held up a hand to stay Ethan's next question. "They won't remember anything. I've already seen to that. As for the patrons . . ." He shrugged. "No one will ever find the bodies. Their names have gone mysteriously missing from the computer, along with their luggage."

"What about the cars?"

"No one will find them either."

Ethan shook his head. "It doesn't seem right."

"Would you rather try to explain that bloodbath to the cops?"

"Hell no."

"Okay, then. Look on the bright side. With Browning gone, we shouldn't have any more problems. Sofie's family seems okay with having another vampire—make that two others—in the family. The town seems to be prospering. What more do you want?"

Ethan scrubbed a hand across his jaw. What Saintcrow proposed didn't seem right, and yet trying to explain the carnage in the hotel would lead to questions better left unasked. "I can't figure Browning out," he remarked after a while. "He must have been hanging around for days, just waiting for one of us to forget to set the wards on the bridge. I could understand it if he came after me, or you, but why kill a bunch of strangers? What did he hope to gain?"

"How the hell should I know?"

"I thought you knew everything."

Saintcrow snorted and then grinned. "If I had to venture a guess, I'd say Browning was looking for someone to end his existence. He was an old vampire. He didn't have the guts to walk out into the sun, so he came here, stirring up trouble, knowing one of us would destroy him."

Ethan thought that over for a few minutes, then nodded.

"He didn't really put up much of a fight," he mused. "But, hell, if he wanted to end it, why not just ask you to take him out?"

Saintcrow shrugged. "Pride, I suppose."

"What about his so-called plan to take over the town?"

"I don't know. Maybe that's all it was, just talk. Maybe he'd convinced himself that was what he wanted, until it turned out to be a lot harder than he thought."

"Would you have destroyed him if he'd asked you to?"

"Sure. Nothing worse than an unhappy vampire. I saved his life once."

"Yeah?"

"A hunter was about to stake him. I staked the hunter instead. Browning was the first vampire I brought here. He'd been here around fifty years when I threw all the vampires out. I'm guessing he was never comfortable out in the real world." Saintcrow stared into the distance, then slapped Ethan on the shoulder. "It's over and done. I'll check into the little girl's family tomorrow."

And then he was gone, as quickly as he'd come.

Sofia woke with a start. Was she dreaming, or was there a baby in the house? And then she remembered. Jenny! Grabbing her robe, she flew up the lair's stairs and hurried into the living room, her eyes widening when she saw Ethan holding the little girl on his lap, feeding her a peanut butter and jelly sandwich.

Ethan sent her a sheepish grin when he saw her.

Jenny blinked at Sofia, smiled through the jelly smeared on her mouth, then held out her arms.

Sofia's insides melted as she took the child from Ethan, then sat beside him on the couch. "Is this her dinner?"

"I didn't know what else to give her. Everything else in the fridge is spoiled."

"I guess we'll have to go to the store. She needs milk. And a change of clothes. And . . ." She frowned. "Wait a minute. Last night you couldn't stand to be in the same room with her. What happened? I thought you wanted her gone."

He lifted one shoulder in a what-can-I-say shrug. "She was crying. I picked her up and she put her arms around my neck and . . ." He shrugged again. "Suddenly, my instinct to protect her was stronger than my hunger."

"I love you, Ethan."

"I love you, too," he said, and then huffed a sigh. "Just don't get your hopes up."

"What? Oh." That quickly, reality came crashing back. Jenny might have kin who had a legal claim on her. Did it really matter? No one would ever know where she was. For the next few minutes, Sofia struggled with her conscience. In the end, her conscience won. If Jenny had kin, she would send the little girl home.

Being the youngest in the family, Sofia had never had any siblings to care for. Looking after a three-year-old was something she had never done, and more fun than she had ever imagined. From time to time, Jenny asked for her mother, but other than that, she seemed happy to play with Sofia.

Around nine that night, Jenny fell asleep on the sofa between Ethan and Sofia.

"Do you think we'd be good parents?" Sofia asked.

"I don't know. I'm an only child. Never been around kids." He stretched his arm along the back of the couch and trailed his fingertips over Sofia's shoulder. "But I'd sure like a chance to see what it's like."

He glanced up, his senses telling him that Saintcrow was nearby moments before he appeared in the living room.

"Well, isn't this is a cozy scene?" the master vampire

remarked. "Sort of like the vampire version of *The Addams Family*."

"Very funny," Ethan muttered.

"What did you find out?" Sofia asked anxiously.

"The kid was born in San Antonio on April 10. She turned three this year. Her last name is O'Neal. Her father was an orphan who ran away from his foster family when he was sixteen. Her mother was an only child. Her maternal grandfather was killed in a car wreck last year. Her maternal grandmother's in a home for Alzheimer's patients."

Sofia stared at Saintcrow. "So . . . ?"

"So she's yours if you want her."

Sofia jumped off the couch and threw her arms around Saintcrow. "Thank you!"

"My pleasure." He wrapped his arms around her and held her close, just to piss Ethan off.

It had the desired effect. Ethan growled at him.

Laughing, Saintcrow released Sofia. "You two are a lot of trouble, you know that?"

"Would you like to be Jenny's godfather?" Sofia asked.

"Me? Are you kidding?"

"I can't think of anyone who would be better or deserves it more."

Saintcrow glanced at Ethan, who shrugged and said, "Fine with me."

"Then I'd be honored. Now that that's settled, I'm going back to my wife. She's beginning to think I'm seeing someone else on the side," he muttered with a wry grin. "I trust I won't have to come back here again for a good long time."

Unable to stop smiling, Sofia said, "We'll expect you back here next year on Jenny's birthday."

"It's a date," Saintcrow said. "I'll even bring a present." A wave of his hand, and he was gone.

"I guess we'd better start looking for a nanny," Ethan remarked, taking Sofia in his arms.

Sofia nodded. She had never been happier, she thought, than she was at this moment. She had an eternity to spend with the man she loved more than life itself. And, thanks to a twist of fate, she had a child to love as well.

Who could ask for more?

Epilogue

Sofia tucked Jenny into bed, then bent down to kiss her daughter's cheek. She could still remember the way her heart had melted the first time Jenny called her Mama. The child had had a few rough nights in the beginning, but she seemed happily adjusted now. After thinking it over, Sofia had asked Saintcrow to do a blood exchange with her the way he had with Ethan and Kadie. It had been partially successful, allowing her to be awake a few hours each day. They had found a wonderful nanny to look after Jenny when Sofia and Ethan couldn't be with her.

It was hard to believe two years had passed since Jenny had come into their lives. So much had happened. Micah and Holly had decided to move back to Morgan Creek. They had built a luxurious home on the hill near Saintcrow's lair. Micah was now in charge of security.

Saintcrow and Kadie were also in residence. Sofia thought it was because Kadie had tired of traveling, but Kadie said it was because she missed the ghosts. Sofia would have kidded her about believing in spirits, but how could she doubt it when a ghost had sent Ethan to save her life? It was comforting somehow, knowing there were good spirits watching over the town.

Ghosts or no ghosts, there was no denying Morgan Creek was prospering. They now had facilities for RVs and tents, as well as a large picnic area and a stable with horses to rent.

Ethan had repaid the loan to Saintcrow and the two had decided to be full-fledged partners.

Sofia loved having her favorite brother living so close by. She and Holly and Kadie had all become good friends.

Next summer, Sofia's family was coming to stay for a week.

She glanced up as Ethan stepped into the room. "Our little girl is already asleep."

He slipped his arm around Sofia's shoulders. "Sorry I'm late. I had to handle a little dustup at the hotel. One of the patrons thought he'd been overcharged, so we gave him a free night to keep him happy."

"World's best vampire innkeeper," she murmured, smiling. "Who'd've thought?"

"Certainly not me." His gaze caressed her. "I love you."

"I love you more."

"No regrets?"

"Just one."

He frowned at her. "What is it?"

"We're still standing here, talking, instead of curled up in bed."

"Handling complaints is what I do best," he said, a husky growl in his voice as he swung her up into his arms. "Just tell me what you want, my love, and I'll see you get it."

And she did.

Read on for an excerpt from
Amanda Ashley's next vampire romance,
coming next year!

HOLD BACK THE DAWN

Newberry Township
1867

The Mothers of Mercy Hospital was located in what had once been a fashionable part of town. Age had whittled it down, leaving the place looking as old and worn out as the dilapidated manor houses that surrounded it. Most of the well-to-do folk had fled the area during an epidemic, though a handful of the wealthy landowners—too stubborn to move on—remained on their estates, closer to what was left of the place.

Roan Cabrera paused on the weed-choked dirt road that led to the entrance. The air was fetid with the stench of horse droppings, rot, and despair. He didn't know which was worse, the stink outside or the smell of disease and death that permeated the very walls of the hospital.

Materializing on the third floor, he ghosted past the nurse on duty, unseen, then continued down the hallway until he came to the room at the end of the corridor. A woman lay unmoving on the narrow bed. Maura Singleterry, age twenty-eight, was the victim of a carriage accident that had killed the driver and two other passengers. She was a pretty woman—or she had been. Now, her cheeks were sunken, her eyes shadowed, her hair limp and lackluster. Trapped in a coma for the last three weeks, she had a bleak prognosis at best.

Entering the room, Roan closed the door, then glided silently to the side of the bed. He stood gazing down at her a moment; then, taking her limp hand in his, he sat on the edge of the narrow mattress, his mind delving through the darkness that kept her trapped in unconsciousness.

Opening a mental link between them, he murmured, *Hello, Maura.*

Roan?

Who else? Where would you like to go today?

My wedding day, but first . . . I want to know about you.

What would you like to know?

How is it we can talk when I can't communicate with anyone else? Are you real? Or just a fever dream?

I'm real enough. 'Tis a gift I have, being able to speak with those who are lost in the dark.

I can't find my way out. She whimpered softly. *I try and try, but I can't get through the darkness.*

Roan stroked her brow. *I know. That's why I'm here. Put your questions away for now, Maura, and I'll take you back to the day you wed.*

He closed his eyes, his mind searching hers until he found the memory she wished to experience again. He gave it back to her, not as a dream, not as a faint memory, but as if she were living it again. . . . She mingled with everyone who had been there, recalled each word spoken that day, each thought that crossed her mind, the love she felt for her new husband, the taste and smell and texture of the food she ate, her nervousness as she and her husband left her parents' home, the carriage ride to the inn where they had spent their first night as husband and wife.

It was a rare gift he had, being able to grant those who were dying a chance to relive their most cherished memories. It cost him nothing, and he took but little in return for the pleasure he gave.

An hour later, Roan kissed Maura's cheek in farewell and left the hospital. He felt a brief twinge of regret in knowing she had only a few hours to live. It seemed unfair that such a sweet-natured woman should be taken before her time. Unfair, he thought again, that one who had everything to live for should be brought down in her prime while he, a man who had no reason to go on and no one to mourn him when he was gone, had existed for centuries.

Connect with 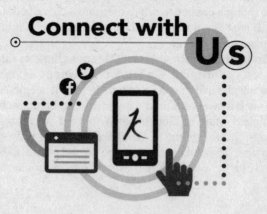 Us

Visit us online at
KensingtonBooks.com
to read more from your favorite authors, see books
by series, view reading group guides, and more.

 Join us on social media

for sneak peeks, chances to win books and prize packs,
and to share your thoughts with other readers.

facebook.com/kensingtonpublishing
twitter.com/kensingtonbooks

Tell us what you think!

To share your thoughts, submit a review,
or sign up for our eNewsletters, please visit:
KensingtonBooks.com/TellUs.